Screen Door Jesus
&
other stories

Screen Door Jesus
&
other stories

Christopher Cook

HOST PUBLICATIONS, INC.
AUSTIN, TEXAS

Layout and design: Joe Bratcher

Cover design by Mary Lou Williams

Photograph by Alan Pogue

Library of Congress Catalog Number: 2001 135530
ISBN: 0-924047-21-6

Second Printing

CONTENTS

For those who ask questions,
for those who resist,
for the doubters and seekers:
the honest ones . . .

 . . . and for Betty

"Why, sometimes I've believed as many
as six impossible things before breakfast."

—the White Queen to Alice

"For we are made a spectacle unto the world,
and to angels, and to man. We are fools
for Christ's sake."

—Paul the Apostle
I Corinthians 4: 9 - 10

"Men never do evil so completely and cheerfully
as when they do it from religious
conviction."

—Blaise Pascal, *Pensées*

Arc of Flesh, Ascending

She had been once to West Texas, and all the way to Tucson, and knew from that time the world possessed great circumference. In those alien reaches, distant arcs fell away far beyond the eye's ken. She planted her feet in scrabbled crust, the weight of all that desert sky held her down. The earth: rough brown parchment laid thin beneath unfathomed blue. Everywhere depth without surface, skinless bones. The human soul seemed puny in that endless space, and bared to it. She felt naked there, without substance, yet could not rise.

Back home in East Texas, in the piney woods, she floated. The world was tightly circumscribed by the color of green and the density of trees, the places between filled with a profusion of undergrowth, climbing vines, flowers, so that space did not waste itself on emptiness. Instead, it gave over to a chaotic intertwined abundance — wet, humming, tangled thicket — and the eye could not travel far except upward, nor the soul. Try to move horizontal through that damp impenetrable web and you snagged up quick, had to back out. Up was the only way to go. So she ascended. Rising like smoke, weaving blueward through forested fissures, weightless. Gliding up there over the dark green canopy, a kestrel slipsliding gravity's embrace, her nakedness felt private.

She was trying to get to God.

The reason she'd gone to Tucson, transversing West Texas

1

en route, was the baby. She perched on a vinyl upholstered seat in the Sunset Limited gazing out the window, the sway-hipped locomotive gripping narrow iron rails over low hills then plains and deserts, between ragged mountains and bloodbruised buttes, an emptiness unlike any she'd ever conceived, unless that in her own soul had been hers. It wasn't, not yet. She was too young to claim it. Seventeen, with child, on a journey to join the man who begat it unknowing until the phone call. "Well, come on out then," he'd said, "you need traveling money?" She didn't, had borrowed it already from her parents, her mother weeping, father resigned, as if they hadn't driven her to this escape, this train ride a mere final proof.

He was an enlisted man, yet a boy himself, a swaggering know-it-all from her own home town, with a temper, and careless. Too young to know it, too young to care if he had, but already taking one fork over another as if it didn't matter. He was stationed at the Air Force base outside Tucson, and she rode the train two days and a night to reach him, carrying the child with her, embedded in her flesh like a secret tumor. She did not know what it would come to as she crossed over the eastern range into that sunscorched desert valley among the creosote and ocotillo and towering saguaros uplifting long arms through the flames as though they were rich men beseeching Lazarus for a drop of water.

Her name was Winona, his L.C., short for Lonnie Charles, his father's name. He met her at the station and that was the best she ever got of him. A new name, Winona Crowder, and a child, William, after her own father, and a decade's misery packed into one year that left her beaten. Standing in the tiny barren yard before the aluminum Air Stream trailer, her belly swollen as round and smooth as a prickly pear tuna, she fixed her eyes beyond the wasteland on distant mountains: the jagged high-shouldered Catalinas, the snaggle-toothed Rincons, the Santa Ritas ranging southward, all of them rattlesnake dry and roughskinned, harsh: and she wondered who he was, and who he might become, and what she'd got herself into. This not about the child, but about the husband.

2

Within the year she learned what emptiness was, found that which bounded her in every direction reflected that which lay within, conceived even at her own birth, an inheritance. She could run from it or claim it or ignore it, but it was hers. He did not love her or himself, she was alone. And then she urged forth the crying infant and he set upon them both. L.C., an angry man, resentful of what his pleasures wrought, wanting things without paying for them. He couldn't fill her emptiness, wouldn't try, merely expanded it, pushed the edges out farther than she could comprehend, so far they threatened to collapse. After the child was born, she knew they both would die of thirst if she stayed.

She stood in the yard holding the sunshaded infant studying those bone-dry mountains. She might have been gazing upon Mount Horeb from the Desert of Sin. The price one paid for a moment's naked lust, a lifetime. Though her very substance sloughed away to commingle with air, evaporated into that vacuumed space, she could not rise above it.

So she wrote a letter, borrowed more money, and went home. East Texas, her parents' house, town of Bethlehem on the Sabine River, the Louisiana line. The cloistered green, thicket and bottomlands. She took the boy, and discovered a month after her arrival she was again with child, had brought it with her, another long journey with an embedded seed, this time unknown even to her. She named him Horeb.

Moses had found God on that self-named mountaintop. Or God, Moses. Either way, she cast her eyes about for a burning bush.

Twice an escapee, yet still imprisoned. Between her mother's concealed shame and a father's self-constructed dignity, Winona tracked and backtracked the bars of her cage, the two boys in tow, looking for a way. She worked as a truckstop waitress, sold Avon door to door, fried donuts on the predawn shift. Men flirted, told her she was sweet, leaned on hard redboned elbows and winked. Nasty mouthed Breen Pratt offered to lick her neck, and on Saturday nights she sat on the front porch near the moonlit wisteria wondering if anything smelled so sweet as those lavender blooms, even love. The house sat back off the paved road where the town ran out, in a sandy grove of leaning loblollies, a sycamore, two magnolias, a small clapboard house with two bedrooms, one for her and the boys, and the porch where she found solitude once they were snugged in bed. Saturday nights she romanced possibility.

Sundays they went to church, the five of them, all in a row on the narrow pinewood pew, spitshined for divine inspection. The Holiness Tabernacle, a small ramshackle structure on concrete piers and windows along the sides, an elevated wood rostrum up front with a lacquered pulpit and the baptismal tank, a fair rendition of Calvary painted on its back wall. Forty people on a good Sunday, righteous Holy Ghost preaching, singing. Singing hymns to the Blood of the Lamb. Seeking salvation, seeking relief. Testimonials of trials, of tribulation, of answered prayers, and long trembling laments over children led astray, cancered relatives, plain bad luck. Folks feeling poorly limped forward, received the holy anointing of oil, heard their names called out to Jesus, shuddered back to seats whimpering from the joy of it, the restless anticipation. Sometimes we are healed. She called out as the rest did, begged for the hem of His garment, saw it passing out of reach.

Where was He?

The boys were trouble from the get-go. They took after L.C. and she watched in terror to see the power of the flesh. The older one started out like her but the younger was the stronger and Billy bent Horeb's way. The grandfather held no influence, keeping character intact, silent. The grandmother sought solace more in brooding than affection, justifying worst fears. She was a worrier, a nag, a talker by nervous habit saying nothing of interest. Winona worked, the boys grew wild, she knew they needed a father.

One Saturday night she felt so lonely she let Breen Pratt lick her neck. She borrowed the family car, her own beyond repair, and drove mindlessly to the Pressure Cooker, a lowslung sour honkytonk tipped down the cypressed riverbank, found his nasty mouth there and turned him loose. She got no pleasure from it but shame, but it was a start. Praying hadn't helped. Repentance soon followed and she felt close. Folded over the low bench during altar call the next morning her guts gave way and she wept for an hour, everybody else ready to go home, hungry, her refusing until she got an answer. She thought the sweet breath of Jesus had come upon her when the hairs at her nape riffled in a breeze. She lunged and whirled to see none other than Mother Maguire waving a Bethlehem Funeral Home fan to cool her down. "Keep it up, child," the old woman urged, toothless, sagging mud-cracked jowls, "He gonna answer someday."

"When?" she cried. "When?"

"Someday."

Years passed in this way. Years.

She felt old. She felt tired. She lay in bed in the small room added to the house-back, her room, the boys by now too old to have certain urgencies witnessed. Too old for a father, as well, their own energy too much in young rut, Horeb a pure amoral force at thirteen, the elder Billy a step behind. Both headed for a bad middle, a worse end. She worked at the nursing home now, the evening shift, cleaning up the senile mess, propping up despair with kind hands, gentle words. With the boys these proved useless. Soft things fell away from those hard surfaces like raindrops on rock, as wind over stone. She would not live long enough to see a change. The world was very old, the elements in those young unyielding bodies ageless. She watched, terrified. She was moving as quickly as care permitted, trying to head it off, but saw reflected in their intractable faces that she was barely in motion. Life was too long, too short.

By night she began to walk. Coming home from work into the yard, she veered off from the porch and first by impulse, then desire, tunneled into the forested darkness surrounding, followed slim trails of whitetail and coon and armadillo through the underbrush, discovering deep within the woods small unbrushed clearings ceilinged by starlight, by moonlight. She sat on a deadfall stump and combed her hair. Leaning her head to one side, then the other, she combed slowly, listening to midnight mutterings of restless dreaming birds, the footsteps of creatures passing among the dead leaves, signaled owls.

She felt close again. Who could stop her?

In his sixteenth year Horeb killed a man. A boy, really, his own brother. An accident, he offered, and no request for sympathy. He was aiming the gun, Billy turned into it. You don't turn into a triggered gun, already pointed. Everybody knows that. Everybody. There followed a closed casket funeral and no charges. People die hunting, it happens. You cry for a while, or hold it in, repeat the lesson: Don't turn into a triggered gun, already pointed, ever. Then you hunt on.

She registered no surprise. It knocked her flat, but it didn't surprise her. When Horeb disappeared shortly after — not one contact thereonward, not a postcard, not a phone call — she did what a person did. She kept putting one foot in front of the other, leaning against time. The grieving had come before, precocious. Events were mere facts now, verifying truths long known.

She moved on. Still working, still going to church, still combing her hair under pale traces tumbling downward through latticed leaves in a wooded clearing, now by morning light as well as night. Her chapel, she called it. Where she worshiped. Church she attended by habit, hauling her shrunken parents. Nothing happened there but misery shared, a collective groaning. Her own mother the loudest complaint, the choir's shrillest voice. She'd never found peace in it, never would.

You find God when you quit searching.

*   *   *

As a young girl, she'd floated. During that slow arc between sleep and first thought, during moments misplaced among governed hours, standing still in the deep woods as a doe marks time, an eternity lost in an eyeblink, she'd floated. No effort, none. Effort counterproductive, the self-conscious mistake corrected by forgetting. She'd carted no weight then, no burden of regret, sinless, a wide-eyed young pilgrim unmarked by possession, not even the tenderest bruise of want. It wasn't until she was older she learned that wasn't right. "The true way is narrow and hard," she'd been told, "and you don't deserve any better. Carry this, and this, and this." And they had loaded her up, nodding sagely while she sank, her eyes rolling with fear. She was drowning.

Even in that distant desert so long ago where rivers revealed barren gulches, where a saguaro begged a drop, she'd drowned. All that time, what she'd wanted was to rise up, glide on the lightness all around, sail on unseen currents coaxing her upward as if she'd sprouted wings, might fly. She'd believed then it was the sky pressing her downward. It wasn't. The earth deserved that onus. It had pulled her back, nailed her feet, anchored her distended belly to the sunparched soil, heaving dry sand over her head until she smothered.

Now she sat naked in the arbored chapel at twilight, comb in one hand, remembering. That, and what came after. The first child, home flight, the second coming, endless yearning for the touch that would satisfy. Desire for holy breath, a sign, any kind.

What might peace feel like, if it existed?

Around her cicadas hummed, crickets cracked kneebones. Sunset in western retreat, deepening shadows. The gap torn overhead through which a ragged patch of sky cascaded lay awash with pink, maroon, burnt umber. She lifted her chin, fixed searching eyes on a single startled dimlit star, calling. The tangled thicket closed in, palpitating vine and feeler, treetrunks shuffling gnarled toes through shallow dirt,

7

enveloping her. Thus embraced, she closed her eyes, awaiting ascension. If patient, she would rise like smoke. Up there soar with eagles.

Had He not promised?

Come fly in the midst of heaven, gather yourselves to the supper of God that you might eat the flesh of kings, eat the flesh of mighty men. And small ones, too.

Screen Door Jesus

When I was thirteen my old man spent a year for the oil company in Saudi. My mother went with him so I stayed with my maternal grandparents, the Ogdens. They ran a photography shop right in the middle of those piney woods and bayous up in East Texas, in a little country town called Bethlehem. Sawmills and chicken farms, mostly, folks stripping out what timber that remained or mass-producing eggs for Denny's. Also, a little scratch oil. Once in a while you'd pass an overgrown field outside town and see a drilling rig going in, someone feeling hopeful.

My grandpa was a machinist for a pipeline company until he hurt his back and they cut him loose. The pipeline was a division of either Texaco or Chevron, I forget which, you know how those big companies are. All heart. He'd given them thirty years and like that, he's out on his tail. Never was bitter about it, though. People in his generation learned to accept things. Instead of brooding, he took stock of the situation, noodled it through, then rented a storefront on Main Street near the courthouse. Bethlehem was the county seat, so there was a downtown of sorts around the courthouse square and running off east a couple of blocks toward the Dairy Queen. If you kept going past the Dairy Queen a mile or so you hit rank wooded bottoms and crossed the Sabine River into Louisiana.

My grandparents opened their photography business not long before I arrived. Grandpa had always enjoyed taking pictures. The attic was stuffed with old cardboard boxes filled with slides and snapshots — family scenes, fishing trips, kids opening Christmas gifts. A vacation to the Grand Canyon, a two-headed snake in a toilet bowl. And so on. Most of the pictures were bent and faded, and after he died it took us a month to sort them out. I found a picture of a naked woman smiling in one box, a real looker. Don't know who it was, but I guarantee you it wasn't Grandma.

In the store Grandpa sold Kodak cameras and film and whatnot. After the screen door incident he built the stock up and had some nice equipment. But early on it was slim pickings. His severance pay from the pipeline company was zilch so he started from scratch, not even a darkroom. It was a tough go. He sent film down to Beaumont for developing and printing. Grandma worked in the place, too, only she refused to learn the stock. Too technical, she said, all those questions about exposures, f-stops, film speeds. Mostly she just watched the counter and talked. Business was slow, so that meant the telephone. Always on it. Yak, yak, yak.

So there I was, thirteen years old stuck in a small country town after living all my life in Houston. Bethlehem wasn't a metropolis, and that's a fact. A dogfight was a big event. Mostly what they did was religion. A church on every block. Soon as one built up to a hundred members they'd fall into a fight, as if there was some critical mass beyond which people couldn't get along, and they'd form two new churches, like molecular division. Such disputes were said to be doctrinal. But Grandpa observed that if you peeled away that notion and looked underneath, what you'd find was a clash of personalities and American democracy in action.

I noticed right away how those churches kept the town life humming. They were always organizing events. Revivals, missionary sermons, fundraisers, gospel singings, picnics, youth nights, you name it. Keeping people busy. Idle minds avoided, chinking up cracks in time to keep the devil out. My grandparents were Pentecostal, holy rollers. That meant tongue speaking, shouting in the aisles. Sounds more interesting than it was, actually. It was mostly my grandma's doing. No beer. No tobacco. No cussing. A no-nonsense rule for every situation.

My grandma made me go to church Sundays, and I soon
got to know the other kids in the congregation. Those kids
couldn't do a thing worth doing or go anywhere fun. TV was
sinful, so was dancing, movies, pinball machines and roller
rinks. If you're on a date, what's left? Make a quick run through
the Dairy Queen and head down to the riverfront park. Sit in
the car getting hot and bothered, fogging up the glass. Touch,
touch, kiss, kiss. Pretty soon it's off with the clothes, hanky-
panky time. La-la, boom! There you are. People got married
young. They had to. You'd think the preachers would catch
on. But that was Bethlehem, sanctified and holy. A regular sex
factory. If I'd been old enough to drive it might've been okay.
But by the time I got my license I was back in Houston, begging
girls to cop a feel just like all the rest. I missed that little old
town then.

Anyway, I got there in January, shirtsleeve weather in those
southern piney woods. Afternoons you could chunk your shoes.
Right away I met RobRoy Conroy. That was some kind of
name. I thought he was kidding until he showed me his birth
certificate. Named for an uncle who got killed invading some
place in Vietnam. RobRoy's old man had recently put a pool
table in their garage. He was a guard supervisor at the state
prison farm and said it would keep the boy off the streets, as if
Bethlehem was a seething cauldron of gang activity. The
Conroys lived next door to my grandparents.

Each day after school I got free ice cream in Turk's
Drugstore downtown, at the counter fountain. Scoop of vanilla
with chocolate syrup. RobRoy ate one, too, then paid for both.
Afterward we'd go to his house and shoot pool and I'd win the
next day's ice cream. That went on for several months, then
all of a sudden RobRoy learned to shoot. Practicing when I
wasn't around, I figured. One day — the first day of summer
vacation, as I recall — he beat me several times in a row and I
said all right, double or nothing. I lost, said okay, double that
or nothing. I lost again. That went on until I owed him six
months worth of ice cream. We walked over to the drugstore
where I reasoned with him. RobRoy was all right, flexible. I

11

bought him a banana split with extra toppings and he let me off the rest.

As we left the drugstore we saw a big crowd down the street. It turned out the old lady who lived behind the Western Auto Store had discovered a miracle in her back yard. Mother Harper, we called her. An old widow woman. She was hard-shell Baptist but friendly all the same. Sat on her front porch and waved to everyone. Always cooking, taking food to the shut-ins and sick. Real thoughtful, she was. A Mother Theresa type, a philanthropist. Candy for the kids, green beans from her garden for the grownups. Always with a smile. Piling up the good works, headed in a beeline for the pearly gates, everybody agreed on that much. She was plump with pink skin and crinkly green cat eyes and that silvery blue-colored hair old women wear. The color of a bluejay on a brisk winter day.

Mother Harper was standing in her back yard watering the gladiolas — in addition to her vegetables, she was a nut about flowers, her back yard resembled a picture in one of those gardening magazines — when she looked up and saw a picture of Jesus on her screen door. She almost fainted, she said. She called over Mr. Lott who owned the Western Auto and he saw it, too. Word spread quick. Pretty soon half the town was there. That's when RobRoy and I walked out of Turk's Drugstore and saw the crowd. We made tracks to see what the fuss was, hoping maybe the house was on fire or someone was having a heart attack. You never know. Maybe somebody robbed the Western Auto, RobRoy said, and shot Mr. Lott. We were both optimistic that way. But when we got up close everyone was yammering about the screen door.

We pushed our way through the crowd and there it was. The usual kind of back screen door sitting atop some rickety wooden steps, a little long in the tooth like its owner. The wood frame was warped. The aluminum screen had stretched from getting pushed on and it bulged and sagged here and there. The sunlight came down through the foliage of a pecan tree in the back yard to hit the rumpled screen at an angle. That's where the image of Jesus was, dappled on the screen. RobRoy claimed he saw it plain as daylight but it seemed awfully vague to me, like the man in the moon. I turned this way and that, looking. After a while, I thought I saw something that might pass for a face. With a little imagination, on a slow day, it might resemble Jesus.

"Lookit that!" RobRoy exclaimed.

"I am," I said.

"See it?" he asked.

"Reckon so," I said doubtfully, "there it is, right there."

You know, I've often wondered why God just doesn't come down and get on television and make a speech, like the president. Or show up at half-time in the Super Bowl. Make an appearance, tell everyone to straighten up and fly right. That'd be the simple and straightforward approach, it seems to me. But no, instead He's got to play cat and mouse, hide the thimble. Wants you to look under the rug, behind the couch, like some joker leaving clues in unlikely places. It reminds me of a picture I once saw of an electron. Nothing but a trail of bubbles where the electron had been. No electron, mind you, just its trail, cause the light from the camera excites the electron, shoves it out of the frame. Say smile and there it goes, with the scientists right behind, hot on the track. That's how God is, I suppose. But why? Seems like He could step right out in the open, say *Boo!* Instead, you got to go looking for Him, like a game of hide and seek. But I'll say one thing for those folks in Mother Harper's yard, they were looking hard.

Standing there with RobRoy, watching those believers milling around beating their gums, yawping with excitement, I wanted to crack a joke. Only something held me back. Even then, without realizing, I intuitively understood that people lack a sense of humor when it comes to religion. Several years later I bought a 3-D picture postcard of Jesus at an interstate truckstop outside Dallas. On a whim I sent it to my Aunt Mildred in Arkansas, who'd always eyed me with suspicion. She evidently considered me a smartass. A devout Southern Baptist, she returned the postcard with a terse note enclosed.

"When are you going to grow up?" she wrote. "You're just like your father. An apostate. A blasphemer. I'm praying for you both."

A day later, RobRoy and I were back in Mother Harper's yard, observing the screen door Jesus with casual interest, our attention mostly consumed by all the rubberneckers swirling around us. Some were clinging to Bibles, half were praying out loud. One old fellow with an aluminum walker was trying to get healed. RobRoy nudged me, said he was Benny Thibodeaux's great-grandpa. "Man," he said, "I thought that old guy was already dead." The Thibodeaux family ran a broken down chicken farm out on Sarah Jane Road.

I studied the old man. He must've been ninety if he was fifty, shriveled up to a hunchbacked nothing, toothless and drooling. He leaned over his walker grabbing with one hand for the screen door. Mother Harper was beating him back with a broom. "Let it alone!" she hollered. "Quit! You gonna ruin it!" The old man fended off the broom and grabbed but she stood her ground on the porch steps, swinging. It was the first time anyone had seen Mother Harper act that way. But who could blame her? The scene in the yard was loony.

A bunch of Catholics — Cajuns who'd come from across the river in Louisiana — were putting lit candles around the steps, sticking them to the steps when they could, mumbling and fingering rosaries. Baptist, Church of Christ, Assembly of God, Jehovah's Witnesses, United Pentecost, they were all there. Even some Nazarenes. The Methodists were hanging back at the edge, watching, not sure what to do. The Pentecostals were weeping and speaking in tongues. There was everything but Mormons and Jews. RobRoy said he reckoned they just hadn't got wind of it yet but they'd be coming.

"I don't think so," I said, "least not the Jews. They don't believe in Jesus."

"Not yet, they don't," RobRoy allowed. He gave a sly nod toward the screen door. "But wait til they see that."

The following day the crowd was twice as large and people

were beginning to act silly, to my way of thinking. Even RobRoy was starting to smirk. They were crying, singing, shouting. You couldn't take three steps without someone shoving a Bible tract at you. We climbed into the pecan tree to keep from getting walked on. The view was panoramic. One go-getter with an ice chest was selling cold soft drinks in cans. In the blazing summer heat, people were buying. A young guy with an accordion showed up, tried to organize folks into gospel hymns until he tripped and fell. The accordion groaned like a piano dropped off a rooftop. RobRoy and I got the giggles but we held off laughing. We weren't stupid. When people are feeling the spirit, the spirit can turn mighty quick.

Crowd control was zero. Mother Harper, stationed on the back steps, was having a time of it. Her yard was disappearing fast. People traipsing through the garden, flowers getting crushed. Before it was said and done — I mean several weeks later — her back yard resembled a lunar landscape. I reckon Mother Harper regretted the day she looked up and saw that screen door.

That evening at suppertime my grandma never shut up. You'd have thought Lourdes had come to East Texas. It was a sign from God. Chariots in the sky. A burning bush. Water into wine. The Resurrection was going to take place any moment. She was really cranked up. But Grandpa was quiet, faraway like. You could see those gears turning. Click, click, click. In his thinking mode. My grandmother didn't even notice.

After supper I met RobRoy outside and we hoofed it back to Mother Harper's place. It was dark by then. People had flashlights, were singing and praying, people on their knees moaning, everyone slapping mosquitoes. One woman wore a headlamp like rabbit hunters use at night. Of course, you couldn't see anything, just a warped aluminum screen. "Takes natural light!" Mother Harper kept yelling at them. "Go on home!"

The next day there was an article in the local paper. Within a week it was national news. We never saw the reporter but I guess he came by because Time magazine printed a story and photo. Everyone complained the picture was out of focus. RobRoy agreed. All it showed was a blur. It looked accurate enough to me, but by then you kept such views to yourself. The Time reporter called Bethlehem "a bleak southern sawmill town." That comment made the mayor mad and he wrote a letter to the editor that didn't get published. The council discussed banning the magazine but couldn't decide because of the Constitution. Then the controversy blew over, forgotten. Things were moving too fast.

So many people were drifting in that RobRoy and I held a contest to see who could find the most out-of-state license plates. I stopped at thirty-two, got tired of counting. Folks even arrived from overseas. A group of Germans passed through speaking what I supposed was German, though RobRoy said they were sick and clearing their throats. Turk down at the drugstore said they were Lutherans, named after the guy who started up the war between Catholics and Protestants. Then came a group that looked Italian or French. RobRoy claimed he even saw a Chinaman but couldn't prove it. Lou Dawson, the police chief, announced in the paper that more than a thousand folks a day were passing through Bethlehem.

Along about then a heat wave hit. The mercury topped a hundred, the humidity was close behind. Turk's Drugstore ran out of ice cream. The guys hawking iced sodas were getting rich. People converging on Mother Harper's shrine passed out in droves but it wasn't the Holy Ghost. Plain old heatstroke. Mr. Lott complained no one could get through to the Western Auto, his own store. Cars parked in the lot and everywhere up and down the street. All those people in town and he was losing business. That's when my grandpa put up his sign, glued it to the back of the Western Auto building facing Mother Harper's yard. It said:

Pictures of screen door
Ogden Photos
Two blocks west

After that, if locals wanted to buy a camera or film they drove an hour south to Beaumont. No way to get inside my grandparents' shop. It was worse than an Irish bar on St. Patrick's Day. People wall to wall. The place felt like a sauna and smelled like a weight room. There was a line clear out the front door, folks buying those pictures. They shoved and pushed and got into fistfights. Good Christian people, too. And loud, loud. You couldn't hear yourself think. My Grandpa opened early and closed late. If not for the counter he'd have been crushed. He was working like a dog, my grandma was too busy to ask questions or discuss the particulars. That almost killed her. Even worse, she couldn't shake loose to spend any time in Mother Harper's yard. She yearned to be part of it, what she called The Great Awakening.

My grandpa stayed up late every night printing photos. His screen door Jesus picture wasn't any better than the one in Time magazine, I noticed, but people snatched it up anyway. He only charged fifty cents a whack. Some people bought five or six. One lady from Indiana showed up wanting a gross. She paid in advance and we mailed them to her later. That's when Grandpa thought about mail order. He put an ad in the Pentecostal Herald and the orders rolled in, he couldn't keep up. It was running him ragged. He didn't have a regular darkroom. Every night he'd close the bathroom door at home and set up the enlarger on the commode seat. Developing trays in the bath tub, rinse trays in the sink. Drying lines with clothespins stretched all over the house. He was so overworked he showed me how to print and offered me a nickel a picture. But I kept screwing up. He finally told me to beat it. I'd lay in bed and listen to Grandpa stumbling around in the dark.

Meanwhile, Mother Harper was going nuts. By then her pretty yard had turned into a dirt pit. The garden was a memory. All the flowers were gone. Even the pecan tree was sagging. All day long and most the night there was a revival meeting in full swing behind her house. Then one afternoon Benny Thibodeaux's great-grandpa finally got hold of the screen door and claimed it healed him on the spot. He threw down his walker. Half an hour later he was yelling for it back, but that was long enough. The word went out.

People showed up in wheelchairs. A man with emphysema got hauled in on a stretcher. His daughter walked alongside carrying the oxygen tank. Mothers showed up dragging kids born with club feet, cleft palates, Down's syndrome. We had muscular dystrophy, multiple sclerosis, diverticulitis. There was gall stones and kidney stones and people with personality disorders believed to be demons. It was a regular Oral Roberts crusade. Deaf people, mutes, deaf mutes, blind folks, name anything lame or defective and there they came, a live-action encyclopedia of the infirm, physical and mental. Anywhere you looked you saw one Boo Radley or another. One lady brought a dead cocker spaniel and laid it on the porch steps and started bawling. Even RobRoy admitted that was a bit much. Kind of pathetic, he said.

Naturally, it wasn't long before someone heard Jesus on the screen door speaking. It was a big, bare-footed, pie-faced woman from up the country, from back in those riverbottoms. "I heard Him!" she hollered. "He's talking! Praise Jesus! Said He's coming back soon!" After that people came with tape recorders. A man carrying a fancy video camera showed up and announced he was a documentary filmmaker for TV shows specializing in supernatural phenomena. When he started talking about poltergeists and ESP, the crowd ran him off. To tell the truth, he barely got away. He was hoofing it down the street with a torn shirt last we saw of him. Me and RobRoy hung around and watched all day long. We'd stopped shooting pool altogether.

As you'd expect, Mother Harper hadn't visited any sick folks since discovering the miracle. They all were in her yard. She finally quit standing guard duty on the back steps, but she didn't sit on her front porch waving at people, either, except to try and wave them on past. She even stopped going to church. Instead, she stood at the kitchen window watching her yard disappear inch by inch, getting aggravated, feeling meaner and meaner. It was wearing her down. You could see her head through the window. Mother Harper was aging quick. Her hair that was blue had turned whitish-gray and she looked haggard. No sleep will do that.

Of course, all this time, Lou Dawson wasn't getting any sleep, either. As police chief, he was supposed to keep the peace and protect private property. But all night long he was getting phone calls from Mother Harper about the people in her yard. All day long he was trying to do crowd control, just him and one deputy, Walter McAfee, and Walter was more interested in Jesus than he was in crowd control. Between the law and revelation, he was confused. When it comes to duty, where does a person draw the line? Walter was youth director in a Baptist church where he doubled as the Boy Scout leader. He was wider than he was tall, with a huge hanging gut that drew your eye — you couldn't help but stare — a role model for youth.

In short, the crowd was out of control and the law was confused. Mother Harper finally got so fed up that she decided to charge admission. Only that didn't work. She couldn't keep track. She put up a sign and folks ignored it. She strung up a rope and they tore it down. They resented her efforts, you might say. Some of the more outspoken were moved to condemn her. They called her names — Salome, Bathsheba, Jezebel — and consigned her to Hell. They compared her to the money-lenders in the temple. Real colorful, they were. It was strong stuff. As I said, the spirit can turn mighty quick.

Then one day without warning Mother Harper just stood up on her hind legs and fought back. She came out the door onto the back steps, both eyes shooting flames, and told them all a thing or two. That nice old lady cussed a blue streak. She told them where to go and when to get off. She used words I'd never heard, RobRoy either. Up in the pecan tree we were taking notes. She blistered their hides. Those people were falling back on their heels. Then she turned right around and went back inside. And there she stayed. After that, nobody saw Mother Harper for days at a time, although Mr. Lott claimed he saw her old Oldsmobile parked at the Crying Shame, a beer

joint out on Sarah Jane Road, one night. No one believed him.
But RobRoy said he thought it was possible, even likely. He
reckoned the close proximity to a religious miracle had brought
out her true nature and turned her into a reprobate.

Now here's where we come to the good part. I haven't even
mentioned Old Man Nickels. He lived right across the street
from Mother Harper. A tough old geezer, as skinny as Abe
Lincoln and about that tall, only beardless, unkempt, and stoop
shouldered. He had long white hair falling over his ears, and
sunken black eyes, sullen and fierce. Always wiping his mouth
with a dirty wrinkled rag. He chewed plug Red Man's and spent
days in his garage with a table saw making purple martin bird
houses. Sipping home-made whiskey, too. First thing my
grandma had told me when I got to Bethlehem was stay away
from Old Man Nickels. She insinuated there was something
off-kilter about him. Her tone vaguely suggested it had to do
with sex. "Don't never, and I mean *never*, get alone with him,"
she'd said.

The aura of corruption Grandma cast over the man
produced the natural effect of increased curiosity. RobRoy and
I used to stand in the road in front of Mother Harper's place
and watch Old Man Nickels moving about his garage, leaning
out the front door now and then to spit tobacco juice. I told
RobRoy what Grandma had said and he said the guy had never
tried anything funny on him. If he noticed us in the road, the
old man would yell and shake his fist, then turn his back and
sip whiskey from a Mason's jar. RobRoy said Old Man Nickels
was just a little bonkers, that's all. Living alone, making bird
houses and drinking whiskey, what's wrong with that? Sure
beat going to school, and I agreed. Some of those houses of
his were real pieces of work. Triple-decker with chimneys,
porches, front stoops, everything but a jacuzzi. He sold them
on commission through the Bethlehem Feed Store. RobRoy
said that other than making the bird houses, the old man had
been retired since about age twenty-two.

Old Man Nickels had let it be generally known that he
considered the screen door Jesus a lot of hooey. He was alone

on that, or at least the only one willing to say it out loud. He snorted and grinned, told people they were full of malarkey. Then he collected their money. Because he was located across the street, he charged people to park their cars in his yard. Dollar a shot. Except they didn't give him any guff like they did Mother Harper. People who acted snotty got a flat tire. After Jesus showed up, the old man stopped making the bird houses. He just stood in his front yard stuffing the profit down his pants. Every once in a while he'd disappear into his garage for a swig of shine.

Reason I said this is the good part is because everybody knew Old Man Nickels and Mother Harper weren't on speaking terms. It went back to when Mr. Harper was alive and he and Old Man Nickels got into an argument. No one even remembered what about. Religion probably. Mr. Harper was a city councilman and a Baptist deacon to boot. Morally principled and always right. You've met the type. But when he died his widow and Old Man Nickels just kept on not talking. Nothing malicious about it. Just nothing there, nothing to discuss, not even a howdy-do. It was a matter of tradition or, we reckoned, just ingrained habit. But that's what made it so unlikely, what we found out later.

It was early in July. I remember because the Fourth of July parade went around the courthouse square and headed down Main Street where it got stuck in the crowd overspilling Mother Harper's yard and Lou Dawson like to have never got it straightened out. What with all the patriotism and religious fervor flying simultaneously, a serious mess developed. An explosive situation, Lou called it. His deputy, Walter McAfee, was no help at all. Caught squeezed between God and country, Walter froze up. When a fella like that has to choose between the Pledge of Allegiance and the Ten Commandments, he just craters. Walter stood around slack-jawed and helpless while Lou did all the work. But right after that is when this thing happened that threw the whole town off stride.

Early one morning before dawn, Lou Dawson was making his rounds. He usually wasn't up at that hour. It was maybe

21

four-thirty and still dark but he couldn't sleep. He said Mother Harper hadn't called all night and that kept him awake. He was driving down Main Street past the Western Auto when he caught something in the headlights. It was moving across the road kind of slow and jerky. Dark and hulking, he said, but way too big for an armadillo or possum. More like an upright bear, or a giant zombie, or Bigfoot. Lou said he started shaking all over when he saw that shape. Something about it gave him the willies. He slowed down and loosened his gun in the holster, but when he got up closer he saw those smoldering black eyes of Old Man Nickels staring into the headlights, all wild and crazy. His head was twisted sideways, the white hair disheveled and hanging in his face. The old man was wearing his pajamas.

But what Lou couldn't tear his sight from was what he was carrying. A human body was slung over his back. Lou gawked through the windshield, stricken dumb, his skin crawling. He gradually made out a pink nightgown. One of those nylon see-through jobs, he said, with lots of layers so you can't see through it. He finally realized it was a woman riding piggyback. And not just any woman, but Mother Harper.

Old Man Nickels stood there blinking into the headlights, staggering under the weight. He bent almost double, Lou said, and his legs started to buckle. He was barefooted, the long white hair stringing down, clinging to his neck, his face covered in sweat. Finally the old man just sort of kneeled forward, real slow-like, and rolled Mother Harper onto the road. She was dead as a doornail.

Not much happened after that. Lou Dawson tried to keep the incident quiet. He helped Old Man Nickels carry Mother Harper's body into her house before calling Doc Jacobs, who served as county medical examiner on the side. But either someone keeping an all-night vigil at the screen door saw them, which was possible, or Lou couldn't keep a secret, which was more likely. In any case, the facts got out.

It seemed that once he recognized what it was in his

headlights, after Old Man Nickels laid the body in the road, Lou Dawson exited the patrol car in a hurry. "Good God Almighty!" he shouted, "What you gone and done now? Kill 'er?"

"Naw, hell naw," Old Man Nickels gasped, on his hands and knees, "we's just sharing some comfort," and he flailed one arm upward weakly, "when the ol' biddy hollers 'Mercy!' and conks out. That ain't a killin'."

Lou stepped back, realized then the old man hadn't been carrying Mother Harper toward his house. He'd been carrying her back home. That this wasn't a matter of kidnap or murder. That Old Man Nickels, as Lou politely put it, had been interpreting a Good Samaritan's duties beyond the usual range.

"My Lord," he muttered, "Holy Mother of Christ," which was the way the police chief talked when he wasn't in public.

Meanwhile Old Man Nickels climbed to his feet, breathing hard, his fierce bony features lit in the headlamps. "You gonna stand there gumming your teeth," he griped, "or help me fix this situation."

So Lou helped him, only he must've told someone later because the details of what happened, particularly about what got said and what was in Lou's mind, are awfully specific.

As for what followed, Mother Harper's relatives sold her house quick to an Assembly of God evangelist while its value was at a premium. And almost immediately the screen door image started looking less and less like Jesus and more and more like a badly warped aluminum screen. Mr. Turk at the drugstore pointed to wear and tear from the long summer heat as the culprit. "That and other conditions," he said, making room for Mr. Lott's theory of relative humidity. Of course, there were others who argued that what caused the image to disappear was Mother Harper falling into her spiritual backslide, punishable by death. That was RobRoy's theory, and I didn't argue. We were back on the pool table by then, betting ice cream sundaes, with me focused on learning bank shots and trying to stay out of debt.

Still, for months afterward folks continued to appear in Bethlehem looking for the screen door Jesus. They were still dribbling through when my parents returned from Saudi and I moved back to Houston. Those pilgrims would stand in the yard staring at the screen, disappointed, while its new owner stood off to one side preaching latter day fire and brimstone. My grandpa's sign was still posted, though, and a few people drifted up the street to buy pictures. Then that ended, too.

The following summer, when I returned for a week's visit, RobRoy said he hadn't seen anyone behind Mother Harper's house in months. It was a rent house by then, the preacher had moved on, the yard was still bare, the dirt too packed to grow anything. He said Old Man Nickels had gone back to making purple martin houses.

That evening at supper I asked Grandpa if he'd sold any screen door pictures lately and he shook his head. A miracle don't last forever, he said, shrugging. Only he wasn't referring to Jesus, in my opinion. I'd overheard my father remark that Grandpa made more than $5,000 on those screen door pictures. That's what saved his business. Up to then, he'd been going broke.

And I Beheld Another Beast

Mr. Cunningham was on the roof and wouldn't come down. His wife, a tall high-waisted woman with a prominent jaw, stood in the back yard holding a cocked fist against one hip, chin rammed forward. Beside her stood Mrs. Puckett wagging her head, going *unh-unh-unh*. Both women gazed upward toward the roof where Mr. Cunningham wrestled an armful of aluminum poles and wires. He favored an actor in a farce assembling an unruly tent frame.

"Earl, come down from there," Sister Cunningham called out. Her tone was deliberate, as if speaking to a headstrong child. "Come down before you fall down."

The man ignored her. He lifted one metal tube connected to another by a hinge, set it in place and let go. The piece dropped. He grunted, perplexed, then one foot abruptly shot from beneath his haunch down the steep slope, boot sole sliding over asbestos, an awful sound promising catastrophe, like tires skidding sideways on a graveled curve. He quickly leaned upward into the pitch shifting his weight and grabbed the roof ridge with a free hand.

Down on the ground, Mrs. Puckett sucked her breath. *Unh-unh-unh*, she moaned. Propping an elbow in one hand across her stomach, she pressed the fingertips of the other hand to her chin and swayed forward as if the Thinker statue, upon seeing something terrible, had lurched to his feet.

"Earl, you listen to me," said Sister Cunningham. "Get

25

down from there. Right now. And bring that thing with you. You hear me?" She kicked at a knot of nutgrass, exasperated. She was not worried. Her husband was a husky man but coordinated. He was good with his hands and liked to build things and had never fallen off a roof. But she did not intend to have that contraption on her house. "Get down before you fall," she said.

Atop the house, twenty feet up with a bird's-eye view of the yard, of his wife and Mrs. Puckett standing below straining their necks, of the rippling topside of the camphor tree — its big limbs stretching outward, almost touching the roof gable — and of the green summer garden in rows to one side and the empty quail hutch leaning on three legs next to the fig tree, the half-finished beehive beyond, the wheelbarrow loaded with wet sand he meant to spread and a stand of pesky tallows along the back property line he hadn't been able to kill, with a clear view of all that and more, Mr. Cunningham carefully lifted his right leg to straddle the ridge.

He heard his wife again, glanced down, saw her long pale face tilted back, the outthrust jaw. Sometimes he thought of Vernalynn as a bulldozer missing reverse gear and with nowhere to go but straight ahead. Earl Cunningham felt an unaccountable urge to spit, not on her, but near, close by. "I don't want to have to climb up there myself," she said, "I mean it, Earl." A sharp edge burred into the words, her I'm-just-about-fed-up voice.

Looking right and left, he could see the tops of houses along Myrtle Street. A red Frisbee was stuck in the Hebert's rain gutter, Henry Mitchell needed a new roof. Farther away stretched the dark green treeline along the Sabine River bank and all of East Texas, it seemed, rolled out beneath a taciturn summer sky, endless. He laid the folded TV antenna across his thighs, wiped his forehead on a khaki sleeve, thinking he should've checked it on the ground first. Always run an equipment check first, he knew that. He cast an eye about for the boys. Earlier, when he climbed up the ladder, before his wife and Mrs. Puckett appeared on the scene to direct traffic, they'd been standing in the yard watching. After a moment he spied their feet. They were hunkered beneath the fig tree in the shade.

Down below, Mrs. Puckett backed up several steps for a better view, heard a rustle behind. She turned and bent at the waist to see under the lower fig tree branches. She stared at the two boys wearing short pants, barefooted and shirtless, eating ripe purple figs. Snotnosed brats, to her mind, old enough to know better. Sister Cunningham canned those figs. When they saw Mrs. Puckett's face, they scooched back. With a loud snort meant to say it all, she straightened her narrow back and returned to her vigil. Mrs. Puckett observed Mr. Cunningham astride the rooftop grappling with the antenna again. *Unh-unh-unh*, she murmured, as if she'd never seen such a sight. He was gonna put her in the ground from nervous tension, just watching.

Mrs. Cunningham, closer to the house, set both clinched fists against her hips and called out, "I've already told you, Earl, I'll not have that wicked thing on my house. If I have to, I'll shoot it down." Threatening now. It sent a shiver down Mrs. Puckett's back, imagining her neighbor with a gun, blasting away.

The boys crawled over to one side to better see around Mrs. Puckett's stick-like varicosed legs. From the musky shade they studied the scene, silent, chewing the bright pink fig meat, tender and swollen. They'd been eating the succulent fruits and watching the tug of war for a week now, in one form or another, between the grandparents. To date, neither side seemed to be winning, although their grandfather sometimes gave the impression of a defeated man, as though the mere existence of the contest and his role in it equaled a surrender. It was an ongoing skirmish with Mrs. Puckett acting as referee, more or less. The sort of referee you saw on televised wrestling, who managed to stay in the vicinity but was careful not to get too involved. She was a tall skinny woman with facial warts whose predatory eyes skittered like pinballs until they located a suitable object to settle on and bore into. The boys thought of her as a witch and were careful around her lest she cast a secret and malicious spell. Being from New Orleans, they'd heard about voodoo plenty.

The two women and the boys watched as Mr. Cunningham pulled a pair of pliers from a back pocket and began twisting nuts. The balky hinges squawked in protest. They weren't galvanized, a design error like those Mr. Cunningham noticed more and more frequently. Cheap merchandise keeping the economy afloat. Frowning, grunting, using pieces of copper wire off a coil in his shirt pocket, he slowly jerry-rigged the old antenna into shape, got it upright in place. He realized he hadn't heard from Vernalynn in some time. He looked down and saw she'd gone inside the house. Next door, Mrs. Puckett was sitting on her back steps drinking a Dr Pepper, watching. So were the boys, the little boogars. Lying on their backs by the fig tree, both half naked, idly gazing his way and scratching mosquito bites. His youngest son Marlan's boys. Marlan lived in Louisiana, instrument man for an oil exploration firm. He made good money, raced speedboats, married and divorced women. Mr. Cunningham had lost track of the wives and maybe Marlan but not the grandkids. These two arrived each summer for a three-week visit: Daryl, who was nine, and Conway, a year younger, the one digging for agates up his nose. Earl grinned and shot them with the pliers, they waved back.

Earl Cunningham had worked for the power company since returning home from the army, when he had to choose between the GI Bill and regular employment. Not a man to waste time, the day he got off the bus he'd gone over to Gulf States Power and hired on as a lineman trainee. A month later he met Vernalynn at the Dogwood Festival dance. She wasn't a pretty girl but she looked ready, tapping both pumps, he couldn't resist. Vernalynn told him he was a fine dancer for a man with two left feet. Earl respected a woman who spoke her mind and married her soon as he could. Due to appearances, she demanded a three-month engagement. After marriage he taught her to make sauerbraten and say hello and good-bye in German — he'd been stationed there overseas — and after that Vernalynn chose not to learn another thing from him. This was how he told the story to the fellas at the deer camp. In mutual company, though, with Vernalynn listening, he recollected how he'd returned from Germany aiming to catch the prettiest fräulein in East Texas, and danged if he hadn't.

Vernalynn raised the kids and Earl, except for five early years when he traveled, covered the hometown county district, climbing step by step as he gained seniority until he was no longer asked to scale utility poles or handle live wire. Nearing retirement now, he worked in the company's Bethlehem office but refused to wear a necktie. Vernalynn was disappointed, said a tie lent dignity. Let them boys just starting out wear a noose, he replied, I'm too old for ambition.

When Daryl and Conway asked what he did all day, he told them he monitored the grid. Daryl, who wanted to be an NFL quarterback, took this to mean he was a higher up with a football league. He'd heard sports announcers refer to the gridiron. Conway planned to race cars, fast ones. His favorite movie was "Smokey and the Bandit," which he'd seen fourteen times. He said the best show on TV was "The Dukes of Hazard," and Daryl agreed. It was that conversation which prompted the antenna.

"We don't even have a TV," Vernalynn said once he told her his plan, "and we don't want one. Nothing but sin on those things."

"Plan to borrow one," he'd replied. "Henry Mitchell's got a set he don't watch, stuck in his garage. Saved the antenna, too. Just while the boys are here."

They were sitting in lawn chairs beneath the camphor, back yard early evening, the western sky a washboard of rumpled rufous clouds. June, and humid, the sweet green aroma of newly mown grass. A slight breeze up from the coast scatted a heatwave, cicadas whirred in the overhead foliage. Vernalynn fanned herself with a folded copy of the weekly Bethlehem Bugle. According to Abner Huckaby, the editor and owner, economic policies recently implemented in Washington by the federal reserve confirmed certain predictions in the Book of Revelation. She'd interrupted this unsurprising news to hear Earl's plan.

"Brother Odom preaches against TVs," she said, swatting away a fly. "Henry's boob tube can stay in that garage where it belongs."

Vernalynn watched the boys shooting one another with sticks by the garden. Running around, flinging themselves in the grass like they had bees down their pants. Pretty soon they'd be scratching. "Stay off my bean plants!" she hollered. She wished they'd wear shirts, wasn't like they were toddlers.

Her husband gazed at her. His mouth twitched, the pearl wideset eyes flickered. Either amusement or irritation, she couldn't tell. After all these years, you'd think to know. But Earl was odd that way.

"Boob tube," he said. "Where'd you hear that?"

"Church. You, too, if you'd listened." She bent her head to one side making a face and swatted again at the fly. Missed. "If you went more often." She hated the way they landed on your arm, crawled amongst the hairs.

He swung his eyes and fixed them on the two boys, now playing by the beehive. The little monkeys were swordfighting with sticks, both in spreadlegged positions, standing in close, wildly swinging the sticks. Conway ducked and Daryl smacked him on the back. *Splat!* You could hear the sound all the way across the yard. The boys froze, waiting to see if Daryl would cry.

"You gonna poke out an eye!" Vernalynn yelled. "You want a glass eye?"

The boys turned to stand side by side scratching bellies, two miniature naked soldiers at parade rest scrutinizing their grandmother as if she'd just made an intriguing proposal.

"The TV's not for us anyhow," Earl said, "it's for them boys. They get bored come evenings. Lollygag around, get to fussing. It's what they do at home, watch TV. Keeps 'em occupied."

"They not at home."

"No, they're not."

Neither spoke for a while as they watched the purple martins come swooping in, shoveling up unseen insects from the air. The martins nested down the street in a birdhouse behind the Collins house. Lorraine Collins liked her birds. They shot past like black parabolic bullets, gliding and darting, lifting sideways without detectable motion to ascend and turn for another pass. Swallowing mosquitoes, gnats, whatever was handy, more than their body weight each day, according to Abner Huckaby, who promoted purple martins in his newspaper. An alternative to pesticides, he'd written. Daryl and Conway came running up huffing with sticks pressed to shoulders. Each dropped to a kneel and pointed skyward rat-tatting loudly at the slender soaring missiles.

"My Lord," Vernalynn said, watching the boys, "they'd kill anything."

"Marlan ain't trained 'em yet," Earl said. "Plus you could watch those religious programs. I heard that's all they got Sunday mornings, one sermon after another. Ever denomination you can imagine."

"I'm Pentecostal, and I don't need comparative shopping. I'm in my own church Sundays anyhow."

"Except I hear they got 'em on all week long now. They got these special channels with nuthin but preaching and gospel singing twenty-four hours a day. Healing services, testimonials, missionaries talking about cannibals and pygmies, you name it," Earl said, "they got it. Some folks never even leave the house, all they do is watch them shows and pray."

Vernalynn slapped a mosquito and stood up, said it was getting dark and she was going in. She set the newspaper under her arm, declared, "And there ain't no use putting up that antenna cause we're not bringing a TV in our house." She said it matter-of-factly in no uncertain terms, then strolled away through the damp grass toward the back porch door. She could just imagine Brother Odom driving past to see a TV antenna on her roof. From the steps she called back, "I'll have supper ready shortly. Daryl, Conway, you boys come in and wash up."

Earl sat in the dusk and considered. Ever since he and Vernalynn had joined the Holiness Tabernacle ten years ago, once they'd discovered how liberal the Church of Christ was getting, she'd become more and more opinionated. And hardheaded, as if she'd discovered the final answers to mysteries he could hardly articulate. God's plan, the road to salvation, traffic commandments and rules of passage, what clothes to wear and which buildings to stay out of — no movie theaters, for instance, no pool halls — what sort of jokes you could make, the list was endless. And specific. Where'd they get all that stuff? No smoking or drinking was fine, wasn't healthy anyway. Wasn't in the Bible, either, not that he'd ever mentioned it. But no TV? It hadn't bothered him when they got rid of the old one way back when, nothing worth much on it, to tell the truth, except the news maybe. And he hadn't missed that, either, mostly who shot who and how awful things are. Who needed a TV to know that? All the same, he didn't see the need for a rule about it. And now the boys were here, they liked TV.

Plus he'd looked at the listings in the TV Guide at the Market Basket stand. "Smokey and the Bandit" coming on night after next, right after "Dukes of Hazard." The boys' favorites.

No joke, Vernalynn was getting worse. Maybe it was age. Seemed like the bulldozer was missing reverse, as it always had, but now it didn't even own a neutral. He had a good mind to start back to the Church of Christ. That'd fix her wagon. Start a war, too. "No use in that," he muttered into falling darkness. He got up and went toward the house. Fine, he wouldn't change churches again.

But the antenna was going up.

Mrs. Puckett sat in the kitchen with Sister Cunningham, listening. In the other room she heard the TV, a loud motor with lots of tires screeching and somebody hollering, "*Yaaahooooo!*" She glanced at her watch. It wasn't quite yet eight o'clock, so that would be one of the Hazard boys, Bo or Luke. They both were cute as bugs. In a few minutes, of course, there'd be Burt Reynolds in his best movie role, to her point of view. She might just beg a headache, sneak on home. In the meantime, she was acting neighborly, as good neighbors should. Sister Cunningham — she called her that even though they didn't attend the same church, Mrs. Puckett was Southern Baptist — had invited her over, so here she was. Drinking Dr Pepper over ice at the kitchen table. Being neighborly.

"That TV sure is loud," she said, aiming to get right at the nub of things. "I know you're disappointed."

"Yes I am," said Vernalynn. "It tears my heart up. To think judgment day'll come and I'll have to account for things not my doing."

Mrs. Puckett tasted her Dr Pepper. Fortunately for her, she didn't have a husband to run up any bills in the Book of Life, not since Sanford passed away. She sighed thinking about it, his bad prostate and then the cancer, how he'd just shriveled up to nothing, like an old dried prune. Complaining the whole time, naturally. She said, "I know Sanford was relieved to die. He suffered so."

"Well, I'm not about to die," Vernalynn said. "I'm in good health."

Mrs. Puckett's eyes scattered, got interested in the wall cupboards, the way the glass knobs were set against the doors. "Them's nice knobs," she said, "they come from the hardware?"

"I haven't the slightest idea," Vernalynn said. "Earl built those cabinets. You'd have to ask him."

"I'll wait 'til another time," Mrs. Puckett said politely. "He sounds busy." She heard a car crash, a siren. Sheriff Hawg probably thought he had the Hazard boys cornered, he was in for a surprise.

She presently pulled her attention back to her neighbor, who was speaking. "Course those kids in there've never had a chance. Marlan won't stay interested in kids. He likes his women, one after the other. It's a sad thing to watch, the way they come and go. Like musical chairs. Wasn't for the women those boys wouldn't get any guidance at all. Not that they get much." Vernalynn raised her glass of apple juice and sipped. She did not partake of caffeine. "I s'pose they've never seen the inside of a church."

Mrs. Puckett didn't move. This was the first time she'd ever heard Sister Cunningham speak of her youngest. If not for the grapevine, she wouldn't know Marlan had been married five times, was employed by an independent oil company with reputed ties to the mafia, had crashed two new cars and three speedboats and almost died the last time. Burns over both arms, she'd heard, if not for his relative youth and vigor he might've died. Of course, the vigor didn't surprise her, the way he chased women. It explained why his mother never mentioned Marlan, though. Until now. Though her hand on the Dr Pepper glass was getting awfully cold, Mrs. Puckett held still, unwilling to disturb the direction of Sister Cunningham's thoughts.

"I mentioned Moses the other day and they didn't know who I was talking about," the woman continued. "I asked then if they'd ever heard of the Ten Commandments and they said no. Then Conway said yes they did, they'd seen the movie. He helped Daryl remember. It was full of thunder and lightning, they said. But they'd never heard of Abraham or Isaac or even King David ...."

Mrs. Puckett was thinking about Charlton Heston. She'd never considered Moses in a manly sort of way until Charlton Heston. Ever since, when she heard Moses mentioned she usually got a picture of Ben Hur, and vice versa. Mr. Heston worked for the NRA now, protecting the right to bear arms.

"So then I thought, surely they know the New Testament. So I began talking about Jesus, God's only begotten son, how he came into the world to save us, how he was crucified. And I'll be if they didn't act a little vague about *him*."

Mrs. Puckett clucked her tongue. She couldn't help herself. "Unh-unh-unh," she said. "My, my."

"And I *know* they haven't been baptized."

"Why, that's just awful," Mrs. Puckett declared, not thinking, "a father ignoring his children's welfare that way!

I'm surprised the authorities —" and her voice suddenly dropped. She glanced away, weakly concluding with, "Well, I'm just surprised no one's noticed."

Out of the corner of her eye she saw Sister Cunningham draw her shoulders back and wipe the table hard with a dishcloth as if there were crumbs to be found. "Well, not all children are as perfect as some others," she said stiffly.

Mrs. Puckett assumed she was referring not to her own other children, but to Mrs. Puckett's middle child, Eldon, who was languishing in the state prison. He'd accidentally stumbled into some bad company who got him hooked on drugs. Next thing he was robbing a 7-Eleven, not even aware of what he was doing. But serving five-to-ten all the same on account of the gun. Which he never would have fired if it hadn't been for the drugs. She wrote him regular. Eldon wrote back, saying he was fit as a fiddle, doing dandy, having a great time. He sounded bitter.

"How about Bible tales?" said Mrs. Puckett. She tried to sound chipper, not an easy task. But let no one say Malva Puckett talked back catty or harbored a grudge. "I got this children's book, just one story after another. It's the one I used on my own kids. Illustrated in color."

Vernalynn wasn't listening. Elbows propped on the table, she leaned on interlaced hands, the dishcloth hanging between them. Her mind seemed far away in dreamy land, and Mrs. Puckett saw by the wall clock it was ten after eight already. From the other room came the sound of Burt's voice. Then a car door slammed and an engine varoomed, squealing tires and banjo music. She heard the boys laughing, Mr. Cunningham's, too, a low rumbling belly chuckle. She abruptly stood up.

"Well, I better be running along, Sister Cunningham. Got a ton of things to do. Why, I haven't even swept today and here it is almost bedtime. 'Preciate the Dr Pepper, it sure was good."

Mrs. Puckett eased toward the door, had it half open before Vernalynn snapped to. "Oh, thank you, Malva. Thanks so much for coming over. You have a good evening, now."

"Yes, ma'am, and you keep your chin up. Just remember everything goes for the best. That was Sanford's philosophy, and I don't declare if the man wasn't right, bless his heart."

Outside, she trundled down the porch steps and across the yard, her meager legs churning the grass. With all those commercials, she couldn't have missed much. The way Burt swaggered and grinned and fooled the police just tickled her to death. That's the one thing she'd never understood about the Holy Ghost crowd, the way they talked against TV. Without hers, she would've been the loneliest person in the world.

Saturday night, Vernalynn interrupted the TV watching long enough to make her announcement. She marched into the livingroom, was pulled up short by the sight of Earl sprawled in his recliner laughing like a kid. The boys lay belly down on the floor giggling. Her eye roved to the picture tube. Here came a teenage girl riding a bicycle, not paying attention, she hit a curb and went flying over the handlebars. Good grief. Earl and the boys guffawing like it was a fun thing to see someone hurt. A young man appeared then on the TV saying welcome to America's funniest home videos. Next a grown man smoking a cigar drove a golf cart into a pond. Lord have mercy. Vernalynn closed her eyes. The things people would do for entertainment.

"Earl," she said sharply, "you, too, Daryl, Conway. Listen to me. If you're not too busy watching people injure themselves I have an announcement." Her husband said, "What's that, dear?" One eye lingered on the TV as if he might miss something. The boys didn't even look at her. She went right to the set and turned it off, the boys groaned. She squared off. "Tomorrow morning we're all going to church," Vernalynn said flatly. "I'm telling you now. All of us. You'll get up, get dressed, we're going. I don't want to hear a word about it except thank you, ma'am. You understand me?"

They gazed back blankly. "Alright then." She reached to switch the TV back on, jerked away her hand. Let them do it. She would not abet corruption.

The next morning she rousted the boys early and made pecan waffles, their favorite. Thinking she did not want to seem harsh. If the boys associated church with pleasant events it couldn't hurt. She put a pile of her special canned figs on each waffle and listened to the radio tuned to the Sunday Morning Gospel Hour on the local AM station. Gospel hymns set a nice Sunday tone. The Happy Goodman Family, for instance, who sang harmonies. All the Goodmans were stout as cornfed sows but they weren't ashamed to be Christians, she could give them that, they weren't afraid to be happy.

Once Daryl and Conway had eaten she checked their hair and ears. Conway's was full of wax. He squirmed like a garden snake but she got him clean, told both boys to sit in the livingroom and wait until she was ready. "And don't move," she said. Meaning stay off the floor, don't go in the yard.

Mr. Cunningham backed the Chevrolet out the garage, the others climbed in, a few minutes later they pulled under a stand of yellow pines in the churchyard. The Holiness Tabernacle was a simple clapboard building set on concrete piers, whitewashed, unadorned by pretense or steeple. An humble home, Brother Odom called it, for the humble children of God. Inside the single room lit by windows along both walls were two rows of narrow wooden pews facing an altar call bench and the rostrum. On the slightly elevated rostrum stood the pulpit; behind it a baptismal tank was set into the wall. On the inset wall behind the tank a painted picture of Calvary. The dry scent of floating dust, slanting light. Vernalynn often thought how plain the Tabernacle seemed compared to the brick Church of Christ, where people were more concerned with outside appearances than what lay within.

They sat in the third pew on the right, the Cunningham pew. Following song service and healing prayers, Brother Odom preached on the end times, touching on last week's article in the Bugle proving the fulfillment of Revelation prophecies. A retired maintenance man for the city, Brother Odom often mispronounced words and lacked ministerial training. "I am not an eddicated person," he admitted, "but I

know my Bible. The Saviour's own chosen was no more'n
fishermen, not a banker or professor in the bunch." Besides,
anyone who cared to read would understand Revelation. "The
first beast rising outa the sea with ten heads and a lion's mouth
is godless communism," he said quietly — Brother Odom was
not a screamer — "with the coming Antichrist either a Russian
or a Chinese, we ain't sure yet. And the second horned beast
which is a dragon, that's the Roman Catholic church, the pope
astride its back," and here he raised a cautionary hand, "while
the Mark of the Beast, six-six-six, that stands for computer
numbers we each'll receive as identities, like inmates in the
state prison. Gonna rig this thingamajig to your brain and track
you through TV sets." He paused for effect and Vernalynn
wagged her head along with the others; they let out small
anxious murmurs of concern. "So you better get prepared,"
Brother Odom concluded, "cause that's what's coming down
the pike. Are you ready? Are you saved? When the Rapture
comes, will you go? Won't be no second chances. And it's just
around the corner, signs of the times everywhere. Read your
Bibles, folks. Be one to say you stood up from the mud and
looked around."

Vernalynn thought it'd been a fine sermon, and timely,
though a mite complicated for Daryl and Conway. She'd have
preferred something less deep, something simpler, such as Jesus
walking on the water or healing the lame. Both boys had acted
bored. They'd wiggled and fidgeted throughout, she'd jerked
Conway's finger from his nose more than once. A bad habit,
she'd noticed. Recalling Marlan had been the same, always
digging, usually eating what he'd found.

When service ended and Mr. Cunningham stood and
jangled the car keys, saying he'd go warm the car motor while
Vernalynn said her howdies and byes, his wife told him they
weren't leaving yet. "We're staying long enough to get these
boys baptized," she said, "I've already spoken to Brother
Odom." She saw the peculiar look come over her husband's
wide face. Mouth twitching, the flickering eyes.

"You talk to Marlan about this?"

"Why, of course not," she replied, tossing her head. "Why'd I talk to Marlan? Wouldn't care one way or the other anyhow. That's his problem."

"He's their daddy."

"And I'm their grandmother."

"Well," said Mr. Cunningham, "that's why."

She leaned forward, spoke low between clenched teeth. "You listen to me, Earl Cunningham. You bring a TV into my house, put up an antenna anybody in town can see. Sit there and watch it, sound all over the house. That's the kind of example you set. We're the only chance these boys got, and look at you," and she thrust her purse beneath one arm and the Bible beneath the other, saying, "Besides, this is between me and my Lord. These boys are going to get baptized."

Daryl and Conway watched, curious to know which way it'd go, wondering what baptism meant. Daryl noodled the vague idea it had to do with Mrs. Puckett. He'd heard her brag she was a Baptist. Presumably, the term referred to magic of some evil sort, smoking pots and bullfrog's eyes, a crystal ball, maybe little demon monkeys with wings that snatched at you. He didn't want a thing to do with Mrs. Puckett and discreetly tugged at Conway's shirtsleeve. They sidled away toward the side aisle. Their grandmother swung around like she had eyes in back and told them to stay put. "You're going to get baptized this morning. You know what that means? Brother Odom—" and she cranked her head about for the preacher, found him and pointed, "he's going to stand you in the baptismal tank and dunk you under water."

Conway's eyes ballooned. He muttered something she didn't hear.

"What?"

"Said he can't hardly swim," Daryl spoke up. He put an arm around Conway's shoulders. "Me neither."

The two of them shifted weight from one foot to the other, uneasy, poised for flight like fawns caught in headlamps. They watched their grandmother give their grandfather a sharp knowing glance, as if to say, "Listen to that. What did I tell you?"

Mr. Cunningham shook his head frowning. "Marlan never taught you to swim?" They both shrugged. "Told us he would," Daryl offered, "only he ain't. Not yet."

"Well, you needn't worry," Vernalynn said in a comforting tone, taking them by the shirtsleeves, pulling them forward up the aisle, "cause this water isn't deep. Chest high maybe. Plus we'll be right there watching. We'll put you in a robe, and Brother Odom will say, 'In the name of the Father, and of the Son ...'"

Earl Cunningham went out to the car to wait. He didn't want any part of it.

For three days they'd been calling one another Father and Son. "Let's go catch some bees in a jar, Father," Conway would say, grinning, and Daryl would reply, "Sounds good to me, Son." Conway being the Son because he was younger. They had not yet decided who was the Holy Ghost. If they were to get a Shetland pony, he'd be the Holy Ghost. But their grandmother had nixed the idea, saying where were they gonna put a horse. Once back home, they decided, their step-mom Rouella's poodle Frenchie could serve as the Holy Ghost. In the meantime, they let it ride and amused themselves with Father and Son. "Hey, Son, wanna go down to the river and throw at turtles?" Daryl said. "Yeah, let me get my rocks, Son," Conway replied. Both of them smirking, careful Grandma Cunningham was out of earshot.

Mrs. Puckett overheard them. She was coming over the yard to see Sister Cunningham at noon — they'd not seen one another all day — the boys were playing with the water hose by the garden. She saw the older one hang his thumb over the nozzle and spray the younger, calling out, "Look out, Son! In the name of the Father, you're getting baptized!" The other one jumped up and down with his mouth open, swallowing water, then shouted, "Hallelujah, Father!" and fell writhing to the ground. Both of them were stripped to underwear, naked as jaybirds practically. She could see their dinky privates through the wet cotton shorts.

My word, she thought, and scrambled up the back steps to knock at the door. A minute later she was watching Sister Cunningham dress down the holy little terrors while they dug into the grass with their toes. The boys nodded and said *un-huh* and *yes ma'am* and shot Mrs. Puckett evil glances. For her part, she thought Sister Cunningham was letting them off easy. Thinking she ought to take a belt, tan their hides good. If she herself had done that more often with Eldon, he might not've got in bad company, ended up in confinement. But no, she'd let Sanford handle the discipline. He'd never had her backbone.

"That's the end of it, and I mean it," Sister Cunningham was saying, "now go inside and change shorts, the both of you." The boys shambled past. They gave Mrs. Puckett a final spiteful glance. "They don't like me," she said.

"You told on 'em," said Sister Cunningham, as if that justified a lack of courtesy. "It sure is boiling." She squinted against the blazing midday light, wiped sweat from her cheeks with both fingertips. "And sticky. Anyway, they'll be leaving in a couple of days. Marlan's picking them up Saturday." She sighed.

"Well, at least they're baptized," Mrs. Puckett observed, always one to see the bright side. "You done everything you could." She raised her gaze toward the roof, studied the antenna outline against a powderpuff cloud drifting past. "Surprised you get good reception with that ol' thing. Must be a hunnerd years old."

Sister Cunningham didn't bother to look up. Said, "It's coming down Saturday. You want something to drink?"

"Why, I surely wouldn't mind, thank you. Dr Pepper if you have it. A person works up a thirst in this steambath."

They went up the steps, Mrs. Puckett commenting on the heat, that she'd heard a report this summer was expected to be the hottest in a decade. Scientists thought it was ozone, which worsened in summer. Something about a missing hole. "And then comes hurricane season," she noted. "They say this is s'posed to be a busy year for hurricanes."

41

Half an hour later in the kitchen Mrs. Puckett was still talking about hurricanes when the telephone rang. "I recall when Carla came through, remember it like yesterday," she was saying, "how that water come up so fast, dirty water smelling like death. And then those winds. Mercy! You know it pushed a broom straw through a two-by-four in the Hebert's back yard? Seen it myself afterward. Just imagine the power, that little bitty straw. I told Mr. Hebert, 'You oughta take a picture a that and send it to the paper. They might even pay you sumthin,'" and Mrs. Puckett hesitated, recollecting, "only he never did, didn't act that interested. Being a banker, maybe he didn't want the publicity. And then that other one hit a ways down the coast three, four years back. Below Galveston, right after Sanford died. Betty, it was, or Dean, I forget. Course all we received from that one was rain —"

And then the phone rang.

Sister Cunningham answered in the livingroom. Mrs. Puckett heard her say, "Marlan." Then she said *okay* and *I understand* and *that'll be fine* several times between pauses. Marlan probably calling to say he wasn't coming Saturday, asking if the boys could stay longer. Which would complicate the crisis over the the TV, that was Mrs. Puckett's first thought. When Sister Cunningham returned directly, her face expressionless, Mrs. Puckett was studying the knickknacks on the window shelf above the sink from her seat. "That sure is a cute ceramic," she said, motioning with her chin, "it come from the Dollar Store?"

"What's that?"

"That hen and chicks group. Has lots of detail, you don't hardly see that anymore."

Vernalynn sat down without looking. The ceramic figurine had been sitting there for at least five years. "That was Marlan," she said, "calling from the road. DeRidder. He'll be here in an hour or so for the boys."

Mrs. Puckett couldn't decide whether this was good news or bad, so all she said was, "DeRidder, Louisiana?"

Vernalynn ignored the question, the DeRidder across the Sabine River in Louisiana being the only DeRidder in the world, so far as she knew. "He and his wife got some time off, they're taking the boys over to Houston," she explained. "Go to a ball game, spend a day at Astroworld, Marlan said, which they've never been to. He said there's some speedboat races outside Houston on the weekend." She sipped her apple juice. "I sure hope he's not racing."

"I thought he was injured with two burnt arms," Mrs. Puckett blurted. She couldn't imagine a man racing boats in that condition. Marlan Cunningham must be some sort of racing fiend, all she could say. She noticed she was being closely observed by Sister Cunningham. The pale face was unpleasant, the eyebrows dipped in a vee.

"Where in tom hill'd you get that notion?"

The question startled Mrs. Puckett. She'd never heard Sister Cunningham use such language, it flustered her. She recoiled in the chair, feebly replying, "Well, I don't rightly recall, now that you mention it. I reckon it come from somewhere unreliable."

"It certainly did," Vernalynn said. Thinking the one thing that aggravated her most was incorrect hearsay and rumor. This was because she'd once had the habit herself but had overcome it through self-discipline and prayer. *Who shall abide in thy tabernacle? He that backbiteth not with his tongue.* Right there in Psalms fifteen. She'd rather cut out her tongue than spread malicious gossip. She'd often noticed the tendency to this defect in Mrs. Puckett but out of charity had never pointed it out. Setting the facts straight, she said, "Far as I know, Malva, the only thing Marlan's ever burned is bridges."

Mrs. Puckett felt tempted to ask which ones but the firm carriage to her neighbor's mouth decided against it. "Well, we've all burned bridges," she said cheerfully. "Lord, I know I have." She smiled wanly, as if to express the regret she sometimes felt at having done so, though she really couldn't think of any bridges she'd burned or even crossed. Her life had been fairly uneventful except for Sanford's long illness and Eldon's ordeal.

Then Sister Cunningham excused herself to begin supper, saying Marlan and his new wife Rouella planned to stay the night, leave for Houston the next morning. That way they'd get to visit with Mr. Cunningham after work. This would be the first time either had met Rouella, she said. All she knew was that her daughter-in-law was a registered nurse and worked long hours.

"Is that right?" Mrs. Puckett said, swallowing the last of her Dr Pepper. Personally, she'd heard Marlan's latest worked at a clinic, an abortion clinic, even though she was Roman Catholic, being a Cajun, and was divorced from a gynecologist who'd lost his license. Rouella. Mrs. Puckett hoped she got the chance to meet her. If the opportunity presented itself, she planned to ask when, in her opinion, was the moment the spark of life began. The exact point when you became a person.

Vernalynn had a big pot of chili cooking on the stove — she planned cornbread and a side salad to go with — when she heard a car pull into the drive. Before she could call the boys they blew past her through the kitchen and out the back door hollering, "Dad! Dad!" She wiped her hands on the apron and fussed with her hair and followed.

Marlan stood in the yard near a sparkling new cherry red Thunderbird with Daryl and Conway clinging to his legs. They each balanced on a shoe, right and left, and he stiff-legged forward like a man on stilts while they tried to hold on, laughing. Off to one side, a dark-eyed olive-skinned woman with blunt features and curly black hair smiled and crossed her arms, watching. She was short and full-bodied with prominent breasts, wore an apricot yellow sundress decorated with colorful parrots and open-toed sandals. Vernalynn thought she looked dressed for a luau.

"Hey! Hey!" Marlan protested, "you boys're getting heavy! Whatcha been eating, lead taters?"

"Figs!" Conway shouted, "thousands a figs!"

"Mrs. Puckett put a spell on us," Daryl said, "turned us into stone."

"Oh, she did not," said Vernalynn.

"Hey, mom." Marlan grinned. Getting husky as his father, she noticed, with the same wide face and gray eyes. His hair styled in a crewcut. "Mom, this is Rouella." He turned his grin on the olive-skinned woman. "Rouella, mom." They nodded and smiled, Rouella said, "Those boys are a handful, aren't they?"

"Who? These squirts?" Marlan grabbed a head in each elbow and squeezed, the boys yelped. "What you fellas been doing?" His eyes scanned the yard, lifted briefly toward the antenna on the roof, back down.

"Watching TV," Daryl said. "Seen Smokey and the Dukes all in one night."

"I learnt to swim," said Conway, not to be outdone.

"You did not," retorted his brother, "all they done was dunk you."

"Almost drownded, too," Conway announced proudly, "and Frenchie's gonna be the Holy Ghost." Still perched on a shoe gripping a pants leg, he leaned backward to look up at his father. "I'm the Son."

Marlan bumped him on the forehead with a knuckle and chuckled. "Sounds like you boys been to church."

"Yeah," Daryl said, "now we're Baptists."

"Oh, you are not," said Vernalynn.

Rouella had come up beside Marlan and the boys. She put a hand on her husband's shoulder and stroked Conway's head, then Daryl's. "Speaking of which, we're going to start going to mass every Sunday," she said. "Your daddy and I discussed it and he agreed."

Marlan closed one eye and made a wry face at his mother. "Just listen to her. She's gonna straighten me out yet, I swear."

Vernalynn didn't hear. At the word *mass* something had gone out of her, left her bereft, frozen cold as ice, as though the word possessed the power to suspend time, and motion too. Her mind had come to a halt, then clicked forward one notch to the words *Roman Catholic*, and locked in place.

"Mom? You okay?"

Marlan speaking. She jerked awake and saw her son standing there in the yard with the boys and the dark-eyed woman who was his wife holding Conway's jaw cupped in her hand, gazing at him, saying, "You'll go to the catechism Saturday mornings for a while. Know what that is?"

"We gotta get baptized again?" Daryl asked. "They gonna dunk us?"

"Why, whatever do you mean?" Rouella said.

"Grandma already got us dunked," the boy replied, "last week at the church, what I was saying. They gonna do it again?"

Marlan grinned, said, "Well, I'll be, Rouella, mom already took care of that part, looks like," but the younger woman had already fixed her black eyes on Vernalynn to say, "You went and baptized these boys?" Hot disbelief in her voice. "Without asking?"

Vernalynn's knees felt weak. "Why, they're my grandsons," she said, mustering a frown. "Marlan's boys."

"Into that holy roller crap?" Rouella demanded.

"Rouella," Marlan said.

"Is that what you done? Is it?"

The questions hammered Vernalynn, she felt a little dizzy. Then she caught hold, straightened her back, thrust her jaw forward. "Now you just listen here, young lady —"

"What? You gonna tell me I'm not their mother?" Rouella tossed her head and took a sudden step forward, almost a lunge. Vernalynn stumbled back from the force of it, as if she'd been shoved. The woman's face loomed in front of hers, a threatening thing full of outrage and heat and two flashing eyes. The hard pointed voice drilling in further. "So I don't have any say? That what you mean?" The younger woman stopped, threw back her shoulders, her olive-skinned throat darkly flushed. Her full mouth was wrung with scorn, with exasperation. "I just don't get it. Of all the *nerve*."

Marlan put a hand on his wife's arm, said, "Rouella now, take it easy, sweetie-pie."

She shook him off angrily. "Don't fool with me, Marlan, not now."

Vernalynn felt a sickness in her belly, and fear. She wanted to bolt, get away, she couldn't believe this horrid scene was occurring, with her smack in the middle. Trembling, she garnered every ounce of strength to hold her ground. "Those boys needed it," she said, "they need taking care of."

"That's right," her daughter-in-law retorted, "and I aim to do it, Marlan and I both do, and we don't need some busybody sticking their —" She whirled around to the boys, told them, "Go get your things, we're leaving. Now." A direct order, beyond any dispute, and Daryl and Conway jumped and scooted into the house. Rouella turned back to face Vernalynn, her body seeming to radiate a power that was of itself and nothing else, no need for appeal elsewhere, self-contained and absolute, Vernalynn thought, it was frightening. "You listen to me," the younger woman said, "don't you ever, *ever* mess with my family again."

Before Vernalynn could absorb this latest blow the woman turned to Marlan and said, "I'll be in the car." She marched away. A moment later a car door slammed.

"My Lord," Vernalynn murmured. Tears welled in her eyes. The way the girl talked, like she owned the world. "My Lord, I never ..."

Marlan blew his breath out and rocked on his feet, rubbing both eyes. "Whooee," he said, "didn't think we'd get into all that." He tugged at his pants, snapped the fingers of one hand into the palm of the other. "Listen, mom, I been meaning to mention Rouella's temper. But I thought I'd ..." and he shrugged helplessly, "just sorta wait, you know. See how it went." He glanced up the drive toward the car. "She's a spicy little Cajun pepper, I'll tell you that much, she got cayenne in her blood."

Vernalynn looked away from him, brushed a wisp of hair from her forehead. "My Lord," she said weakly, "I just never ..."

"Aw, mom, you can't take Rouella seriously, not right now, she's just upset. It'll go better next time. I'll see if I can't get her to ... well, look, maybe we'll stop by Sunday on our way home."

Vernalynn felt as if someone had yanked her guts out.

"You're not leaving? Why, you can't leave, your dad isn't even home yet."

"Well, I think we better," Marlan replied, shaking his head, "for now anyhow."

"I cooked supper," she said, reciting in a daze, "the beds are made up. Your dad —"

But her son was still shaking his head no. "You seen Rouella, mom, there just ain't no use in us staying. Not this time. Tell dad I'm sorry he missed me," and he tilted his head, the wide gray eyes apologetic, saying, "She's a good woman, mom. And real family oriented. Just a tad strongminded."

The boys tumbled out the back door and down the steps fussing, bumping their carryalls, telling each other to get out of the way. They came up to Vernalynn to offer cursory hugs and mumbling good-byes, then rushed off toward the Thunderbird arguing over who'd sit where. Marlan gave her a quick hug, too, saying, "Thanks for everything, mom. Tell dad I'll give him a call," and then he was at the car, as well, opening the door. It was all going so fast, Vernalynn couldn't keep up. She thought she might fall over but for the fact it was spinning around her, holding her upright by some centripetal effect on the paralyzed axis of her defeat. She heard Marlan shout. He was grinning and pointing upward, toward the roof. "See you got a TV!" he yelled, then he was in the car backing out into the road and the Thunderbird disappeared down Myrtle Street.

Vernalynn stood motionless. Why, it'd been like a dream, a bad dream, where everything happens so fast you don't have time to think before another bad thing is happening, and it goes like that until it ends, one thing after the other, until you wake up with a jerk breathing hard going *My goodness, what was that?* She stood in the yard fingering the apron, thinking if she stayed put, didn't move, the world which had so recently flown apart would collect itself again. She would just stand there until it did.

Next door, in her kitchen, leaning against the sink cabinet peering through the cracked venetian blinds, Mrs. Puckett said *mmm-mmm-mmm.* What had all that been about? Thinking the other woman must've been Rouella. Thinking she probably wouldn't get to meet her now, ask that question. The woman had flat out waded into Sister Cunningham like a cyclone, too, way it looked from here. *Mmm-mmm-mmm.* Ran right over her, could see it plain as day.

Mrs. Puckett sipped her Dr Pepper, peeking through the blinds at her neighbor. She still hadn't moved. Poor Sister Cunningham. Probably in shock, one of those post-trauma things. Maybe she ought to go next door, see if she was alright. At such times it was helpful to talk.

She did not want to talk. When Mrs. Puckett came over the two went into the house where in the kitchen Vernalynn told her neighbor to help herself, cold drinks in the refrigerator, and then she went out down the hall into her bedroom, closing the door. Mrs. Puckett sat at the kitchen table drinking Dr Pepper in case she was needed.

In the bedroom, Vernalynn stretched out on the bed fully dressed, an arm laid over her face, eyes closed. Her mind went round and round, snagging on words like *mass* and *Roman Catholic*, playing terrible images of Marlan and the boys on their knees cowering below a great smoking beast, a huge roughscaled reptilian predator, a dragon with two horns and enormous razored teeth. It opened its mouth, flames shot out. The scorched air smelled putrid with decay. Marlan and the boys scrambled to their feet and began to run, glancing backward, horrified, the beast after them. She watched as the figures retreated into the distance, becoming tinier and tinier until they disappeared altogether. All the while, her voice calling to them, useless. Her breast heaved and a stabbing sob rose into her throat, stuck there. Something was returning across that empty landscape, coming toward her ... looming larger ...

And she saw then it was the scarlet colored beast and as it neared she saw astride its back a half-naked woman arrayed in purple and crimson scarves, wild black hair flying and her dark nippled breasts draped in precious stones and pearls, her hands covered in blood, the blood of Jesus and the blood of ancient martyrs and the blood of her own children dripping down the glistening naked thighs. And Vernalynn saw the numbers burnt into the woman's forehead, 666, and gazed into the fierce laughing face with its blunt features and the black flashing eyes and saw it was her daughter-in-law. The mouth flew open, there came a long hysterical shriek; Rouella's tongue split into a dozen writhing snakes. Vernalynn raised her arm and pushed down into the bed mattress, trying to get away.

Later, when Mr. Cunningham got home from work, he found Mrs. Puckett sitting alone at the kitchen table. The house was quiet. "Your son Marlan and his wife come for them boys," Mrs. Puckett said. "Sister Cunningham's in the bedroom resting." He stood there expressionless scratching the corner of one eye with a forefinger as he took in this news. Mrs. Puckett fidgeted with her blouse collar. She had not ever been alone in a room with Mr. Cunningham, or any other man, since Sanford's death. She felt awkward and thought perhaps she might should leave. "I was just staying 'til you got here," she said, rising.

He nodded and ambled down the hall to the bedroom, opened the door and went inside. Vernalynn was lying on the bed asleep. She looked small. He had never known her to sleep at this hour, and no dinner on the table. When he removed her shoes she stirred but did not awaken. He closed the door softly and in the kitchen fixed a glass of ice water and took it outside.

The sun was lowering in the west like a dark red balloon sinking in slow motion and the heat was giving way to early dusk beneath the camphor tree where he sat. He felt tired. A cicada took up its evening chant, others joined, the purple martins would arrive soon, and the crickets. His gaze roamed the back yard, lighted briefly on the beehive, passed on by the three-legged quail hutch and the fig tree loaded with ripe fruit and back past the pale light coming from Mrs. Puckett's kitchen window. But for the humming of insects, a hush had fallen over the yard, as if the entire world was surrendering in its fatigue to a small temporary death.

He lifted his eyes in the settling gray and studied the dim outline of the antenna on the roof above the end gable, decided he would take it down tomorrow, leave work early. In the gathering twilight, if he tried it now, he might lose his footing.

He might fall.

The Serpent

This happened —

In early March, grandmother dreamed my aunt had become a serpent.

Spring was breaking along the East Texas bayous. The winter rains had passed, the days grew warm. Beneath tangled cascades of Spanish moss, spiked funnels of hyacinth spread lavender blooms over mud-colored water. Creeper vines encircled tupelo trunks overnight. Sweet honeysuckle, swollen green and tender, clung to the brushy bayou shoulders.

The honeyed sun enveloped this tumescent landscape, draped it in succulent warmth. My aunt, the wife of grandmother's son, was given to simple pleasures. She could not resist. She began taking long strolls in the afternoon wearing only a shortsleeved sundress and sandals. The family's beliefs forbid such an unchaste display of flesh. My uncle warned her. She, undeterred, merely smiled.

Nakedness is shameful to a righteous woman, grandmother said just before she dreamed.

By April a scaly growth had begun to creep over my aunt's feet. The local physician prescribed a variety of lotions and my aunt applied herbal gumbos, but they proved useless, just as grandmother predicted. The red rash turned gray and dry skin peeled away, revealing still more of the disease underneath. My aunt sat quietly in a rocking chair by her bedroom window. She gazed outward, sometimes humming softly. The smell of sickness soon pervaded the room, and my uncle sent once more for the doctor.

The doctor examined my aunt. Perplexed, he stepped away and packed his leather bag. He went with my uncle onto the front porch where he stood silently smoking a cigarette. Afterward, he walked to one end of the porch where the wild wisteria hung trellised. He caressed the dark green leaves. This time of year, he said, things grow so quickly. He suggested yet another lotion, then left muttering beneath his breath.

On Easter Sunday, Brother Odom preached on Christ's transfiguration. The miracle of the Ascension, he said, was that Jesus had thrown off the cloak of flesh and become the luminous Spirit of God. My aunt, unable to walk, stayed home in bed. The flesh of her calves had become the neon green of ruined meat in the market. Grandmother said the Lord's judgment is quick for the transgressor. Over Easter dinner, we prayed for my aunt who lay in a fever next door.

The doctor returned. He stood on the porch smoking, said there is so much we do not know. So much, so very much. Frowning, he prescribed sedatives, suggested more prayer, and left.

My uncle denounced Lucifer and reaffirmed his life to Christ. He wore a path between his mother's door, where he begged her to intervene on his wife's behalf, and the bed where his wife lay delirious. But grandmother refused to intercede. We've done all we can, she said, she must rebuke the devil just as you did. Christ needs no mediator.

My uncle, chastised, bowed his head. Sleepless and miserable, he returned to his wife.

Sedatives were ineffective by the end of May. My aunt cried out fiercely, clawed her legs, her belly. We tied her arms to the bed frame with sheets after she tore flesh from her thighs. She lay motionless between violent fits, as if in a trance. She appeared lucid but said nothing and refused to eat. My uncle paced the room quoting scripture.

By midsummer the disease had reached her breasts; the stench drove away all but my uncle, the doctor, and me. Half mad in the heat from misery and fatigue, my uncle resorted to writing with charcoal on the walls of the room. He scrawled *Get Thee Behind Me Satan* in large bold letters above the head of the bed. He sat hours on end on a low stool reading the Bible aloud, mumbling when he fell into fitful naps. Once he cried out in a dream, Lord Jesus Christ have mercy on us!

Throughout the house the fragrance of perfumes and alcohols diluted the pungent odor of rotting flesh. Despite screens on the windows flies swarmed the room. The doctor came daily to bathe my aunt in alcohol waters, but still the eggs hatched and maggots appeared between her toes. She moaned and struggled against the bindings. She broke free. With a terrible cry, she lacerated her feet before we subdued her.

The doctor spent evenings poring over medical journals. His research proved fruitless. He wrote to a skin specialist in Houston, who replied he should amputate immediately. Amputate what? he fumed. It is everywhere. Desperate, the doctor applied a strange platinum colored paste that caused my aunt to scream for an hour. My uncle held his head and ran from the room. The flesh turned black from mercury and lead but continued to decay.

During this time, grandmother visited my aunt only once. In late September, after the summer heat subsided, she stood in the doorway and silently gazed at the figure stretched across the bed. She stared for a long time. I am not the Lord, she finally uttered, and she is not Lazarus. Then she took my uncle aside. He gathered his things and moved into his mother's house. Before leaving, he stood above his wife and raised his arms to the ceiling. I commend you to our Saviour, he cried, and he fled.

The doctor, too, never returned. He spent a week in the neighboring county fighting an outbreak of influenza, then went fishing. We have reached the limits of science, he wrote, and now it is up to God or Satan.

By All Saints Day my aunt was blackened head to toe. She no longer struggled against the bindings, so I untied them. She wet her lips with the flick of a slender tongue. Except for the flickering tongue and two fierce reptilian eyes, she appeared a corpse. Her eyes remained fixed on the ceiling above the bed where her husband had scrawled *We Suffer As Christ Suffered*. From between her lips came an intermittent hiss.

It was a brisk November morning when she slid from the bed and slithered across the floor. She curled up behind a trunk in the corner and hissed. Her head swung back and forth, her gleaming, tar-dark eyes lingered on mine. I slowly stood and backed from the room, closing the door.

The crisp autumn air was loud with the sound of blackbirds. Trees glistened orange and red in sunlight, and the cool aroma of cypress and cedar spread over the morning. From high overhead tumbled the soft squeaks of snow geese heading south in great V-shaped flocks. I went to grandmother's house. The transfiguration is complete, I said.

Grandmother and my uncle kneeled at the sofa, the family Bible spread before them. We are consumed by evil, but by His Grace we are forgiven, grandmother said.

They went next door then, she with the Bible and he with an axe. From the yard, I watched. They stood on the porch and my uncle pushed open the door. The serpent came swiftly and struck at grandmother's ankle. She screamed and turned, raised the Bible aloft as the axe fell heavily across the serpent's back.

My uncle and I buried the corpse beneath a willow beside the bayou. We labored in silence, gave no eulogy and left no marker.

Grandmother lived until Christmas.

Star Man

Doss picked up Little Red at his trailer in the late afternoon. The bruised winter sky lay punctured in the treetops bleeding gray drizzle and they dropped down Highway 87 out of Bethlehem in the gathering dusk. They shot through the deep green woods, running parallel to the Sabine along sandy riverbottom ridges until they hit Deweyville in a light rain just after dark. On Christmas Eve the wet streets were empty, the stores unlit. The small country town seemed deserted.

Doss turned off the main thoroughfare between the Diamond Shamrock and a closed pit-smoked rib stand. He geared the growling truck down, asking, "This the road?"

Little Red leaned forward looking. He scraped the back of a freckled hand along his chin, then waved it at the wrist. "Up there, past that bridge."

The tires burped over road joints crossing the narrow creek draped in bone-white fog and Doss pulled into a muddy lane beneath dripping loblollies and oak. He stopped in a clearing with a sixty-foot trailer and attached carport. A single strand of red Christmas lights framed the trailer door, blinking aimlessly. He honked twice before Luther Broussard came loping out in his coveralls and welder's cap gripping a canvas carryall and a metal lunchbox. Little Red scootched over. Luther squeezed in, shoved the gear beneath his long legs, kicked it back with a steel-toed workboot.

"Hoo-whee, we got some weather, us."

"Better'n snow," said Little Red.

"Temperature drop we get sleet," Luther said. "That rig ice up, then we be crying for snow, yeah."

"My kids, they're crying for it right now," said Doss. He twisted his neck around backing the truck into the trees, a burly thick-chested man with a wide face and blond crewcut under a Gulf Drillers gimmee cap. "They never seen snow."

"Been in it asshole deep myself," bragged Little Red.

"That so?" Luther grinned. "Was maybe a foot deep, huh?"

"Don't even start," the younger man replied. Short and wiry, with small blunt hands, he rolled his shoulders and reached a can of Skoal from a flannel shirt pocket, saying, "Crack that window, you skinny coonass, I want some air."

They were quiet until the truck was back on the four-lane headed toward the coast, the three of them thinking about the next several hours of passage — coursing the coastal prairie southwest around Galveston Bay, sluicing the wetlands between Houston and bayside refinery towns sinking into swamp, following dark coastal roads all the way down to a field outside Freeport where the drilling rig waited. They'd had most of Christmas Eve for a holiday, now three more men on the distant rig were biding time, impatient for relief, eager to bust off at midnight for Christmas Day, the best tradeout a working oilfield roughneck could expect.

The men in the pickup rode in silent anticipation, their thoughts already filled with caustic smells of raw crude and the tang of salt air and sulfur, with the bright soaring image of the waiting tower of clanking rain-slicked steel and pipe, a lighted shrine to honest if dangerous labor. Three working men on their way to earn the daily bread — Doss, the lead man and driller, Little Red the derrick man, Luther who worked the platform floor.

At Beaumont, Doss took an exit into a twenty-four hour Chevron and bought cups of hot coffee and stale jelly doughnuts, thrust them into the cab saying, "Merry Christmas, podners. Hope Santa Claus fed you better back at the house."

They drove into the dense curtain of mizzle shrouding the landscape trading stories about the dinners they'd eaten earlier in the day, Luther explaining why the usual Cajun meal was less fattening than East Texas redneck fare. "That seafood," he said, "all them shrimps an' crawdads, that's why, them frog legs an' fishes. Seafood healthier'n cow meat, you bet."

"My momma roasted a turkey," said Little Red, who was recently divorced and childless and lived with his parents. "She makes a fine giblet gravy, better'n that greasy coonass gumbo." His voice dared anyone to argue.

Luther laughed, stroked his long rooster neck. "Uhn-uhn, *cher*, Christmas Eve, day baby Jesus born. Ain't gonna say no thing. Peace on earth, tha's right." He reached up a big rawboned hand and flipped his welder's cap around backwards. "Time to be giving."

The younger man grunted but let it go.

Doss drove through the gleaming darkness, fallow rain-drenched rice fields flanking the highway unseen to either side. Down south forked lightning seared the horizon. He listened to the wiper blades beating time, squinted through the windshield at the floating mist twin-silvered in the headlamps. "Speaking of which," he said, "the wife give me a bicycle for Christmas." He lit a Camel straight with his Zippo, shoved the wing window open. "You see me on a bicycle?"

"Not lately," said Little Red. He breathed deep, inhaled tobacco smoke and night air filled with the smells of black dirt fields and flecked winter grass and rain. "It got them skinny tires?"

"Nope, big round ones." The driller made a circle with thumb and forefinger to show. "Twenty thirty gears, comes with a manual. Plus it ain't got fenders, slings shit up. Went once around the block? My back's covered with mud. Told the wife thanks a lot."

"Damn. She musta wanted a bike, huh?"

Doss shrugged.

Little Red retrieved an empty Styrofoam cup off the dash and put it to his mouth, let a dark gob of juice slide inside.

"Had this tricycle when I was kid. Ten years old, I'm all scrunched down, my knees knocking the handlebars, embarrassing. I wanted a real bike. But my momma, she's a fretter. Wouldn't let me cause this cousin of mine drowned on one."

Luther shifted his bony haunches, turned sideways against the door to look directly at Little Red. "Say what?"

"Said he drowned. What it sound like I said?"

The lanky floor man closed one eye thoughtfully and jerked his head, then leaned back in the seat with both hands on his thighs, satisfied. "Yeah, alright, drove that bike off in the river, un-huh."

"Naw, that ain't what happened. That'd make sense." Little Red peered into the spit cup, set it back on the dashboard. "What happened, his bud got a brand new one-speed Schwinn. Big sucker decked out with chrome and paint like a custom Harley, saddlebags and handlegrip streamers, a speedometer, bulb horn, red reflectors, wide seat don't eat up your asshole. Cost like a thousand dollars, today's prices."

"I wouldn't mind that seat," Doss said.

"Merwin, my cousin, takes one look, he's salivating. All he got's an old clunker, bent frame with bald tires. So his buddy, showing off, says to Merwin, 'Hop on back,' and off they go down the road. Half hour later the kid comes back alone yelling for help, a logging truck done run 'em off in a ditch."

Luther wagged his head. "Them logging trucks don't watch for no damn thing, no."

"Kid hollering cause my cousin done flew off sideways, hit his head on a rock. Knocked him out cold. Kid done come back for help." Little Red hesitated, rubbing one knee. "Merwin laid in that ditch and drowned. Three inches of water maybe."

"Hoo boy," said Luther. "All it takes, for a fact. Three inches, can drown in a bathtub. You still got that tricycle?"

"In the garage. My momma, she don't throw out nuthin."

They thought about that a minute, about all the people they knew who were packrats, then Doss said, "Your momma worries, podner, she better not see you on a rig. Scrambling around up on that monkey board unracking pipe."

"She thinks I walk around with a wrench turning little valves on and off." He scratched the back of one hand with the other, hard. "Never did get no damn bike. They give me a stupid wagon with 'Little Red' on the side. Where I got my name."

"Can drown in a wagon, too," Luther observed, "if you be trying."

"Well, that's what I got," Doss said, "a bicycle. Better'n what I usually get. Must have six bottles of aftershave hiding in my sock drawer. Me, I try to give sumthin useful. Gave the wife a Beach an' Hamilton blender from Wal-mart. Says she's gonna make fruit juicies, lose weight."

"Have her call my ol' lady," said Luther, "she due for a wide-load sign. Claims it's having them four kids. I let her buy one of them exercise machines off the TV ad? She don't use it. Dries diapers on the handlebars." He reached up to knead his left shoulder. "Reminds me of my Uncle T-Paul."

"Maybe he's got a eating disorder," said Little Red.

"Naw, I mean that bike story. Uncle T-Paul got killed on one over in Breaux Bridge. Shoulda known better, yeah, he was magnetized."

Little Red laughed.

Luther ignored him. "Uncle T-Paul and lightning, they don't get along, no. He's on the bayou fishing in his pirogue, here come a storm off the Gulf. All them other boats around, the lightning pick him out ever time, like he wearing a bull's eye. Him hit buncha times that way, we lost count. Him and a buddy out fishing an' a storm come up, his frien' go right over the side. Gonna swim to shore cause he know where that lightning gonna strike."

Little Red said, "Hell, you gotta stay off open water in a storm. Basic boating safety."

"For true, only he ain't got time. Them Gulf storms, they on you right quick like a bad temper. Here it comes. Tawk! That electricity be jumping around on his skin like a science fiction movie. Smoke coming off his britches, you bet, smell like a brisket. Maybe he pass out but he snap right back. Never do kill him, no. But it change him. Get near a field compass, that arrow turn around and point to Uncle T-Paul like he due north. Pick up a watch, hands spin like crazy. Magnetized."

Luther squeezed his welder's cap, lifted it, ran a hand over his thin brown hair. He stared out the side window into the falling rain, into passing fields along the highway shadowed in darkness.

Removing the small round tin of Skoal from his pocket, Little Red unscrewed the lid, laid a fingerful under his lip and worked it down. "That's mighty interesting, hoss. Right outa Ripley's unbelievable."

"Better chance of getting hit by lightning than winning the state lottery, what I heard," observed Doss. "But you can't tell nobody."

"Uncle T-Paul, he don't never win nuthin," Luther said. "Unluckiest man I ever seen 'cept with a fishing pole. Can't stay outa that pirogue, no, he want them flounder. Fish by his lonesome there at the end, nobody go with him. He come back the dock, people don't ask, 'You catch sumthin?' They say, 'Lightning getcha today?' Like they running a pool, laying down bets."

"Better than the lottery," Doss said, "that's what I'm saying."

"Then one time he's visiting his grandchil'ren, they got a new bike, all excited. 'You try it, PawPaw,' they say, so he gets on. He maybe a block down the way, other end of the trailer park, wobbling back and forth, everybody laughing. And down comes this thunderbolt and fries him like a jumbo shrimp. Big ol' fireball, yeah. I mean it welds him to that bike like they one factory product. Gotta use a hacksaw to cut him loose."

"Geez," said Little Red.

"Yeah, otherwise Uncle T-Paul be buried with a bike in the coffin. An' I tell you what, *cher*, they ain't a cloud in the sky when it happened."

For a while the three men were silent, picturing the incident, pondering the inexplicable mystery of it.

"Metal in that bike," Doss finally offered, "plus him being magnetized."

"Maybe so," said Luther, shaking his head doubtfully, "only where that lightning come from on a clear day, huh?"

"God, most likely," declared Little Red. "Only explanation that makes sense. He wasn't living right, what I'd guess. I heard about this lawyer got hit on a golf course that way. Sunny day with blue skies and he's telling his buddies how he's atheist. Dares God to strike him down if he's wrong. Arrogant sumbitch is grinning, head back, throwing up his arms, yelling, 'C'mon, do it! Do it!' Next thing happens, a thunderbolt comes down outa nowhere slicker'n a whistle and pops him right in the head. Whole body explodes like a watermelon with a grenade stuck inside. Nuthin left of that lawyer but sunshine and a burnt spot on the grass, a little dab of grease."

"Mercy," Luther said. He whistled low.

Doss touched the brim of his cap. "Well, there's some justice in the world, I reckon. Just don't see it much."

Luther shook his head intently, raised both hands as if warding off an attacker. "Lord, that ain't me talking, nossir. I don't make them accusations, me. My Uncle T-Paul a good Catholic, goes to mass every Sunday."

Little Red, raised Southern Baptist, started to remark upon the misguided notion that churchgoing equaled salvation, a typical Catholic notion, but Doss cut in saying, "Stick around this ol' world long enough, you hear some amazing things, yessir, that's a fact. I heard this story just the other day that'll twist your head around."

"Somebody about to die?" asked Luther.

"Nope, but it does involve a lawyer. Wouldn't believe it myself except my wife's brother said his boss knew the guy's cousin. Lawyer over in Huntsville, who it was, in the middle of getting a dee-vorce. The wife caught him cold at Motel 6, saw his Caddy in the lot. Kind of guy buys a new Seville every year whether the old one's dirty or not. She sees the car, drives straight to another lawyer and files on him."

"She already been t'inking on it," Luther said.

"Maybe, only he don't want it. He's crying, saying he's sorry. She says damn right he's sorry, he's got more excuses than the Dallas Cowboys and she ain't buying. They go back and forth like that, he's moaning, living in a studio apartment, she's got the house, playing him like a broke fiddle. Files a peace warrant on him. I mean, she cuts him off clean, no sweet stuff for daddy. Then Christmas rolls around."

"That stuff's hard on kids," said Little Red. "They got any kids?"

"Didn't hear." Doss shrugged. "Probably growed and gone, this guy's middle age. Anyway, here comes Christmas. Songs on the radio, TV specials selling holiday cheer. People start feeling good, having nice memories. The wife calls 'em childhood tapes, she read it in a magazine. People get warm and fuzzy, act friendly with folks they wouldn't say boo to last week. It's the season, them tapes kicking in. And this guy knows it. He's been laying low, typical snake in the grass husband, right? Plus he's a lawyer, like I said. So he's on the phone with his almost ex-wife and works the conversation around to where she ends up asking, 'What would you like for Christmas?' 'Oh, you don't mean it,' he says. 'Sure I do,' she says, 'just name it.' So he says he wants a full night of wild sex in the location of her choice."

"Naw!" Little Red exclaimed, incredulous.

"That's right."

"Did she do it?"

"Sure she did," said Luther. "Women are dumber than you t'ink, yeah. Just like us men. Keep listening."

Doss shot the tall man a quick glance, then said, "It's them tapes. Make a person act funny. Anyhow, they end up at the Shamrock Hotel in Houston, room costs like five hundred dollars a night, suites extra."

Little Red whistled. "That ain't no Motel 6."

"No, it ain't. Now, the lawyer knows that night's gonna be his last best shot to get his wife back. He's burning brain cells, figuring the angles. What's he gonna do?"

"A gift certificate to Sears," Little Red said, "what I'd do."

"The man's rich," said Luther.

"Okay, a fur coat. Or a diamond ring."

"She already got all that," said Doss. "No, what he decides is, give her the kind of sex she'll never forget. Kind that'll have her coming back for more. Except he ain't no spring chicken. Sometimes he can hardly get it up with her, part of the problem. His wife's a looker, only he's been looking for twenty thirty years now, it don't take like it used to."

He paused a moment, him and Luther both nodding, knowing first-hand how that can happen, the younger man between them thinking how his marriage only lasted a year, he'd never got used to a single thing about it and then his wife insisted on an abortion for no other reason than she wasn't ready. Then get ready, he'd told her, I want a family. Next thing he knew they were divorced.

"So what he did, he went to the doctor and got a prescription for Viagra," Doss continued. "The big night comes, they go out for a nice meal. He eats a sixteen-ounce T-bone in about five minutes, sits around an hour drumming the table while she picks at a Caesar salad. Finally they get to the room, got a bed bigger'n this pickup. She strips naked and crawls in, pats the mattress. Says straps on your spurs, cowboy, come and get it."

"Oh man oh man oh *man*," Little Red exclaimed, pounding his thighs. "So what'd he do?"

"This ol' boy takes one look and ducks into the toilet, pops four of those Viagras for backup."

"Four," said Luther.

"Uh-huh."

"Damn."

"That's right, and these are the strong ones, the heavy-duty boogars." Doss cleared his throat and shrugged. "Anyhow, that's what he did. You can guess the rest."

Luther grunted and said he reckoned he damn sure could. Little Red waited a minute, frowning, then said, "Well, hell, I can't. I ain't read up on that. What happened?"

Doss steered with his elbows and cupped his hands to light a cigarette. He leaned back in the seat, blew a cloud of smoke out the cracked window. "First thing happened was, that ol' boy got a hardon that wouldn't quit. Like somebody spiked his T-bone with a pound of Spanish fly. So he jumped on it and the wife, she was happy several times, real enthusiastic. Calling out his name like he hadn't heard in years. He's feeling like a number one stud duck. Figgers he's got it wired, figgers reconciliation's just around the corner. This goes on for like three hours."

"Wow," said Little Red, "whoa-ho."

"What I'm saying. Only every now and then he has to back off, catch his breath. Then he's ready to go again. 'Cept after three hours it's like Marine Corps training camp. His eyes are crossed, arms give out. Finally she gets sore. He says all right, just a minute, he's almost there. But no jack, he can't get off. Now she's complaining. He says okay, no problem, and rolls out the sack, hits the toilet to take the situation in hand. One quick look, though, and his eyes bug out. His whacker's thick as his wrist, redder'n Oscar Meyer at a wienie roast. Still harder than a railroad spike, too, that's for a fact."

Doss took a long, slow drag off the cigarette. Luther said, "Ain't had one like that since I was eighteen, yeah. When you eighteen you can drive nails with it."

"Nuthin lasts forever," said Doss. "You get a little more cautious with age."

Luther said, "I sure did."

Little Red drummed his thighs. "C'mon, what happened to the guy?"

Doss straightened his cap and peered through the windshield. "Well, podner, last I heard, he still ain't nuthin but a big lonely prick."

"What?"

"I told you he's a lawyer."

Little Red shut one eye, thinking. Then he groaned. "Aw, *man.* I shoulda known."

Luther chuckled and Doss grinned, tossing his cigarette

butt out the window. "Why you gotta watch what you ask for," he said, "Christmas or any other time."

Little Red, shaking his head, dipped another finger of Skoal, muttering, "You sorry sumbitch."

They didn't talk passing through the industrial towns fringing Galveston Bay, the refineries and petrochemical plants strung out like glittering carnival midways hunkered low in the marsh, smokestacks strung with countless lights upthrust into the night belching orange coils of flame and black curdled smoke. Back in the west, the yellow glow of Houston proper spread over the horizon reflected off lowrider clouds. The air stank of sour gas and industrial waste oil, of smoldering acid in a rotting swamp.

Passing through Baytown and La Porte, they abstractly studied the closed strip malls and shops, each man balanced precariously between familial memories of Christmas Eve and thoughts of the approaching rig, the long hazardous hours when they'd wrestle slick pipe into the wet heaving night, risking lost hands and arms, broken backs.

Nearing Alvin on State Highway 35, Doss suggested they stop and stretch their legs, have a cup of coffee. He parked at a Waffle House and they went inside past a green plastic wreath with bells on the door, took a corner booth. A solitary red and silver foil garland looped along the wall beneath the window glass. The place was empty. They blinked in the bright light, rubbed road-weary faces into the palms of their hands.

"You boys want coffee?"

They looked up at the waitress, saw a stout young woman with a protruding belly and scarlet pimpled cheeks, bobbed dishwater blonde hair and a silver stud through one nostril. She wore a striped uniform dress with short sleeves and black Doc Marten boots. Braided blue tattoos encircled both wrists. Little Red stared at her nose and grimaced. "Don't that hurt?"

"Little bit at first," she replied, smiling. "No more'n these." She held out her tatooed arms for a close look, then crossed them over her big belly.

"When it's due?" Little Red asked.

She frowned. "Huh?"

He tossed his chin toward her midriff. "The baby."

She put a fist on one hip and cocked her head. Her pale blue eyes opened wide in the broad red face, half serious, flirtatious. "Hey, dude, are you riffing on me?"

Little Red flushed and looked away, grabbed his nose between a thumb and forefinger, pulling on it.

"Never mind him, honey," Luther said, "boy's always digging holes and jumping in. Don't know any better, no. Just bring us some coffee."

"Menus?"

"Sure, I done worked up some hungry. Been listening to these boys tellin' lies."

"Them?" She grinned at Doss and Little Red.

"They just look innocent," Luther said. "Must be low woman on the totem pole, you, working Christmas Eve."

"That's me, all right," she sang. She winked at Little Red and walked away, heavy boots clomping on the tiles. Luther watched her hips rustling the striped cloth like locomotive pistons. "Mmm-hmm, " he said, "whole lotta woman in there trying to get out."

"Hope it don't," the younger man said, rolling his eyes, speaking low. "See that plug in her nose? Must be some kinda fashion statement."

"What it is, all right," Doss said. "See it everywhere. My daughter wants a ring in her belly button. I told her when she gets old enough to pay for her own roof. We ain't some Africans on National Geographic."

"Trying to express theyselfs," said Luther, straightening his cap. "Discover who they are, yeah."

"Good luck," Doss replied. "Almost forty and I ain't figured it out. Ever time I get an idea it changes on me. Know who you are, Little Red?"

"Sure do. Rufus Jackson from Bethlehem, Texas. High school graduate. Member of First Baptist. Derrick man for Gulf Drillers."

"I count t'ree, four selfs right there," said Luther. "What you buy your momma for Christmas, huh?"

Before Little Red could answer, the waitress brought the Pyrex coffee pot and mugs and menus and they all leaned back in the booth watching her set the tabletop. "What Santa Claus get you, hon?" Luther asked. "Sumpin good?"

"Well, it wasn't much fun this year, I got to admit," she answered, filling the plastic mugs. She kept her eyes on the hot coffee she was pouring. "My boyfriend got busted off parole, he's back in the pen. Shoplifting."

"Gettin' a Christmas gift for you," Luther guessed.

She nodded. "Then my folks, they live in Arkansas and I couldn't afford to take off. Already a month behind in the rent. So it was just me and my son, he's three today." She smiled, her small white teeth skewed at odd angles, one missing down front.

Luther clucked his tongue. "My, my, a Jesus baby."

"Best Christmas gift I ever got," she said.

"What's his name?"

"Star Man. Two words."

"That right? And you gotta work his birthday."

She lifted her broad, round shoulders. "It's okay, I get tomorrow off. Least it's slow tonight. Ready to order?"

Doss and Little Red said they weren't hungry, Luther ordered eggs over easy with bacon and a biscuit, cream gravy. "What's your name?" he asked.

"LeeAnn. One word."

"Well, Miss LeeAnn, you a good woman, yeah. That Jesus baby lucky with you."

She smiled again and went off. "Look at them clodhopper shoes," said Little Red, speaking low to Doss out of the side of his mouth. "She's one of them punks you hear about. Messed up on drugs, most of 'em, into cults. Betcha Star Man's some kinda Satanic name."

"Listen you, tha's a good Christmas name," said Luther. "Come from a Bible story, them t'ree wise man." He pointed a long, dark brown hand upward at a steep angle and his gaze took its aim. "What them men be following."

Doss lit a cigarette and stirred his coffee, said, "Luther, you are full of surprises, podner. Here I thought you was just another ignorant coonass."

"Got more'n one self, me," he replied, tilting his narrow head, "just like Brother Jackson here. What you buy your momma, huh?"

Little Red was trying to explain how a reflexology foot massager works when they heard a scuffing noise and turned to see a small child astride a tricycle pushing his way over the tiled floor toward them. He had pale blue eyes set wide between an enormous forehead and fat round cheeks, a small mouth with thick pink lips. He wore a pair of faded yellow pajamas with built-in feet and was sucking his thumb. When the tricycle drew alongside the booth, the child stopped and stared at the three men. His head seemed grotesquely large.

"Oh Jesus, where the hell he come from?" Little Red said, recoiling. His mouth closed tight in a grimace, one nostril flared. He jerked his head around searching the diner.

"I bet tha's Star Man," said Luther. "Whatcha wanna bet?" He put out a long arm with a forefinger extended and the child gripped it with both stubby hands without expression. Doss and Little Red watched Luther wiggle his finger saying, "You the Star Man, punkin?" The child tightened his hold, his blank gaze focused on the tall man's grinning face. "What I t'ought, yeah," Luther said, and he leaned out the booth, reached over with his other arm and gathered up the child, pulled him close and sat him on a knee. He bumped the child up and down on his leg, singing, "Star Man, Star Man, first Star Man I see tonight."

The child's broad face broke into a round wet smile. Luther laughed and tickled him on the belly and the child squirmed, gurgling.

Little Red watched, frowning, as if observing a man play with a dangerous pet, a coiling viper or a ferret. "Sumthin's wrong with that kid," he protested. He drew away in the booth against the wall. "I'd be careful there, Luther, I sure would. Look at his head. He ain't regular."

"Cause he's the Star Man," the man said, dandling the child. "You get that trike for Christmas, sugar? Santa Claus bring it?"

Doss nodded toward the tricycle, told Little Red, "Be nice and maybe he'll let you ride it."

"Ha-ha," the younger man retorted, his face flushed, "that's real funny."

The other two grinned and the child gurgled and threw back his massive head, his wide pale eyes roving the overhead lights.

"Something wrong, I'm telling you," cried Little Red. "It ain't regular. Good Lord Almighty, just look at the —"

"Star Man! There you are!" The waitress came rushing from behind the counter carrying Luther's order and set the plate on the table, saying, "I *wondered* where you went, you little boogar. Got mommy all worried. Out here bothering the customers again, I swear." She wiped sweat from her brow with the back of one hand and reached for the child, apologizing, but Luther said, "It's all right, Miss LeeAnn, he gonna help me eat. Ain't that right, *cher*?" He put his face down close to the child. "You like them biscuit an' jelly, huh?"

"You sure?" The young woman twisted a button on her blouse. "I couldn't find no babysitter on Christmas Eve."

"Sure, I'm sure," the man replied. "I got myself four chil'ren my own at home, me." He pulled the plate near and opened a biscuit with his free hand. "You just go sit your self down, take a load off. We gonna take care of Star Man."

"Well, o-kay." She went behind the counter and fiddled with silverware and dishes, watching out of one eye while Luther bounced the child and shared his breakfast, talking nonstop while the other two men looked on. The heavyset blond man smiled, sipped his coffee and smoked. The smaller man, the younger one with red hair and freckles, fidgeted with his ceramic mug and a can of Skoal and made awful faces like he'd swallowed his snuff. She refilled their coffee several times.

Half an hour later Doss said they'd better hit the road, and Luther gave up the child. LeeAnn put him on the tricycle and rolled him behind the counter, his feet playing hit and miss with the pedals. She rang up the bill. "Hope y'all have a Merry Christmas," she said, smiling. "And thanks for paying attention to Star Man. Not everybody feels comfortable that way. He liked it."

"Shoot, that sweet baby done made my Christmas," Luther told her. "You a lucky gal, Miss LeeAnn."

They went out the door. In the lot near the pickup, Luther stopped, asked the other two men each for a ten dollar bill. Little Red caught his drift. "Hey, no way man, I already left a fifty-cent tip on a dollar cup of coffee. Pay my tithes at church, too, I ain't owing nuthin."

Luther looked him in the eye. "Don't bring no shame down on your Baptist self, you."

Doss handed over a ten and Little Red took out his wallet, griping. Luther pulled a twenty from his own wallet and took the folded money inside the Waffle House. They watched through the glass wall as LeeAnn accepted it, her big red face registering shock and gratitude, then Luther was back sliding inside the cab, saying, "Hoo-whee, cloudcover's done passed over. Not raining anymore, no. Gonna have a clear night."

The other men bent forward and peered upward through the windshield and saw it was so. "Well, I'll be," Doss said, "wasn't even paying attention." He started the truck and pulled onto the highway headed south. Little Red fished in his shirt for the Skoal can, grousing. "You don't just up and hand no stranger forty dollars, not where I come from."

"You young yet," Luther said, "you don't know where you from."

"Tell my momma."

"She ain't listening," Luther said, "prob'ly too busy foolin' with that foot machine you buy her."

Doss drove while Luther and Little Red dozed. The highway furled inward beneath the headbeams, straight as a concrete rail and flat as sheet iron, the tunnels of light catching rabbit eyes or possum in the ditches. He saw blue and white lightning marbling the sky in the east but the wind was pushing north and overhead it was clear all the way to the coast. He turned the radio on low, listened to an FM station out of Houston playing country Christmas carols. His attention went ahead, drew down on the drilling job, wondering whether the well might come in, how soon, how deep they'd have to go. Hoping the weather stayed dry.

Outside Angleton, he awakened the other two and told them they'd be at the rig in half an hour. "Want anything from the 7-Eleven in town? Potato chips? Candy?"

Rubbing their eyes, they shook their heads no and he drove on. The humid air through the vents smelled of salt and fish and brackish vegetation decaying far back in the marsh and he knew they were near. Shortly after he turned right into a shell lane and they saw the derrick in the distance. The night tower of light rose from the dark coastal prairie like an electrified ladder leaning against the sky.

Luther rolled down the window and hung an arm out. The pickup tires crunched the white luminous shells, a cool moist breeze rustled the sawgrass. "Tell me, Brother Jackson, you believe in Jesus, you?"

Little Red threw him a skeptical glance, said, "Hell, what kinda question's that?"

"Ain't no trick, no. Doss, you believe in Jesus?"

"Yessir, I do."

Luther nodded his head. "What I thought. Brother Jackson here, he a believer, too. Me, I believe. The president, he a believer. All them congressmans, they believers. Rich folks gonna say they believe. Ever'body on the street, whole country, you ask, they gonna tell you, 'Sure, I believe in Jesus, you bet.' All that believing ... " He shook his head. "So why the country in the mess it in, huh?"

"Got me," said Doss, braking the truck in the lot beside a portable storage building. He shut the engine down. The noise of the nearby rig bit into the night, the clanging of steel on steel. "I don't have no answers. I'm just an oil driller. Strong back and a weak mind."

They climbed down and stood alongside the pickup watching a platform hand hosing mud off the derrick floor. Above the lone, silhouetted figure the iron frame rose, thrusting upward, pinnacled, converging high on a single pointed light. Above that, the black velvet heavens spread in a silver-sprinkled dome from one midnight horizon to the other.

"Reason for the mess, seems to me," said Little Red, speaking up, "is cause we got a choice. People go and choose what's wrong, that's the mess. Only Jesus forgives us, and that makes it all right. Long as you believe."

Luther took off his welder's cap, studied its narrow brim. "Maybe you right, *cher*. Maybe so. Me, I'm holding that child tonight, Miss LeeAnn's. Whole time I'm t'inking, this baby ain't never gonna believe, no."

"Well, special case like that —"

"An' he don't have to," Luther said, "*pas du tout*. Cause Star Man, he is baby Jesus, for true."

The tall thin man lifted both arms and gazed at what had so recently held divinity, then put on his cap, pulled it snug over his head and walked off toward the rig, saying, "Baby Jesus, right there in my big ol' ugly hands."

Little Red tugged an earlobe, watched the lanky form striding over the shell into the yellow light. "You reckon that's one crazy coonass?" he asked Doss.

"I sure hope so," the driller replied. "Cause we get up on that rig sticking pipe, my life depends on him." He raised the worn pair of oil-stained leather work gloves he held in one hand and slapped them against the younger man's chest. "On you, too, podner. We all in this together. Christmas on a rig's like any other time."

"Yeah," the derrick man said, "reckon so. You watch my back, I watch yours. Right?"

"That's the way I read it. Just don't forget to look at what you're watching." He cupped his hands against the wind and flipped the Zippo, lit a Camel straight. Saying, "Things ain't always what they seem."

A Tinkling Cymbal

The Sunday Brother Wiley preached on the Good Samaritan, George Thomas Hebert raised the subject of the sermon at dinner afterward, as was his habit. The parable intrigued him, he said, each time he heard the story it sparked a new idea. "That's aside from the obvious interpretation," he observed, "the one we always hear. And what did you learn?" he asked George Thomas Jr. "I'm sure we'd like to know." The boy sat hunched over the table between planted elbows, gnawing on a fried chicken leg. His pale blue eyes scattered left and right, briefly converged at some haphazard spot on the linen tablecloth near his plate, then dispersed again. He shrugged. "I dunno. Help others, I guess," he said, "even if it's a nigger or a Mexican or sumpin. Or maybe a Jew."

George Thomas Sr. froze with a forkload of mashed potatoes halfway to his mouth. He frowned. He'd asked him not to use that word less than a week ago. "They call each other that," the boy had retorted, "don't see why we can't. Oughta see their videos on TV." Later George Thomas Sr. watched some on cable. The boy had been right. "All the same," he'd told his son, "I don't want to hear you saying it." An order which obviously had not worked. The boy at age sixteen seemed to listen less and less.

The father now put down the fork and wiped his mouth with a napkin. He pursed his lips, decided the trashy comment was a provocative ploy meant to distract him. Well, it wouldn't work. "No, you missed the point as usual. What that parable is about is prudence," he said, speaking carefully, as if his audience might be feeble-minded, though his tone indicated a hard-won restraint on the verge of collapse. "The man beside the road looked dead. The priest and the Levite both passed without stopping because they were apprehensive. If any Jewish priest — and that's a Levite — touched a dead man, he violated the religious law. They were acting prudent."

Across the table, George Thomas Jr. paused with the chicken leg to his lips, peering from beneath a double flying buttress of bony arms. One eye squinted, he sniffed. "You mean they was doing right?"

"I mean they did what they *thought* was right. Only it wasn't."

"Well heck, how they supposed to know then? Shoot," the boy said, shaking his head, "a fella's supposed to do what he think's right. Ain't that what you always said?"

George Thomas Sr. straightened his shoulders and picked up his fork, satisfied. He stirred cream gravy into the mashed potatoes and took a bite. At least he had the boy thinking. "The gravy's delicious, Lorraine," he told his wife. She sat across the table next to their son, eating quietly. She appeared to be leaning the boy's way a little. The two of them resembled, with straw-colored hair cut close and robin's-egg eyes, thin-faced, tall, with narrow slope-shouldered frames. Both had long slender necks, which looked natural on Lorraine, who floated through life with swan-like grace. She was the most even-keeled woman he'd ever met. Whereas George Thomas Jr. intended to thrash his way forward, it seemed, though he hadn't made much progress. All elbows and angles, the boy never sat still. He twitched and jerked without letup. "Yeah, good gravy," he said.

"Why, thank you both," said Lorraine. She winked at the boy, leaned a little more his way. George Thomas Sr. watched. He firmly believed his wife was overprotective. Lorraine disagreed. With her mouth set in a stalwart line of defense, she maintained any boy should be allowed to enjoy his youth, which came only once. Her husband thought the idea sound in theory. But he was a realist. Regarding his son, he found it impossible to grasp how the squandering he saw might equal enjoyment.

"So I reckon there ain't no use trying to do right," the boy now concluded, "cause you can't know."

Lorraine bent forward, stirred the gravy in the serving bowl, inspecting it. "The texture's right but it tastes a little salty to me," she remarked to her husband, "and I always thought the Samaritan parable was about being a good neighbor, dear, like George Thomas said. In his own way, naturally. Where did you get the prudence idea?"

"Because I've been thinking about it," he replied crisply. "Any good parable has more than one meaning. Take those priests, they had certain obligations. They were trying not to act irresponsibly" — here he planted a piercing eye on George Thomas Jr., who of course wasn't paying attention — "one might even say recklessly. But in this case it's clear they overdid it. Prudence, like any virtue, can be taken to extremes. It's a matter of context and judgment. As a banker, I would know. Prudence is something I've had to consider inside and out."

"Yes, I suppose you have," Lorraine agreed. She smiled serenely and cocked her head. "Can I get you anything?"

"Tea," he said, "I'd like more tea. Feel a tad thirsty."

George Thomas Jr., hunched low between his elbows, belched.

"It's the gravy," Lorraine said, pouring iced tea into her husband's glass from the pitcher, "it has too much salt, don't you think?"

George Thomas Sr. didn't answer. He was watching his son tear into a fried chicken wing. He was going at it like a voracious dog, oblivious to all else. The boy had an attention span of maybe ten seconds. He hadn't learned a thing. It was pitiful.

Monday afternoon at the bank, George Thomas Sr. was in

his office with the door shut, his feet propped over the desk corner, scanning stock prices online when his secretary buzzed him. He stared at the quote on an Internet startup stock he'd recently purchased on his personal account. To his dismay, it had quadrupled in value the first week. Now its worth had fallen by half since morning. He probably should sell. Except then its value would skyrocket again overnight. Who could keep up?

He put the receiver to his ear. "Yes, Judy."

"A Mr. Collins here to see you, sir."

George Thomas Sr. cracked his neck. "Do I know him? What's it about?"

"He says it's personal, sir. He says he knows you."

"Just a minute."

George Thomas Sr. laid the receiver on the desk top, a vast plane of teakwood on which sat the computer, the telephone, an engraved glass Rotary Club paperweight, a doubledecker in and out tray, and a framed eight-by-ten photograph of himself, Lorraine and George Thomas Jr. He'd been intending to replace it for years. The boy must have been in kindergarten when it was made. Lorraine's hair was cut in a Farrah Fawcett shag. He hiked his pants around the desk to the peephole in the door. Through it he viewed the slightly concave image of a man his own age, mid-forties or so, with a deeply tanned face and bent nose. He stood by Judy's desk tugging the bill of a sweat-stained Houston Astros cap, yanking it lower down his forehead as though the lobby's recessed lights hurt his eyes. A pair of Dickey's workpants patched at the knees abruptly ran out of steam several inches above laced leather workboots. The khaki shirt was streaked with grease, "Collins" embroidered in red script against a white oval patch over the pocket. The gaunt man seemed vaguely familiar. George Thomas Sr. then remembered him in green polyester slacks and a shortsleeved white nylon shirt. A maroon knit tie hanging wrinkled to one side, stuck askew with static electricity. Wearing scuffed cowboy boots with sharp-pointed toes. From the church. Collins.

He buttoned his suit jacket and opened the door, stepped

out offering the brisk business-like smile of a man who was busy. "Mr. Collins, how are you?" The man slid a workboot forward and flexed the knee above, dropped the forward shoulder and cocked the opposite hip. He hooked a thumb in his pants. A countryman's pose. Thus set, he sprung his neck back and forth like a skittish banty rooster saying he reckoned he'd seen better but then he'd seen worse, too, and almost everything in between besides now that he thought about it, so's in the long run it all appeared to come out even. "Or pretty much close to it," he finished. "I reckon I need a minute of your time there, Mr. President."

George Thomas Sr. hesitated, patting his lapels. He meant to put the man off but the titular address had caught him by surprise. Such overt respect was rare, and mildly gratifying. He basked in these musings until he realized he was presenting the impression of uncertainty. He scrambled for a credible excuse, which for lack of forethought he had not manufactured, and the longer he wavered the more he saw that any pretext he now offered would seem more the sham it was than the reason he needed. With a short sideways glance toward Judy, as if to partition the blame for this unexpected trap, he stepped aside gesturing for the man to enter. "It's not the Oval Office, Mr. Collins," he said, prying loose a chuckle, "but I suppose we'll make do. Have a seat there."

Once they were situated across the desk from one another the banker leaned back in his highbacked executive chair and unbuttoned his jacket. "Now, Mr. Collins, what can I do for you?"

Collins shifted in his seat, pulled at the grimy bill of the gimmee cap. He rubbed the side of his nose with a scarred knuckle and blinked, his small mahogany eyes flitting to either side, then adjusted his perch in the chair again, hoisting one oily workboot to rest on the other knee. He leaned forward, plucking at at his cap bill, rolling his shoulders. It occurred to George Thomas Sr. that he was witnessing a baseball pitcher carefully compose himself, running through an arcane rite of precise time-tested motions as he prepared to deliver a critical pitch. The banker waited patiently, his professional expression instinctively constructed of concerned if impartial interest.

Collins had yet to begin speaking. His eyes surveyed the perimeter of the commodious office, the banker followed. Behind him, he knew, the glass picture window gave way to a narrow strip of johnson grass with two spindly azaleas and the parking lot beyond. Elsewhere, the ivory toned walls were hung with a framed bachelor's degree in accounting from Texas A&M and several mounted certificates of commendation from Sertoma and Kiwanis, grouped decoratively, a lacquered redwood Board of Realtors award, and an engraved brass plaque from the Bethlehem Chamber of Commerce naming him "Businessman of the Year". Both wandering men halted on a large photograph, conspicuously placed, of George Thomas Sr. posing with another man. It was autographed with a bold message in black ink. The two smiling men wore business suits, a name tag was stuck to the banker's chest. The second man splayed one hand above his coat pocket as if holding his appendix, wrapped the other arm over his friend's shoulders. The banker thought they faintly resembled one another. He'd stood in line an hour for that prize at the Republican State Convention in Dallas. It had cost him a thousand-dollar contribution, which Lorraine said was excessive, though he knew it'd been a sensible investment. More than sensible: shrewd. Now he nodded toward the picture and said, for his visitor's benefit, "The governor."

Collins turned his gaze on the banker and began speaking as if he had not heard, as though his mind all along had been traveling currents elsewhere and his voice had just now climbed aboard in midstream. "Yessir, I'm a religious man. Leastways intend to be. I try," he said, "I surely do." His voice was high and nasal and carried a flat backwoods twang suggesting his was the first generation come up from the Sabine River bottoms to town, which was surely true.

"Thought I was gonna be a Church of God preacher when I was a boy," he went on. "Had me a callin', yessir. Heard that voice clear as Moses seen a burning bush. The Spirit come on me, told me to get right at it. Preach that Bible, son, thump it good. So's I did.

"Only it weren't long fore I got off track. Had a Hank Williams voice, you see, kinda lonesome-like. Folks pre-chated it. Got me a guitar, learned some chords, started playing them honkytonks. Money was good. 'Cept I got off in the drink right away. Can't hold alky-hol. And women? Yessir, I was wallowing in the filth. Oh I knowed the price of sin, but I ignored it."

The man grabbed both thighs and twisted his chin downward to one side, expelling a short violent bark as though the pain of the memory was too great to endure. "Done wicked thangs I'm too shamed to tell," he continued. "Was going straight down and wouldn't even look. Then come a night I had me a dream with a warning angel and I woked up hollering. Couldn't quit shaking. Liked to scared me to death. So's I quit. Jest like that, walked away from it.

"Come right back to Jesus, come crawling on my knees. 'Cept I couldn't find the callin' no more. Jest couldn't locate it. Done missed my chance, you see, done missed it. That hurt, yessir. Made me feel small, made me feel dirty."

Lifting his hands, the man flipped them over studying first the scarred swollen knuckles and then the oil-grimed palms like he expected to find them yet desecrated with the residue of his abomination, as though he suspected the repentance once proffered had fallen short of that required. He let them fall to his lap, saying "Coulda turned my back and run right then but I didn't. Nossir, went to church anyways, still do, you seen me. Held to the straight and narrow best I could. Took up a trade, learned me auto mechanics. Can't sing or preach but I can fix a car. Like the Good Lord admitted, one thang we can't help. We all fall short." He balled one fist in the other hand and squeezed. "Yessir, we all fall short." The knuckles popped like firecrackers.

George Thomas Sr. waited, his face still in neutral. Being a small town banker, he was accustomed to folks who took the scenic route to business. The stories he'd heard, sitting right there in his office, tales of catastrophic misfortune and personal ruin, he could write a long sad book. He recollected uninsured housefires, sudden bankruptcies, suicides. But now as the silence drew out he perceived the man across the desk was awaiting a response.

"Yes, that's right, Mr. Collins," the banker agreed equably. "We all fall short, we certainly do."

Collins pushed the cap back off his forehead and gave a satisfied grunt, as if the confirmation reconciled some unspoken hope. "Course I s'pose the Lord had His problems with bankers," he granted. "To hear Him talk, I mean. Weren't there myself but I can read. Right there in the book, black and white, zackly what He said. Myself, I believe in the Bible. Ain't like some. I ain't tortured with doubts."

He shot one arm forward and rapped the edge of the teakwood one-two-three, then fell silent again. The banker waited only a moment this time before nodding in agreement.

"Yessir, believe in it word for word," Collins continued. "Ain't nary a wrong word in it. Either you believe it or you don't, ain't no in-between, nossir, that's what I believe. Way I was raised. Couldn't help it even if I wanted, which I don't. My daddy and momma taught me right and I never contradicted 'em, not then and not now. Bible truth's why I fell out with the Church of God folks last year, came over to the First Baptist."

The man came to a full stop as if he expected his listener might want to probe the nature of this scriptural dispute, but when no inquiry was made he plunged ahead. "Yessir, the Bible's God's own truth, plain as the nose on my face," he said, closing one eye to suggest the magnitude of this fact, "and I'll tell you straight out, if'n you doubt that then you're headed straight to Hell."

This final charge spilled out in a fierce torrential rush like an ancient prophetic challenge. Jeremiah himself might've been sitting there in an Astros gimmee cap blasting the adultery of Judah. George Thomas Sr. bristled. The other's barely contained outrage was infectious, and he stanched a surge of indignation to think Collins had barged unappointed and unwanted into his office to put him to some test, as if his faith was suspect and he harbored clandestine Church of God

81

sympathies. He sought to return the man's gaze but found it shifted, now riveted on the computer. "That there one of them computing machines?"

The banker glanced over, saw by the screen it still was connected online. The disruption had made him forget. Irritated, he tapped at the keyboard and signed off, saying, "Yes, Mr. Collins, that's how I was raised myself. Now, what can I do for you today?"

The man pulled himself up and back and sat very erect in the chair, bobbed his head once. "Well, I thought so, yessir. Looked at you in church yestiday and I says to myself, 'Now, lookee there, Harvey Collins, there's a man who believes. He may be a banker but he believes. He can't help who he is anymore'n you can. But you can tell jest by looking he ain't like them others what Jesus condemned. Nossir, he's different.' And I was right."

George Thomas Sr. now rested his elbows on the chair arms and stared at Collins with both thumbs hooked beneath his chin, fingers uplifted in a steeple. He was trying to figure out just what the man was referring to. He tried to recall where Jesus condemned bankers, and could not place it. He'd read scripture all his life, both Old Testament and New, and as far as he knew no such thing had ever happened. Moneylenders in the temple, of course, but they hardly qualified as legitimate bankers.

"Yessir, the Good Lord frowned on users," Collins said. He twisted his head to one side and winced as if the very word conferred a punishing jolt of electric current. Once recovered, he added, "But that was a different time, I reckon."

The banker slowly folded his steeple, squeezed the point of his chin between thumbs and fingers. "Mr. Collins, I believe you mean userers."

"That's right, I do. What I said. Users. Loaning money at a profit. But like I mentioned, them was other times. They was using shekels and such instead a dollars. Ain't seen a lot of dollars myself, not like you. But I ain't *never* seen no shekels. That's how different them times was. Course the Lord's word's one thing never changes, nossir. It's the truth yestiday, today and tomorrer. Ain't changed one jot or tittle in two thousand years. Said so yourself. So I reckon I can trust you. Yessir, I need me a loan."

During this latter pronouncement the words had piled up with increasing volume and speed, with Collins becoming more agitated, his face growing darker and more turbulent by the moment, his eyes swelling in anguish, until the final declaration found him canting forward off the seat with his cap whipped off and clinched in both fists between his knees, shoulders trembling violently. The sudden barrage left the banker stunned. After a bit, he managed to ask, "Do you trade at this bank, Mr. Collins?"

The man swiped one cheek with a finger and dipped his head absolutely. "Yessir, I do. And I was sitting there in church thinking about that ol' boy in the road, the one plumb near dead, how I knowed what he felt like. Now that coulda been Jesus a'laying there Hisself, that idee come to me, He was a man too. But mainly I was thinking it was me. Cause right now I'm more or less in the same position, you see. Not that I'm dying, least not yet" — he offered a brave lopsided grin, with several missing teeth — "but I'm feeling right near it, financially speaking. I need me some help."

George Thomas Sr. said, "A loan."

"Yessir, I ain't asking for a handout. Jest got myself in a hole, ain't too proud to admit it. Why I'm reaching up for a heppin hand. Once't I get climbed out, my aim's to give it back. You can write that down. I'm willing to pay interest. Them's the rules. Only seeing how you a man of God, don't reckon you'll cheat me. I'm gonna trust you. Yessir, that's my decision."

George Thomas Sr. rode out the short speech nodding, indicating he had no desire to dispute the man's trust. Thrust far back into his chair, fingers interlaced, he had navigated the strait of bewilderment some time ago and entered the fathomless gulf of human irony. There he contemplated the startling view: this man who badly needed money had wrestled angels of righteous reluctance and triumphed, discovering sufficient inner resources to entrust him, a banker, with the privilege of extending a loan with interest. The sheer size of the presumption boggled the mind.

"And don't try to talk me out of it," Collins was saying, "nossir, I done thought it through. Never got nuthin free, don't 'spect it now. Paying a little interest won't kill me."

George Thomas Sr. inhaled deeply through his nose and sat upright, bumped up closer to the desk to rest his elbows on top, forearms triangulated upward so that one hand curled over the other at the apex. His eyes briefly roved the room, lit on the picture of him and the governor. He rested them there, saying, "Of course now, Mr. Collins, you realize we'll need to ask you some questions."

"I figgered that. Like the man said, when you in Rome do what them Romans do. You ask and I'll answer."

"And I'll need you to fill out a loan application." The banker spoke the phrase by habit, his eyes lingering on the photograph. He'd never noticed until now how the governor was sighting off to one side, as if his attention was taken elsewhere, his smile practiced. He could see it plain as day all the way from over here. It was embarrassing. How come he'd never noticed that before?

"I already done it." Collins leaned forward and reached behind, pulled a rumpled piece of folded paper from his pants pocket. He unfolded it and laid it over one knee, tried with a rough hand to smooth the creases. "Sorry I got it a little dirty there," he said, handing it to the banker.

The damp loan application was smeared with rust-brown comet trails of some sort of automotive lubricant. George Thomas Sr. mindfully held it above the desktop to give a quick once-over, not really reading. He gave a series of small noncommittal tongue clucks, as was his practice at such moments. "And what exactly is the loan for, Mr. Collins?"

"Auto loan. For my truck. You can call me Harvey."

"Buying one?"

"Nossir, fixin mine. Needs a new transmission. Only I ain't going with a brand new one. Buying rebuilt. Jest as good and costs half as much. Know how to watch after my welfare that

84

way."

The banker cleared his throat. "Well, Mr. Collins ... Harvey ... we do auto loans, naturally, but not for repairs. That comes under personal loans."

"Yessir, a personal loan. That's what I need." The man pulled an earlobe and grinned. "Need me a loan and it's personal, so reckon I qualify."

George Thomas Sr. did not smile. "If possible, we like to secure such loans with collateral," he said. "Something of substantial value."

Collins scraped his jawline with a thumb knuckle, regarded the floor.

"How about your house?"

The man shook his head. "Lost it several years back. Doublewide trailer house, only it had defects. Couldn't afford no lawyer so we jest give it back. 'I ain't paying for that piece a junk,' I told 'em, 'you go get it whenever you ready. Sitting right where you put it, Hickory Hill Trailer Park.' That's flat out what I said. Yessir, we mostly rent now. Out near Blackjack Creek, that address right there." He pointed at the loan application.

"I see." George Thomas Sr. leaned back in the chair with his chin thrown up as if pondering a fallback solution to a difficult mutual problem. "How about the truck itself? What's it worth? How old is it?"

"Twenty years."

The banker evinced a heartfelt grimace.

"But that's jest on the truck, now," Collins put in quickly. "That motor? Rebuilt it ten years ago myself. It's a good motor. Don't use no oil. Yessir, I could sell that Ford pickup tomorrer, no problem, people line up to buy it. 'Cept for the transmission, that's what I'm saying. It's shot. Gotta replace it." His voice slammed to a halt. Then, almost in a whisper, "That truck's all I got, Mr. Hebert, it's my work transportation."

George Thomas Sr. nodded. "All right, Harvey. You give me a little time to look things over. I'll need to clear anything by my board. Call me in a couple of days."

"Wednesday?"

"That'll be fine."

At the office door, Collins wiped his right hand on his pants leg and thrust it outward, his shoulders pulled back. He probed the banker's face intently as if memorizing it for future usage, his dark eyes shining, almost defiant. "I was right to come," he said, "Yessir, knowed right there in church I could trust you. God bless you, brother." He pivoted and strode away through the lobby, his bootheels leaving small black crescents of grease ground into the carpet.

George Thomas Sr. sighed. What he'd said about the board wasn't exactly true. In fact, it was a baldface lie. They'd approve any decision he made, always had, usually after the fact. But the fiction made it easier to say no when it was no that needed saying. It was standard banking practice everywhere. Still, he hated doing it. And he intended to give Collins the loan if he could justify it in any way. The man needed some help or he wouldn't have come in.

That night at dinner he told Lorraine it was likely some high-tech stock in which he'd invested five thousand dollars would either make them a bundle or provide a tax break in capital losses, he couldn't predict. She replied she had full confidence in whatever he thought best, investments was his bailiwick. He called the present market a guessing game, she said his guess was better than hers. In passing, he mentioned a member of the church had come by the bank. "Harvey Collins, you probably don't know him."

Lorraine closed her eyes to search for an image, said, "No, I evidently don't."

"I do," George Thomas Jr. announced. His mouth was full, green beans squirreled into both cheeks. He forked another load in. Both parents watched, transfixed. After he swallowed, the boy stuffed in a large chunk of chicken-fried steak and resumed smacking with his mouth half open. His father snorted.

"My Lord," Lorraine said, "where are your manners?"

The boy ignored her.

"And how do you know Mr. Collins?" she said.

With a thin upraised hand George Thomas Jr. signaled her to wait. He guzzled most of his iced tea and burped. "He fixed Josh Mabry's Camaro over at the M&M garage."

"Were you racing again?" Lorraine asked. Her anxiety was scarcely concealed. They had bought him a brand new Toyota Camry for his sixteenth birthday, when he got his license, and he treated it like a race car. "Cause your father and I —"

"No, I was just there."

"Cause if —"

"No-o-o-o," he moaned, "I said no. But Josh blew a head gasket coming out of second. Harvey Collins fixed it while we watched. He asked if we knew his wife from the school, and we did. Little ol' skinny woman used to work in the cafeteria. A server but she was always coughing. They fired her cause of it. Harvey said she got the big C. Plus they got a daughter in my grade," he added, "only she quit."

"It's *Mister* Collins," Lorraine said, "don't call him Harvey, that's not polite. She has cancer?"

"Big C, yeah," the boy said. "Harvey said she's dying." He wolfed another oversized piece of steak and commenced chewing, reached beneath his T-shirt to scratch an itch.

"Well, that's just awful," said his mother. "And I don't even know her. She goes to our church?"

Her son shrugged.

"I can't place them," Lorraine murmured. "Of course, if I was to see them ... "

George Thomas Sr. continued eating as he listened to the two talk. Though he declined to participate in common table gossip the information interested him. Collins had not specified his family situation. That he had a wife and daughter was no big surprise, but he might've mentioned the sick wife. They were bound to have medical expenses. He turned to his son. "Does the daughter work?"

The boy grinned. "Are you serious? She's too busy playing around. Sissy Collins is a slut."

"George Thomas Hebert!"

His pale eyes darted and rolled, exasperated. "Well, she is, Mom. I don't know what else you call it. I heard she was dancing topless at some club."

"You did not!"

"What I heard." The boy muttered as if it didn't matter one way or another. "Anyway, she got the reputation. She even went out with that nigger quarterback we had, Rashad" — he sneered and drew out the name out long — "*Raaah-shod* Washington. Only he dropped her once he found out about her."

"Well, I still think there's better terms for some poor girl whose mother is mortally ill," Lorraine said. She knit her eyebrows. "Something less degrading."

"Like nympho?" replied the boy.

"Of course not, that's a terrible word. Actually, I was thinking of ..." She clinked her fork against the china plate rim, frowning, puzzling the matter as though it was a particularly ticklish riddle. "That is, if you insist on even discussing the subject ..."

The term "Jezebel" occurred to George Thomas Sr., followed by harlot, strumpet and floozy. But instead of joining the conversation he excused himself from the table and went down the hall toward his home office. He heard Lorraine back in the dining room say something about "women of misplaced virtue." The boy snickered loudly. He shut the door and sat down at his desk, withdrew the loan application from his briefcase along with some bank records and a credit bureau report. He placed the papers in a pile and began reading through them again. If they collectively proved anything, they proved Harvey Collins wasn't a liar. The self-assessment of his predicament had been accurate. The numbers showed a man in over his head, floundering in a cash flow shortfall and sinking. The Community Bank statement showed no savings and a checking account which hovered near zero except for brief upward blips marking paydays. There'd been several recent overdrafts when checks winged through accounting before a paycheck. Also, Collins in some mysterious way had obtained a Visa account at the bank six months ago. That would've been during the last big push to attract more credit card clients. George Thomas Sr. cringed. Those Visas had been handed out like supermarket coupons, and now the Collins account was maxed. They were making minimum payments, barely covering the high interest charges. The banker laid the paper aside and scanned the credit bureau report. Bethlehem Mobile Homes had filed a default on the trailer a couple of years back, the utility bills frequently got paid overdue. Collins had no credit elsewhere.

He stood up and went to the window, opened the blinds. Outside, cicadas trilled lightly in the oleander hedge. The settling darkness grained a flat dusky sky above the riverbank down the way, low gusting clouds eclipsed a crescent moon through the sycamore. Myrtle Street was empty, he had the impression it would rain soon. Across the road, through the living room window at the Mitchells, the television was on. He abstractly viewed the flickering light for a minute, then returned to his desk. Collins had asked for a thousand dollar loan, to be repaid in twelve monthly installments. That would mean almost a hundred dollars a month. If the bank extended the term to reduce payment size, the man still couldn't make it, not according to these records. George Thomas Sr. could not in good conscience justify approving the loan. It would violate policy, it would be reckless. Refusal was a straightforward decision, the only prudent one.

He shut his eyes and pictured the gaunt rooster-like Collins perched forward on the office chair, practically groveling, desperate. Then during departure standing in the doorway, erect, that dark gleaming expression both defiant and proud, as if the humiliation to which he'd been reduced had somehow raised him up, made him larger. Assuming the loan was a done deal. Calling him brother.

A flash of resentment passed over the banker's face and down his chest like heat lightning to collect in his belly, settled there in a throbbing ache. For a moment, he thought he might throw up. People simply did not understand the kind of pressure such appeals put on a man in his position.

*   *   *

On Wednesday he returned from his weekly Rotary Club
luncheon to find Harvey Collins seated in the bank lobby. He
did not see him at first. Judy caught his attention and tilted her
head, her hazelnut eyes sheering off at an acute angle, and he
spun in that direction to see Collins sitting beside a potted
horsetail fern holding the grubby Houston Astros cap. He
appeared to be wearing the same work clothes as Monday. He
jerked to his feet, saying, "Yessir, good afternoon. On my lunch
hour, figgered I'd jest pop by and save you a phone call. Pick
up the loan check while I'm here."

George Thomas Sr. hesitated, patting his belly — the meat
loaf was resting a dab uneasy — then asked the man to step
into his office. It was a short meeting. He explained the loan
had been turned down and regrettably he couldn't overrule the
board. Collins flinched at the news. He studied the floor
between his feet like a man searching for a fumbled pin, then
lifted his somber gaze. "Well sir, I ain't an eddicated man,
surely ain't. But I reckon to know when somebody says I can't
be trusted."

He reached up a coarse hand to his throat, massaged his
Adam's apple. In the next few moments, his countenance
transmogrified. There emerged a kaleidoscope of distinct
apparitions, one after the other, as if through luminous veins
beneath the drawn rufous skin flowed a spectral liquid
emanating now incredulity, now rage, now grief. In the end,
his face surrendered to lay open like a dark tender wound.
"Nossir, I ain't deserving," he admitted. "Done got on my knees
three times and asked. Asked my boss, and he didn't have it.
Asked the Lord, and he pointed me to you, said you was the
one. So I come and asked. Got on my knees. And if'n I was
deserving it woulda got give to me. And it ain't. Yessir, I
understand. It's on my head now. I thankee for your time."

George Thomas Sr. wasn't sure what to say. He was still

deliberating an appropriate, reasoned response when the man rose, wearily slapped his thigh with the cap and walked out, passing Gabe Wilson in the doorway. Wilson owned the GMC dealership and needed to arrange a larger line of credit for his used car inventory, and the banker was soon caught up in friendly negotiations and forgot about Collins. The man occurred to him once in passing that evening, but only briefly, and he did not think of him again, even on the following Sunday when Collins was not at church and Brother Wiley preached on the faith of a mustard seed. He spoke of how that tiny grain, smaller than any other, when sown in the earth and properly tended, grew up to become an herb surpassing all others, a tall bushy plant shooting out great branches so that the fowls of the air might lodge beneath its shade. At dinner afterward, George Thomas Jr. was made to share what he had learned, which was that mustard came from a bush instead of a vegetable, unlike mayonnaise, which he did not like anyhow. The father observed that so long as they were talking major food group sources, he was relieved to learn his son was capable of converting a fine topical church sermon into chopped liver. His voiced dripped with sarcasm.

Nor did he think of Collins the following week. Or on the subsequent Sunday when George Thomas Jr. once again proved that he neither listened to anyone nor learned from experience, not even his own errors, of which there were many. That he in fact was hell-bent on wasting his young life. His father did not conclude this from a single incident but from an odious aggregation. It was an inescapable deduction founded in close observation over considerable time. The boy spent his evenings running the roads in the Toyota, neglected his schoolwork, fussed with his mother, ignored his father, when made to stay at home did nothing but sprawl in front of the TV patrolling music video channels, looking bored, the volume cranked up to the rafters. All he cared about was his car. To his father's knowledge, he hadn't even shown an interest in girls. The boy was surly, impulsive, moody and graceless. He was headed for nowhere at best, at worst, calamity. George Thomas Sr. monitored the debacle, increasingly furious, and decided it was time for another serious sit-down with Lorraine.

It was the next afternoon, after he'd calculated how best to broach the subject — a tricky back door maneuver using the subject of the boy's college plans, or lack thereof — that the thought of Collins returned. It did not arrive by accident or circuitous association, but was unnaturally thrust upon him. He pulled into the driveway after work and found his son, belly down, precariously balanced over the faded green fender of a Ford pickup truck, upper body disappeared into the engine compartment. The boy was banging metal while his protruding legs treaded air. The father got out and stood in front of the truck's open hood, looking inside. The boy's head and spidery arms, streaked with sweat and grease, were plunged deep into the cavity. There, buried beneath the oily dustcaked motor, he pulled at a ratchet handle and grunted, forcing it. At the end of each crank, the steel handle clanged loudly against some doohickey, a greasy cylindrical thing encrusted with dirt. George Thomas Sr. thought maybe it was the starter, he wasn't sure. His uncertainty created not one iota of guilt. He knew nothing of automotive mechanics. Car problems were why God had created auto technicians who did. "Whose truck?" he asked.

The boy attacked the handle a final time then pushed up, slid off the fender wiping his face with the tail of his T-shirt. The shirt, once white, had suffered a terrible end. He grinned and wiggled the ratchet tool toward the pickup. "Nice, huh? I been wanting a truck like this, a fixer upper. Got all kinds of potential."

George Thomas Sr. scowled, stepped to the side and circled the vehicle. Dented fenders, faded green surface pockmarked with dark rust, the driver's wing window fractured, rear bumper end twisted downward as though it'd tangled with another during rutting season and lost. He faced his son. With a curt gesture, as if dismissing something repulsive, he said, "The answer is no. You've already got a car."

"Yeah, but I always wanted a pickup." The boy grinned again. "Besides, I already bought it."

The father gaped at his son. "What?"

"I used my savings and Mom signed. It's a surprise." The boy squirmed, did a quick tap dance in Keds on the drive. "Plus you'll never believe the deal I made. I got it for a song." His voice cracked with undisguised pride. He reached over and patted the fender tenderly. "It was a steal."

That his wife and son had conspired against him slowly sunk in. Concealed within the shadows of that disaster, though, George Thomas Sr. sensed a larger cataclysm, something monstrous. His eyes were drawn to the truck. He staggered back a step, caught his balance. He felt dizzy. A fly buzzed around in his head in smaller and smaller circles and lighted in his forehead, right behind his eyes. His breath came in short shallow spurts, as if he was panting. For a moment, he thought he might pass out. He realized that beneath the suit jacket his shirt was wet with perspiration. But his mouth felt dry, his tongue thick and swollen. "Where?" he said, barely audible.

The boy shrugged. "Guy here in town."

"Who?"

"Harvey Collins. Runs good, too. He says all it needs is a transmission. And I got money for that, it's only a thousand. Mom said it was okay. Shoot, man, always wanted me a pickup. I'm gonna body-putty the bad spots and paint it canary yellow, get some chrome reverse mags and balloon tires." He stroked the fender again, ran a blackened hand over the curve in a long caress. In the suffused late afternoon light, his thin bony face seemed to soften. "When I'm finished, you know? It's gonna be cherry."

George Thomas Sr. wasn't listening. He stared westward down the street beyond the dark treeline marking the city park. Above it the fat dusking sun hovered at a ravished horizon like a bruised cyclopean eye, massive, dark red and purple. From the sweeping limbs of the sycamore in the front yard came the lazy twilight call of a mourning dove, but he took no notice. All he heard was the fly inside, an enormous horsefly, angrily buzzing as if his head was an enclosed glass sphere from which the insect frantically sought escape. He reeled and went up the walk toward the front door. As he neared the entrance, he vaguely observed that someone was standing in it, holding the door open. He was under the impression it was Lorraine. As he passed through into the house, she might've been smiling and she might've said, "George Thomas needed a project, dear, something to succeed at. I knew you'd approve, seeing him with a concrete goal. Aren't you surprised?" He wasn't sure. Later, though, sitting in his study remembering, he was pretty sure she'd been there, and that's what she'd said.

Before preaching next Sunday morning Brother Wiley announced the church would take up a special offering. The minister paused, lifted both hands to embrace the pulpit. He was stout as a fireplug, a silver-haired dignified man with black-rimmed glasses and shaggy brows and a strong bass voice, earnest with authority. He cleared his throat. Everyone waited. Sometimes a member of the body finds himself or herself in a particularly desperate position, he began, and at such times it is proper to approach the church and ask for assistance. If it's a crisis of faith, naturally, or even advice in a troubled marriage, then better to speak to the minister in private. But sometimes a person needs the whole congregation. Maybe he's suffering a terrible illness, the pastor observed, and needs the prayers of all, or perhaps she's despondent over the loss of a loved one, feeling lonely and requires visitation. Then it's appropriate to involve the entire body. No one should feel ashamed to ask, anymore than they'd feel ashamed to give. That's what the church is about — community. See how the Lord relied on his disciples for comfort even if they sometimes let Him down? It proves that no man's an island, that the gospel of Christ puts us in loving relationship with others. We depend on them, they depend on us. So this morning, the minister concluded, we are going to take up a special collection for the Collins family, who is undergoing an unexpected period of financial hardship. Brother Wiley did not further elaborate, though many would have appreciated some details. Instead, he called the ushers up front to stand while he prayed.

At the sound of Collins' name, George Thomas Sr., who was situated in the fifth pew on the left between his wife and son, lurched in his seat as if someone had poked him. During the prayer, he kept his head half bowed canvassing the congregation. When the surreptitious search turned up empty a wave of relief passed over him. He felt light-headed, realized he'd been holding his breath.

Sister Landry played the piano and sang while the ushers passed the plates. Lorraine leaned his way to murmur, "Well, at least we helped them by buying that old truck. Isn't that them over there?" Without moving, she swung her eyes discreetly to the right. His followed hers like a lowboy trailer in tow to discover Collins directly across the aisle staring at him. The man's small dark russet eyes flashed, he boosted his chin high and nodded. George Thomas Sr. glanced away. As the collection plate came down the pew, he opened his wallet to remove a hundred dollar bill. Lorraine pinched the sleeve of his jacket. "My Lord," she whispered, "we already bought that truck." He dropped the bill into the plate and passed it to his son, who smirked and reached in, grabbing the bill as if he might retrieve it. His father muttered, "I'll break your arm," and the boy jerked his hand away. A dismayed aspect of fear in his narrow face cycled into indignation, then anger. George Thomas Sr. ignored him.

Sister Landry's voice trailed off and the piano stopped. Brother Wiley announced the offering had come to more than five hundred dollars. He did not indicate whether the amount was satisfactory, so George Thomas Sr. leaned back as if to stretch a sore neck and chanced another sideways glance at Collins. The man was wearing the green polyester slacks and cheap nylon dress shirt with the wrinkled knit tie. Maybe he only owned two sets of clothes, one for work and one for church. Next to him sat a girl with thick orange-red hair and pale freckled shoulders in a floral print yellow sundress. The resolute set of her head and shoulders indicated a wish to be elsewhere. He craned farther back trying to catch a glimpse of her profile just as she ducked. Collins had lunged to his feet and rotated to face the congregation. He hitched his pants and wrenched his neck awkwardly in either direction saying, "I thankee much. Yessir, surely do. So's my daughter here" — he yanked a thumb toward the girl — "and my wife what couldn't make it." He stood a moment more, then jerked his head once again and abruptly sat down.

After the service, during Sunday dinner, Lorraine broke the silence at the table by asking George Thomas Jr. if the young woman with Mr. Collins had been Sissy Collins. The boy mumbled, "That's her," continued chewing a wad of roast beef. "Well, she looked nice enough to me," Lorraine commented pleasantly. "She has lovely red hair. And that was a nice dress she was wearing." Her son snorted. "Well, it was," she protested mildly. He lifted and dropped his shoulders indifferently. "And she was well groomed," she added, "without too much makeup."

Her son snickered. "Oughta see her the rest of the time. Shorty shorts and halter tops with no bra and plenty of makeup. She puts this dark purple stuff on her eyes."

"Eyeshadow," Lorraine said.

"Whatever, she gobs it on there. Josh said she's trying to hide."

"I think that's just the style, isn't it?"

"Maybe." He crumbled a slice of cornbread in his plate and covered it with brown gravy, dosed the mound with salt and pepper, concentrating, performing the procedure as a laboratory chemist might mix explosives. Without looking up he said, "Josh had this weird sound he couldn't locate? Thought it was his rear end. We went over to M&M yesterday and guess what, ol' Harvey done lost his job." The boy elevated a probing eye toward his father, who seemed lost in thought. "So how'd you like the sermon?" he asked.

George Thomas Sr. didn't reply. His jaw moved up and down methodically as he worked on a piece of roast beef, his blank gaze resting on the tabletop. He was listening to the fly inside his head. It had returned during Brother Wiley's sermon, hadn't rested since. Spiraling round and round, a high-pitched gyrating hum. Annoying.

Lorraine said, "Penny for your thoughts, dear. Hello there? Dear? Oh, hel-l-l-oooh." He looked up. She said, "George Thomas asked you a question." He turned to his son. "How'd you like the sermon," the boy said.

"It was alright," he replied, nodding slowly, "it was just fine." The buzzing seemed to be getting louder again. Must be a horsefly, it was big.

"So what'd you learn from it?"

He peered into his son's face through the noise and saw the malicious grin, the taunting pale blue eyes. The boy knew. The boy knew he had sat through the entire sermon without paying attention, that he had not listened. That he had not heard a word and hadn't the slightest idea what Brother Wiley had said. He couldn't even remember the topic printed on the church bulletin. The phrase "loaves and fishes" occurred to him. Was that right? No, he was confusing that with another recent Sunday. Wasn't he? He didn't know. Carefully setting down the fork, he wiped his mouth with the napkin and excused himself. He went down the hallway, the fly going round and round and round, beating its brittle parchment wings against the inside of his skull. Somewhere in the rear distance he heard his wife say, "Your father hasn't been feeling well," and his son said, "He acted weird in church." Then Lorraine said, "Ever since that truck," and the boy said, "Unh-unh, no way, I ain't givin' the truck up. But I might need to borrow some money. I think the U-joints gone bad."

In the study, he closed the venetian blinds and sat in the dark. It was quieter that way. Plus flies didn't dart about in darkness, they might smash into something; they roosted somewhere and waited for light. The one inside his head settled in its familiar place just behind his eyes. Without the humming noise, he could think. George Thomas Sr. pictured the man seated in the church pew, the rough mahogany face shot with hardship, the small hot eyes staring his way. With what? Accusation? Maybe. Certainly 'defiance. That lifted chin. And then the brief nod. Grudging forgiveness in that nod, as if forgiveness of some kind was warranted. It was not. His decision had been appropriate under the circumstances, and prudent. He had certain fiduciary responsibilities, he had executed them. Fair to all concerned, therefore innocent. Or not guilty, as a court might say. Without guilt, no need for forgiveness.

He rose in slow motion so as not to unsettle the fly and leaned forward, cracked the blind with his fingers to peek into the yard. A bright June day, oleanders in bloom, heat waffling off the street pavement, not a cloud in the pallid sky. The incoming band of sunlight awakened the fly. It began to spin and keen, its strident wings beating the backs of his eyeballs. So loud, and persistent, painful. He dropped his hand, it fell silent. Must be a horsefly, he decided, it was big as a boat. And getting worse.

He returned to his chair and sat in the darkness, wondering what sort of sickness had come over him.

Doc Jacobs recommended rest and relaxation. "Could prescribe medication and I will if you want," he said, "but it looks like stress to me. You been overworking?" Perched in boxer shorts on a hard plastic chair facing the examining table, George Thomas Sr. wasn't sure what to answer. All he did was sit at a desk eight hours a day seeing clients, talking on the telephone, making decisions. Not much physical activity but he'd always enjoyed his work. "Well, let me put it this way," Doc Jacobs said, "you got something special bothering you? Trouble at home maybe?"

He sniffed. The small white room smelled of Listerine and soap. The plastic chair was cold. He felt naked. "Nothing unusual."

The doctor leaned against the vinyl-covered examining table holding a stethoscope, crossed his arms over the white smock, crossed his legs and interlocked his feet. He was a tall braided pretzel with a square head crowned with a gray wirebrush flattop. "Take a couple of days off then. Stay home. Go fishing, play some golf. Stay away from the office. And if it keeps up, call me."

"Did I mention that sucker feels big as a helicopter?" his patient asked.

"Call me anyway," Doc Jacobs said, "say Thursday or Friday."

George Thomas Sr. said he would.

So on Tuesday morning he played nine holes of golf with the club pro Shank Gibson, shooting badly. The sunlight hurt his eyes through the Ray-Bans, the strident buzzing advanced and retreated at random, he threw up behind the hedge on the sixth tee. When he scheduled another round for the next morning, Shank seemed anxious. "Expect you'll feel better? Upchucking sure puts off a game."

"Be here with bells on," he said, "I'm unstressing."

Lorraine made him tuna salad for lunch at home but he wasn't hungry. He tried to nap in the afternoon. Restless, he called the office several times. Judy said everything was ship-shape, not to worry. He skipped dinner and slept poorly, then quit after the fifth hole Wednesday when the stridulent noise became so loud he couldn't hear Shank's instructions. They crouched on the smooth green diagnosing a twenty-foot putt and he watched the pro's mouth making soundless words, then slid his putter in the bag and walked away, crossing the wide sunsoaked fairways to his car. He drove home. Lorraine, standing at the sink rinsing a flower vase, offered him a bowl of strawberry sherbet, saying he needed to eat *something*. He didn't reply. In the darkness of the study, once the noise subsided, he phoned Judy.

"How you feeling?"

"Fine, fine," he said. He bent forward in the chair with his head between his knees, an elbow propped on either thigh. "Anything there that needs attention?"

"No, it's been a light day." She paused. "That Mr. Collins came by and left a note. He sure is strange. He just walked up, dropped the envelope on my desk and left. Didn't even say hi."

The banker emitted a soft guttural sound, something in the vicinity of a groan. "What's it say?"

99

"Well, I didn't open it."

"Open it."

He waited. After a moment she started reading. "Mr. President, reckon Satan done fooled me again. Twice't now. He's a right smart feller. First time I was a boy, like I told you. Then he had me thinking you was the —" Judy hesitated. "It looks like 'Samatite' but his handwriting —"

"Samaritan."

"Right, okay ... Had me thinking you was the Samaritan but you wasn't. Ol' Lucifer got my wife that credit card too, which I can't pay. So the bank can come at me. Well come on. That church money was too little too late. Now I gotta do what I gotta do. It's on my head, I reckon. But they'll be better off. God forgive me, which He already done. Harvey Collins.

"P.S. That boy done got him a good truck, make him treat it right."

Judy said, "Well, don't that beat all."

He sat in the dark, trying to think. The fly was beating his brains out.

"Wonder what he's gonna do. Think he's dangerous, Mr. Hebert?"

He resisted a jagged impulse to howl or screech, instead said, "What I want you to do, Judy, is make a couple of calls. Call his house, see if his family's alright. And you better call Chief Dawson and read him the note, see what he thinks. Then call me back."

He hung up the receiver, shuffled down the hallway to the kitchen and drank a glass of water, his eyes half closed to hold down the shrill, high-toned buzz. Above it he heard the TV in the living room. Lorraine watching CNN. He went to the bathroom and threw up before returning to the study to wait. Judy called back shortly. The Collins phone had been disconnected, she said. Chief Dawson had agreed to send a patrolman over to the house and check on the situation. "He said he'd call back. I told him you're at home."

"Thanks, Judy."

He opened a desk drawer and felt around until he located a

small penlight flashlight. The batteries were old, the beam a soft glow. From the bookshelf he got his King James and used the penlight to find Luke, chapter 10. He began reading. Thieves beat up the man, left him beside the road. First the priest passed, then the Levite. Progress was slow. Each time the horsefly started up, he closed his eyes and waited until the noise stopped. He'd reached the part where the Samaritan was coming down the road when the telephone rang. He flicked off the penlight to answer.

"Yes?"

"Dawson here. What kind of operation you runnin' these days, George, a collection agency? That ol' boy sounds madder'n hell." The chief's booming voice dropped to a chuckle. "Heard you got a bug. You hanging in?"

"Fine, fine," he replied. He cleared his throat. It felt raw. All the vomiting, the stomach acids. "Just thought we should check it out."

"Well, you done the right thing," the chief said, "never can tell with a note like that. Man goes crazy, might have a list, you're on it. Sent out one of the boys to the house, talked to the woman and her daughter. They said Harvey left town. Packed some clothes in a pillowcase and pulled out. Said he had some business to finish up. They weren't sure what he meant by that. He was afoot. Ain't that his ol' Ford pickup I seen your boy driving?"

George Thomas Sr. slowly nodded.

"I'll take that silence as a yes," said Dawson. "You reckon Harvey's mad about that, too?"

He shrugged.

After a moment's wait, the chief said, "Sure been good talking at you, George. If Harvey Collins shows or you get worried let me know, we'll send a patrol by regular. Get some rest. Talk atcha later." The line went dead.

He hung up, fumbled for the penlight and resumed reading. There was nothing in the parable he had not remembered, nothing to hint what might've happened had the Samaritan not stopped. Presumably, the injured man would not have recovered to go berserk and start killing people. He would've lain there and died. Unless someone else came along. Naturally, they might have helped him. Then he would've lived. That was a possibility. There was no way of knowing, of course, the way the story was told.

Collins' body turned up Saturday.

Late afternoon, George Thomas Sr. was reading in the study with the overhead light on when Lorraine knocked at the door and opened it. The news was on TV, she said. A body had floated up in the Sabine River about six miles downstream, a fisherman in a boat had run over it. The corpse was in bad condition but the I.D. was positive: a forty-five-year old white male, Harvey James Collins, of Bethlehem. "I thought you'd want to know," Lorraine said.

He nodded. He was wearing a pair of casual slacks and a Ralph Lauren pullover shirt and deck shoes without socks. She looked at the Bible open in his lap, glanced away, then fixed her gaze back on it. "What you reading?"

"Book of Job."

"Ah," she said, pursing her lips. "You know, I never have understood that story. Poor old Job. Like he was a laboratory rat in some cosmic experiment. Don't think I could hold up to the strain. Guess that's the point, though. Supper in half an hour." She winked. "Made some shrimp gumbo, your favorite."

"Mmm-mmm," said George Thomas Sr. She smiled and closed the door. He stared at the flat painted surface, his attention focused inward on the spot in his forehead just behind his eyes. The fly wasn't there. That was good. The medicine Doc Jacobs had prescribed the previous day was working. No angry horsefly, no buzzing. He couldn't pronounce the drug, some exotic compound of Latinate syllables, but it spelled relief.

He returned to his reading — Job on the defensive, listing his good works, his friends mocking him — and when Lorraine called him to supper he made small talk while devouring two large bowls of gumbo over rice. His stomach had rebounded, another good sign. Neither of them brought up the subject of the dead man, but when George Thomas Jr. came barreling in late and zipped by toward the bathroom to wash he called out, "You hear about Harvey?" He reappeared with wet hands and plopped into the dining chair, saying, "Yep, they found him in the Sabine all chewed up. The turtles and gar been at it. We was down at the park when they brought him in. Josh missed the whole thing. Man, the smell was awful." He twisted his face.

"That'll be enough," Lorraine said, "after all, we're eating."

"Shrimp gumbo!" the boy exclaimed, rubbing his hands on his pants. He licked his lower lip seeing his mother ladle the dark brown soup into a wide bowl of rice. "Shoot, we ain't had gumbo in a coon's age!"

"Well, with your father feeling better I thought we'd have something special. You want some more, dear?"

George Thomas Sr. shook his head. "No, no. So tell me, how did Harvey die?"

The boy shrugged. "I dunno. Drowned, I guess. He was in the river. Hemp Murphy said he probably jumped off the highway bridge. That's the most popular spot. He said ol' Harvey couldn't swim, what he heard. We seen his wife and Sissy down there. They was in the park waiting for the body. I talked to her. She ain't so bad."

"Mrs. Collins?" Lorraine asked. "She's better?"

"No, Sissy." The boy blew across a soupspoon full of hot gumbo, put his mouth to it and slurped. "I was talking with her last night at the Dairy Queen, too," he said. "She says Harvey sure left them a mess, they're flat broke. Then I seen her again today, at the park."

"Well, maybe he left an insurance policy," Lorraine said doubtfully. "At least a little something to get by for now. There's the money from the truck, and the church collection."

"Nope, nuthin," the boy announced. "They never seen the truck money, and ol' Harvey took that church money when he left. Only it wasn't in his pocket. Guess the river got it. I heard

Mrs. Collins talking to this newspaper reporter? She said they ain't got the rent, plus they owe money everywhere." He glanced at his father. "She said they asked for a loan but the bank turned them down flat."

"Well, I seriously doubt that," Lorraine said, "at least not if a loan was warranted. Your father has never been one to turn his back on a person in need if he could do otherwise."

"Is that right, Dad?"

George Thomas Sr. picked up his iced tea, sipped, set the glass down. "I try to do what's right within the range of both generosity and prudence," he said.

"So you turned him down?"

He did not look at his son. He took another sip of tea, his eyebrows pinched. "I really don't think it proper to discuss another's private financial business, especially when it concerns the bank, and most especially if the person is deceased."

The boy sneered. "Yeah, that's what I thought."

"Hush, George Thomas," said his mother.

"If you'd just loaned him that money," the boy went on, "but you didn't. No, you —"

"George Thomas!"

"Why, you practically —"

"George Thomas!" She was shouting. "You hush right now!"

The boy slammed down his spoon and shoved the chair back, leaped to his feet. "I ain't hungry." He swiveled his lanky frame to face his father, saying, "Ol' Harvey was a good guy," then shot his mother a withering glance and stormed out. They heard the pickup start and back into the street. He ground gears and peeled rubber pulling away.

George Thomas Sr. looked at his wife. Her wounded eyes lingered on the far door, the narrow shoulders shuddered. After a moment she slumped and met his gaze. "He didn't mean that," she said. "He's just upset from seeing the body. He didn't know what he was saying."

Her husband cocked his head as if the matter was of little concern, took another sip of tea. "Oh, he meant it alright. He knew exactly what he was saying."

"No, no he didn't," she pleaded, breathing hard. "It's only that he holds everything in, and when it comes out —" Her voice broke, she raised a slender hand to one cheek. "He's like you in that way."

He laughed caustically. "Like me? Like me?" His voice rose loud and hard, its harshness beating the close air in the room like a hammer. "That boy's never showed an ounce of restraint in his life, Lorraine. How's that like me?"

He rose to his feet, tossed the napkin to the tabletop and strode from the room, leaving her pitched forward in the seat, quaking, the long swan-like neck spilling downward, hands clasped twisting in her lap, murmuring, "You just don't know, you just don't ..."

It seemed to him the medicine wasn't working anymore. He sat in the study wearing the slacks and Ralph Lauren pullover, now barefooted, holding the unopened Bible. He listened. The fly had not returned but now he heard an intermittent clanging, like the beating of a brass gong, and sometimes a metallic tinkling that reminded him of the wind chime Lorraine had hung on the back patio. But it wasn't that, he'd checked. There it was again, indistinct, distant, as if some practical joker was walking along a nearby street banging cymbals. At this hour? He checked his wristwatch. Almost midnight. Unlikely. At least the chimer was less noisome than the gong-banger, which hurt his head.

He did not feel sleepy. Last night he'd slept like the dead. Maybe the medicine had stopped. He hoped not. He'd taken the last pill. That would've been right after Lorraine went to bed, still upset. She'd apologized for the boy again and excused his wild behavior, repeated that seeing the dead body must have distressed him, caused an acute stress reaction. He had listened, silently nodding, not buying it.

Because he knew. He'd studied the boy too closely for too long not to know the sheer meanness that lurked there, the careless and debased indifference, the abject insensitivity to the fact others do not merely exist but constitute entire parallel and equal universes of being in the world. The boy did not know charity and did not care to know. That was his character. Who he *chose* to be.

The tall ceramic beer mug was empty so he opened the door and went down to the kitchen to refill it from the tap. All evening he'd been drinking water like a fish and urinating like a horse. The medicine, a side effect. As he leaned against the sink counter filling the mug the gong began to go off again. *Bong — bong — bong.* He waited for it to ebb, then backtracked to the study and set the mug down, stepped out to the bathroom. He was straddling the toilet bowl when he heard the truck drive up. The front door opened and shut. For a long time he hovered above the toilet surveying the clear thick stream shooting downward, then flushed. Passing his son's bedroom door in the hallway, he heard a voice. He stopped, put an ear close. Apparently the boy was on the telephone.

"Naw, Josh, last night, right after you left. Telling you, man, you shoulda stayed ... yeah, I'm just sitting there with a cherry Coke and fries when she walks in and sits down in the booth, right across from me ... when? Just after you split, you moron ... well I can't help it if you're stupid ... yeah, she said I was cute. Said she's been noticing me. And then she says how about a little fun?"

The boy began laughing. His father stood fastened, his ear to the door. He feared the gongs would go off again or the cymbals reappear but they didn't. The boy's laughter abated, he began speaking again. The voice rang boastful and smug, full of triumphant self-regard.

"So I said sounds good to me, babe, my place or yours ... I did, too ... I don't care how it sounds, man, it worked ... you kidding? With my folks home? We went down to the park, by the river. Over behind them trees. Only then she started telling me how she was broke and needed this and that, I don't know what all, some new clothes, I wasn't listening good ...

"Cause I was excited, dickhead, why you think?... anyhow,

all I give'er was twenty bucks, that was all I had ... yeah, then we got in the bed of the truck and she let me put it in ... course we was nekkid, you dumbass ... the hell we weren't, how would you know?

"Better believe it, she's red downstairs too ... huh? ... well, they was big enough, a mouthful ... naw, man, she was clean, she claimed that nigger never got any ... what? Probably, yeah, if you got twenty bucks ... no way, forget that, I ain't calling her this late. Anyhow, you moron, her old man just died today ..."

The gongs went off in his head as if a dozen muscle-bound Nubian slaves were in there swinging sledgehammers. He doubled over pressing both hands to his ears, pigeon-walked down to the study and shut the door. He switched off the light, collapsed in the chair. The louder racket gradually receded, replaced by a steady tinkling patter of peasized hail hitting an aluminum roof. After a while it tapered off as well and there was only silence. He breathed slowly in the dark. The absence of noise brought relief close to ecstasy, as though an excruciating migraine had suddenly vanished.

He thought about praying. He might drop to his knees and lean over the chair and pray for the soul of Harvey Collins, who had wallowed in filth until an angel forewarned him though he still lost his calling, who'd then recklessly gone into debt and lost his truck, who'd finally lost his life and abandoned his family to impoverishment and to predators like his own son who would exploit them. He could pray for the soul of the boy, if it wasn't too late. He could pray for the soul of his wife and the souls of Sissy Collins and Mrs. Collins and right on down the list of everyone he could think of, even the nameless. Lord knows the world could use it. He could even pray for George Thomas Hebert Sr., maybe him most. Not that he hadn't always used his best judgment. He surely had. In a world of unfortunate circumstances, not all were extenuating. Some decisions are terribly difficult but justifiable.

Not guilty.

He thought again about the boy, who surely was. He might

pray for the boy. He considered doing so and even wanted to but the idea set off clamoring gongs that paralyzed him with pain. In any case, he did not believe his prayers would accomplish much if the boy showed no initiative. No one had those kinds of coattails, not even a father. So he avoided thoughts of the boy and wondered what sort of sickness this was. Doc Jacobs hadn't really known, that was obvious. In the dark he felt on the desktop for the Bible, clutched it as if he might find healing there. He felt unclean. That damned parable.

A roller of nausea broke over him as yet another thought registered, one he'd never considered. The Bible slipped from his hands, tumbled to the floor. He felt sick. If the Samaritan had not stopped, the man probably would've died. That would have been his natural fate.

But in that case, what would have become of the Samaritan?

At some point he must've fallen asleep because he awakened with his face cheekdown on the desktop in a pool of slobber. He slumped back in the chair, feeling drugged. His watch by penlight said five o'clock. Almost sunrise.

He sat rubbing his eyes. The late night conversation he'd overheard came back. It was almost more than he could bear, worse than the gongs, the cymbals. With a sigh he leaned down and pulled out the bottom desk drawer, removed a wooden cigar box and opened it. He took the gun out. It felt cold and heavy in his hand, a lump of smooth steel. He wasn't sure what caliber it was or even the manufacturer, he'd never looked that closely. The gun had belonged to his father when he was an auxiliary sheriff's deputy. It was a six-shot revolver, that's all he recalled. Also, it was loaded. He'd inherited it that way, never emptied it. He'd never fired it, either, or any other gun. Now he gripped the revolver in his right hand and stepped into the hallway. In this, the most silent hour of the day, the house lay preternaturally quiet. He went down the hallway barefooted, heard the refrigerator motor kick on in the kitchen as he turned into the foyer. He opened the front door and stepped outside and along the cement walk, the cold damp pebbles embedded in its surface gouging the soft soles of his feet. He shivered.

Where the walkway curved toward the drive he veered left and tread through the wet grass to the oleander hedge, lay down, rolled beneath it. The crumbling soil was moist and cool. Face down, he squirmed on the sticky black loam, then flipped over and pressed wriggling downward like a worm, pushing against the lower hedge branches for leverage, the gun gripped in one hand. He scooped a handful of wet earth and smeared his face, gobbed it in his hair. He paused, sniffing. A dog must have taken a crap under the hedge. Nasty. He began to giggle.

The eastern sky was bruised a deep purple and bled orange with daybreak and he imagined roosters were crowing somewhere and fish were slapping the dappled river surface in misty shallows along the banks, and somewhere someone was dying and somewhere they were preparing to bury the dead while others tossed in fitful final dreams before rising. Then he rolled to his feet and crossed the dewdrenched yard to the driveway, stopped in front of the Ford truck and pointed the gun toward the chrome grill. He pulled the trigger but it didn't budge. He remembered about safeties and found the tiny lever, moved it. He pointed the revolver again and fired. The gunshot exploded across the lawn and down Myrtle Street through the neighborhood as though a bomb had gone off. A volley of crowjacks rose out of the sycamore and scattered on beating wings. He moved to his left and fired again, into the front right headlight. The roar shattered the glass. He smiled and circled farther and shot the right rear tire, the air came whistling out. In back, aiming toward the center of the O in "Ford" on the tailgate, he pulled the trigger and grunted with satisfaction as a small round hole erupted in the canary yellow surface. He ran to the passenger's side and holding the gun with both hands, crouched, shot the front fender at an angle. The slug whinged along the grazed metal and slammed into the garage door. He hesitated, tried to think what to shoot next. Porch lights came on at the Mitchells and at other homes up and down the street but he didn't notice. First one voice hollered, then others were shouting but he didn't hear for the crashing gongs and tinkling cymbals and the reverberating echoes of the gunshots. He was trying to determine where the gas tank was located because he'd seen vehicles on TV shot in the gas tank explode into a huge fireballs of orange flames and rolling black smoke, rocketing high into the air to fall crashing back to earth, blazing conflagrations of crunched metal. But his ignorance confounded him. When he found nothing that resembled a gas tank he moved to the front again and settled for the windshield. He scowled, pointed the gun, fired a final time. There was a sharp splat and a spider's web of silver fractures spread outward forming a ragged geometric orbit over the wide swath of glass. He stood there in the echoing discharge engrossed, bewitched by a symmetric configuration that vaguely reminded him of a giant bloodshot eye.

The noise in his head retreated and he heard the sirens then, and the screaming. At first he believed they were the same sound but then they separated and the sirens wailed in the distance and he understood the screams came from close by. He whirled to see George Thomas Jr. standing in the walkway in his briefs, hands clinched into fists, face bright red, eyes bulging, his mouth distorted in a strange wide-gaped oval as he shrieked, "What the hell you think you doing! That's my truck! Stop it! Stop it! Stop it!"

Out to the side, Henry Mitchell and his wife and others from the neighborhood were gathered on the lawn in small immobile clots, horror etched on their faces, and fear. Beyond the boy, in the open doorway, stood Lorraine in her nightgown, tall and lovely, watchful, as inert as the statue of a Roman empress holding one hand aloft to her cheek. He smiled and waved, raised the gun as if to point at his son, then reversed his hold and pressed the barrel to his heart with his thumb on the trigger. The boy dropped to his knees wailing, "No! Don't do it! For God's sake, Dad, don't do it! I'm sorry!"

The words stopped him. He believed he heard in them the cry of Harvey Collins, and his own too, and the cries of all those in the world calling out for forgiveness in a great croaking chorus, crying out in anguished grief for the completion of their own failed selves. He dropped to the cement drive, lay back weeping on the damp pavement with outspread arms gazing upward, saw the sunstreaked morning clouds overhead separating and uniting and roiling in golden light like molten iron, heard there the birthing cries of newborn divinities emerging from the collective travail. They gathered over him, luminous and warm, full of grace, enfolding him with tender caresses, petting him, quieting him with soft suggestive whispers. In the gentle embrace of sweet ululations he lifted upwards in their loving care toward the light, unafraid, submissive, peaceful.

Heresies

When his supervisor with Allied Security told him his next posting was the John Shelby Boone Ecumenical Retreat Center, tucked among the wrinkled limestone hills overlooking the Pedernales west of Austin, Hank Jeters was of two minds.

A country boy at heart, from East Texas, Hank was tired of working the office buildings downtown, sterile glass hives where rushing men and women got their ideas from Merrill Lynch commercials. Off in those rough junipered hills flanking the river, where a person could unravel, he was likely to sight some wildlife. A big whitetail buck, for instance.

Only the location would mean an hour's drive each way. That was a lot of radio listening to the same hit songs, most of which didn't even sound country anymore, except for Mark Chesnutt. Plus he'd have to use his own vehicle. The company reimbursed just twenty cents a mile, a stingy amount given the true expenses on a Dodge Ram 2500 pickup.

Practical reasons for refusing the assignment won hands down. Hank took it anyway. If a fella reasoned overmuch, he'd run off to Alaska and become a professional outdoorsman.

The only other thought he had was to wonder what "ecumenical" meant.

The duty roster specified a four-day assignment, Monday through Thursday. His eyes sprung awake beating the alarm by an hour the first morning. He rolled out of bed excited. The

112

prospect of seeing some unsullied countryside had him whistling in the shower. He closed one eye, sighted down a Leopold scope through hot runnels of rain coursing down his face, put the crosshairs on a big ten-pointer, squeezed the trigger. *Boom!*

After coffee and toast with scrambled eggs, Hank packed lunch, hit the outbound road.

The traffic spilling into the city at this early hour dismayed him. The incoming line backed up, bunched and unsprung like a slinky. Maniacs darted out to pass, swerving, risking life and limb to get there first. How could people live this way? Year after year, same route in, same out, listening to the radio, traffic updates and weather reports, as if any of them worked outside and had to worry about rain.

He kept one eye to the road and the other on the low junipers skirting hillsides in thick green clumps, hoping to glimpse a white flag bobbing. Not likely this long after daybreak in July. They'd be hunkered down from the heat.

The whole way out, not one Mark Chesnutt song.

A discrete redwood sign marked the retreat center entrance. The gravel lane off the highway wound through denser stands of sunstroked juniper and live oak — grotesque twisted shapes — circled limestoned outcrops to straddle dry creekbeds, then finally passed between two rock columns indicating the grounds. Hank braked alongside an old GMC pickup facing a low, sprawling cedar siding building. A redwood sign with the carved letters in relief read: *John Shelby Boone Ecumenical Retreat Center.*

He'd never heard of John Shelby Boone. A dead guy, most likely, a rich dead guy, of which Texas had plenty. As for "ecumenical," that'd been solved. According to his neighbor Larry Gentry, it was a word professors used, a high-hat way of saying "economical." Larry worked maintenance at the university. There he overheard all sorts of terms meant to impress the listener and exclude the uninformed. "Like they're running a secret club," he'd told Hank, "and make each other learn these fancy passwords."

He shut the engine and climbed down. An older man in a denim shirt and jeans and scuffed muleskinner boots stepped onto the porch. He wore a cowboy jute with a cutting-horse crease set low. His eyes passed over Hank's beige uniform, hovered on the holstered Smith & Wesson. "Reckon you the security we ordered," he said. "Getting a trifle old to handle terrorists by my lonesome, I told 'em, unless I got cart blank to shoot first. Otherwise get me some backup."

The man was lean as bone, with a windweathered chin etched in hickory, side-swiped nose, ochered coyote eyes. He bent forward over the porch edge and spit tobacco. "Reckon you're it."

Hank touched the bill of his company gimmee cap, nodding, rested a hand on the baton grip at his belt. "Kind of trouble we expecting?" He'd worked security for three years but was young and his question hinted uncertainty. Once in the Texas National Bank lobby he'd smacked a lunatic with the baton. Another time he'd tackled a drunk in a 7-Eleven only to bust his own lip on a potato chip rack. Otherwise the job had been boring. He'd never pulled his gun. "I mean, we all the way out here, middle of nowhere."

"Yes, we are," the bent-nosed man agreed, "and that's how I like it. Been keeping this place onto thirty years now, ever since I quit the rodeo. Ain't never had no trouble 'til them theologians plan a meeting," and he gazed off eastward, squinting against early light. "Now we got us some threats. Phone calls mostly. Gun talk. We'll put you out here on the front porch."

Hank frowned. It was not so much the idea of threats that put him off, threats came a dime a dozen in his line of work and never proved out. What he didn't understand was the reference to theologians. He'd been expecting economists. Some kind of exclusive financial retreat. Lots of talk about national debt and interest rates and such. All weekend he'd figured to see a bunch of middle-aged bald guys dressed in Bermuda shorts and sandals, pale as skim milk, trying to act friendly in that awkward way important business people do under relaxed circumstances. They'd stand around outside between lectures getting sunburned, slapping bugs, drinking gin tonics and munching cashews. Sharing private chuckles while they planned the future of the world. That's what he'd expected.

What was this deal about theologians?

On the second morning they moved him inside, to the back of the meeting room. He assumed parade rest before sliding glass doors that opened onto a shallow cedar deck. The deck overlooked a steep hillside erupting in chalky outcroppings, dotted with scraggly bushes clinging desperately to crevices. At the bottom flowed a rocky spring-fed stream riffling water as clear as glass. Except Hank couldn't see any of it because the drapes were pulled shut. The big rectangular table around which the dozen theologians sat had been moved to the far end of the room. All this because Ace, the caretaker, had climbed down the hill to discover someone with a rifle might enjoy a clear view of the back of the room. The part where Hank now stood. An outside stairwell gave access to the deck. In case of rear attack, he was the first line of defense.

Yesterday, when the trouble started — when, as Ace said, "the horse plopped" — Hank had been posted outside on the front porch. It was that time on a summer day, just after lunch, when he always felt a tad sleepy. To tell the truth, he was dozing on his feet. Drifting in and out, drooling. When a white school bus pulled up from nowhere and spit out a roiling mass of people hollering and carrying signs.

That waked him right up.

The signs were posterboards stapled to picket stakes with scrawled letters saying things like "Homos Hate God" and "Sappho Was Never a Mother". One read "Protect Kids From Perverts". That's when Hank first realized the men inside the center — plus the one woman, a surprise, seeing her there — weren't discussing the usual subjects, like whether the Bible required a Trinity baptism or Oneness. He himself had been raised Assembly of God so he was a Trinitarian, although he didn't make a big deal of it. But the folks who piled out of the bus seemed madder'n Hulk Hogan with a referee beef.

The first decision Hank made was to stand on the top step, blocking the way. The raucous crowd swirled in the yard, waving signs, bellowing. He didn't have time to consider if he was scared, a fact he later pondered and thought the single advantage of having been taken by surprise. On the porch facing the threat with his feet set wide apart, he waited, one hand poised near his baton. It occurred to him if they all came at once, worked up as they were, his ass was sweet grass. A notion that this was precisely what he got paid for winged past, banked away down the hill.

A tall whipsnaked woman appeared then near the front, running back and forth. Wearing a yellow sun visor, a loose blue shift belted at the waist, Reeboks. She yelled, flung both arms upward into the commotion. A shudder passed through the crowd. Right before his eyes, with hardly a flicker, the mob coalesced into a tight-knit assemblage, suddenly quiet. She took up position and chopped the air three times with both hands. They started singing, swinging signs overhead in cadence.

"Can't say as I know that particular one," came a voice. Hank whirled. He was inches from Ace's warped nose, the result he'd said of a wild bronc stomping in Laramie.

"Recognize it?"

Hank shook his head no, listening. It was a slow mournful hymn, as if the singers were wrought with inconsolable grief. Gloomy expressions all around, one woman crying. "Them folks got the redass," drawled Ace, "but they scareder'n we are. Makes 'em dangerous."

Hank glanced over Ace's shoulder, saw the theologians collected on the porch. They stood in a compact clump. They seemed unruffled but for one, a slim man with a black mustache and longish hair peppered gray who bristled with agitation. He edged forward from the group and wagged a pointed finger at the protesters. The guy only meant to chastise them, Hank figured, but the gesture proved provocative. It was as if he'd poked a bamboo pole into a beehive, banged it up and down. The singing abruptly stopped. There followed a brief suspension of all movement, and silence. After which the collective body mutated, became a rowdy swarming mass. Its members broke ranks and surged ahead, shrieking. The porch was overrun in a blink, Hank got pushed down and trampled — he was still limping the next day, a knot on his elbow the size of a plum — but the theologians managed to scramble inside and weathered the assault behind locked doors until sheriff's deputies arrived. In the meantime, as he lay curled on the porch amongst churning legs and grunts and belligerent shouts, as he squirmed to cover his head with both arms, Hank was confounded by the mundane substance of his thoughts. Mostly he pondered how cheap his company was to reimburse only twenty cents a mile for travel. Later, once the deputies had sent the intruders packing, he mentioned the incident to Ace. The old man nodded and observed the human mind is a funny thing. "Reckon you noticed the words painted on that bus," he added.

Hank admitted he hadn't.

"Said 'Faith Tabernacle Evangelical Church'. And there was a invite on it, 'Join Us in Celebrating God's Love'." Ace hooked both thumbs in his back pockets and grinned lopsided, leaned to one side and spit. "Now ain't that sumthin?"

Hank agreed it certainly was, though he wasn't quite sure what Ace found meaningful in it. His knee was throbbing, left elbow aching and raw. Wiping dirt off his uniform, he noticed the other man had escaped unmarked. "Where'd you go?" he asked.

Ace pointed downward. "Ain't the first stampede I ever seen," he allowed. "Only safe place was under this porch. Too old for a rumpus, yessir."

And now, the following day, Hank was standing watch inside, in front of a sliding glass door through which a bullet might explode at any moment. A backup guard, Duane, was posted on the front porch. Duane worked for Allied Security, but Hank'd never met him until this morning. The guy didn't inspire confidence. Mid-thirties, not well groomed, underfed, a chain smoker. Spiky dilated eyes. In fact, it occurred to Hank that Duane, whose forearms sported an assortment of amateur tattoos, had come to work stoned. Hearing about the previous day's episode, Duane had reared back with a yellow-toothed grin, exclaiming, "Holy shit! Far out, man! Think they'll be back?" Hank had replied he didn't know but he sure hoped not.

Then Duane asked another question he couldn't answer: "So what exactly those cats doing in there?"

It was a good question. He'd spent the morning listening, trying to pick up any clues that might explain the fuss. Several words got bandied about repeatedly in an abstract sort of way: grace, charity, tolerance. Also, sin. Nothing mysterious about sin, though. It was everywhere. Except some participants referred to original sin, others just said sin. He heard it variously described as a condition, choice, excess, defect and rebellion. One guy kept using the word "corruption." Several mentioned "casting the first stone," which Hank recognized from the story when Jesus held off an unruly crowd, something he himself had not managed.

Though he listened closely, by lunchtime he'd failed to grasp what they hoped to accomplish. Seemed like they were talking around it, way educated people do. Eating his tuna sandwich on the front porch, he told Duane they were discussing religion.

"No shit, dude, they ain't fuckin' OPEC," Duane replied, scratching a tattooed heart stabbed with a dagger. He smoked a Pall Mall while scarfing smelly Vienna sausages dobbed with ketchup and mustard from tiny fastfood packets. The guy was a blur of nervous commotion, he never stopped moving. "But like, are they talking heavy-duty God stuff? Or is it routine rules and regulations? Or maybe it's the price of rice in China, know what I'm saying?"

Hank said he did. Said he'd get back to Duane on that later, when they had more time. He quickly repacked his lunchbox and returned to the meeting room, determined to discover what was what. Peeking through the drapes, he sighted Ace at his sentry position down the hill. The old man lay on a limestone shelf above the stream, boots crossed, the straw hat covering his face. Taking a nap, looked like. Well hell, that was sure reassuring. When the theologians filed in, Hank resumed parade stance.

During the morning all twelve participants had spoken in turns, but after lunch some began dropping out. Hank could more or less watch faces and tell whose attention was due to fade. The eyes would start wandering the room walls, or the ceiling, the hips sliding down the chair a little, shoulders slumped. Shortly therafter, the person was busy elsewhere.

Hank understood how they felt. It wasn't so much that the discussion was hard to follow, though that was true. It was the way each person rambled on and on, covering far more territory than any one person could reasonably cover at one time — or expect another to listen to — though each speaker's tone indicated he believed his comments not only insightful but absolutely crucial to the objective at hand. Which was the thing Hank could not yet decipher. The overall purpose seemed as vague as the discussion, which sounded in turn like a series of long lectures. He'd heard church sermons exhibit the same flaws, though Assembly of God preachers tended to punctuate main points with shouts, pounding the pulpit. Letting you know when to pay attention.

And so passed Tuesday afternoon and the following morning. Ace quit his position down the hill Wednesday after lunch, said he reckoned the trouble was over. Sheriff's deputies were stationed at the highway turnoff. "And them peckerheads ain't coming in the back way," he concluded, "have to climb hills, wade rattlesnakes. We'll keep you and Duane around though, just in case. Boy's strange. Got the smell of prison on him." Meaning Duane, who at that moment was sequestered in the toilet, smoking.

119

Hank admitted there wasn't any telling. Security companies check records too close, he said, and there wouldn't be any qualified guards. Ace grunted, carved off a chunk of Red Man, slid it behind his teeth. "Know what ecumenical means?" he asked.

"What?" The question startled Hank.

Ace twisted his neck and let fly a juicy brown arc. "Was curious, is all. You learnt anything in there?"

"I'm working on it," Hank said.

Wednesday afternoon, Hank noticed the discussion had pared down to three participants. They held the floor. There was the slim mustached guy with longish hair — the one who'd stirred up the crowd — and a tall gaunt man in black wearing a priest's collar and a halo of iron curls, and the woman. She was hanging tough, especially with the priest, who disliked her. Hank had watched her from the start, curious if she was lez. The bobbed blonde hair and pug nose reminded him of his sister BeeBee, who played contact sports and worked in radio station management. He checked the woman out again. Leaning to the left presented a decent view. Her suit was drab green, just right for a deer blind. The skirt hung low, but when she reached beneath to scratch or adjust, her legs were pretty good. Muscular calves, probably jogged. A deep voice, confident, she spoke with authority. Hank went back and forth: bent, not bent, maybe, hard to tell. He'd finally resolved in favor of gen-u-ine butch when she slapped the tabletop and challenged the priest, "What if your teenage son was gay? What if you had to explain why his legal rights in Austin were less than my son's?"

Hank involuntarily snorted but the sound was drowned by the priest, who leaped from his chair with an outthrust finger yelling, "My son is not homosexual!"

The mustached guy guffawed and the woman smiled, others quickly spoke up with soothing voices. Hank cocked an eyebrow. He knew Catholic priests were wild and those not queer sometimes got caught with nuns, but he'd never heard of one having a son everyone knew about. The uproar settled and the woman spoke again. "I'm not saying your son's gay, but what if he was? What would you tell him?"

Hank decided the priest wasn't Catholic. One of those high-class denominations close to it, he supposed, ones that wore the dog collars. And the woman most likely wasn't lez if she had a son. It occurred to him then what the meeting was about. He'd heard on a radio talk show. Austin was considering a new civil rights law for homosexuals and the city council had asked the local ministers' group for advice. The radio host had said such a law would destroy Christian culture. Hank pretty much agreed but waffled. His sister BeeBee being a good person and all. Not that she'd ever come out and said anything. Not that anyone in the family had ever asked, either. Anyhow, Hank wasn't sure. To his mind, that was the problem with politics, always. Every side had a point.

The priest in the dog collar was talking again and Hank listened up. Something about the difference between God's laws and man's laws. The mustached man broke in, said man's laws should express the spirit of the former. It's a matter of social justice, he said, of spiritual evolution — of God's laws and man's laws converging. The woman said no matter how you cut it all laws are subject to human bias. The priest grunted and threw up his hands.

Later, driving home, with the sunset splayed in the rearview as if the sky was on fire, Hank spied a spike buck hunkered in a creekbed. The radio played his favorite Mark Chesnutt song. The swelling on his elbow had eased up, his knee felt better. It was a nearly perfect summer evening, the kind where you stop at a friendly beer joint and have a couple of beers. Except Duane would probably mooch. The guy was over there in the passenger's seat snoozing, bumming a ride because his van had broke down. An old purple and green Volkswagen with bashed fenders, the kind hippies drove.

Duane stirred, his eyes flopped open. "Wanna beer?" he said. He pulled his bones upright, snapped open his Zippo and lit a cigarette, vented the window. "I'm buying."

They popped a few Buds and shot pool at a tavern off Lamar near Zilker Park. Duane smoked and made bank shots and tricky combinations with casual effort. He mentioned he had a degree in English literature, perfect training for security work. Said he'd studied at Huntsville in East Texas and had a quote from Lord Byron tattoed on his ass. Hank said he was from Bethlehem, a small town in the piney woods near the Louisiana line. Duane said he knew it well, he'd grown up in Blackjack Grove. "That's just upriver from you," he said, nailing the eight ball. "Last name's Crowder. My old man was a Pentecostal preacher. Whipped me ever time I turned around, just in case I needed it. Got two brothers, they fucked up, too."

"Pentecostal," Hank said, "that's Oneness. I'm Trinitarian. Assembly of God."

"Father, Son and Holy Ghost," Duane grinned, blowing a smoke ring, "the three musketeers." He scratched a naked woman straddling his right forearm. "Wanna nuther beer?"

"Reckon so." Hank thinking Duane seemed a mite loose for a holy roller. Backslid, most likely, done lost his faith. All those tattoos, the cussing, the everpresent cigarette. Plus Pentecostals didn't drink beer. Of course, neither did Assemblies. Hank frowned. "Know what a theologian is?"

"Sure," Duane replied, "an intellectual confined in a conceptual straitjacket. A rationalist trying to justify faith. Be right back with the beer."

Hank racked the balls and leaned against the table chalking his cue, thinking. The state prison was in Huntsville. You could learn to shoot pool in prison, he figured, and take college correspondence courses. Get tattos, too. When Duane returned, he said, "How about ecumenical? What's that?"

"Means overlooking religious differences," Duane said, "folks trying to find common ground. Cooperation, unity. Shit like that."

Hank grunted. "Wanna trade places tomorrow morning? You inside, me out."

Duane bared his big nicotine-stained teeth, smoke curling into an eye. "Dig it," he said. "You wanna know what they're doing, right?"

"Sorta." Hank shrugged. He knew what they were doing. What he wanted to hear was what Duane thought about it.

They rode to work the next morning in Hank's truck. Duane rubbed his eyes and smoked, said his VW van needed a rebuilt transmission. "Can't afford one now, though, behind on child support. Got four kids, two exes. Fucked up situation. Prechate the ride, dude."

Hank shot him a glance. Two divorces already. The guy was full of surprises. He said, "You look a little rough."

"Burning that candle, man, on all three ends. Was out clubbing all night. Don't fret though, I'll listen up, pay attention, let you know what those cats are doing."

He did, too. At lunchbreak on the front porch he told Hank there'd been a regular foofaraw, almost a fistfight. "Tall dude with the collar? Curly hair? Some kinda right-wing Lutheran. Woman and another dude ganging up on him. Everybody else is laying low." Duane ripping open a Vienna sausage can, squeezing a packet of Taco Bell salsa over the top. He lit a cigarette and talked and chewed sausages at the same time, saying, "It's about that new gay rights law. They trying to decide if it's cool to suck cock. Big theological issue, critical. God lays awake at night biting his nails, can't decide. Want a wienie? They good with salsa." Duane licking his fingers.

Hank shook his head. The smell was awful.

"So then this second dude, one siding with the woman, he says the apostle Paul was queer. Said that's why — "

"Mustached guy?" Hank asked.

"Ditto. Looks like an ACLU lawyer. Probably Presbyterian, could be Episcopal. Call him Mr. Inclusive. So he says Paul was a nut, a Freudian mess, a frustrated queer. Guy has a point, too. Shit, where's that other salsa?"

Hank picked at his tuna fish sandwich and crunched a Frito. Thinking about the apostle Paul. Man, this was news. "He said that about *Paul*?"

"You betcha," Duane said. "Which pisses off Mr. Martin

Luther. He points out Paul condemned homos. Right there in
Romans, Corinthians, Timothy. You've read it. Unnatural lust,
shameless acts. Fornicators, manslayers, whoremongers,
drunkards, idolaters, thieves, liars, self-abusers, backbiters,
etcetera. And sodomites. Long list of nasties. That's Paul, the
cat liked a good list. Sure you don't want one?" He held out a
pale pink sausage, wiggled it, then thrust it into his mouth,
saying, "Them Hebrews didn't pull no punches, dude. Come
to sodomites, they was into *serious* consequences."

Hank didn't recall about that, wasn't sure he'd ever heard.
He asked what they were.

"Execution, hoss. Put you to death. Read Leviticus."

Hank was about to comment that Duane sure knew his
scripture when the guy added, "Didn't bother the Canaanites,
though, they even had male prostitutes. Anyhow, that feminist
in there — that's what she is, a feminist theologian — she
speaks up now, tells Mr. Martin Luther the other guy's right.
That Paul's caterwauling shows he's a repressed gay. Or maybe
not so repressed, just feeling guilty. She's referring to Romans,
where he says, 'In my flesh dwelleth no good thing. The good
that I would I do not, but the evil which I would not, I do.'
Chapter seven, right?"

"Right," Hank said, frowning. Why not? Wishing now he
hadn't miss the debate, it sure sounded more interesting than
when he was in the room.

"And then Mr. Inclusive piles on, mentions Paul's letter to
Philemon. Paul's sending away this slave Onesimus even
though it's tearing his heart out, ripping his guts cause he loves
the guy. Onesimus. Name means 'Useful,' by the way. But
useful for what, huh? Don't take much imagination." Duane
gave a broad wink, lit a cigarette off a burning butt and blew
several quick smoke rings.

Hank sat on the porch with a mouthful of tuna fish, stunned.
After a minute, he said, "You mean they're right about Paul?"

"Who knows?" Duane shrugged. "They just arguing, man.
What theologians do. Think about it. You got two types in there.
Your evangelical types, the fundamentalists, they afraid to

think. Human mind's the devil's workshop. Then you got these others, been to high-powered divinity schools, they into a whole other gig. They pick scripture apart, decide what's real, what ain't. They scholars, right? I mean, they done researched it. Gonna tell you the virgin birth's folklore, the resurrection's superstition, a leftover from some defunct Middle East religion don't exist no more. They basically anthropologists, man. Studying the Bible like ol' Bulfinch studied Greek mythology. One man's God is another man's Zeus."

The idea of it sent Hank's head spinning. He'd never conceived such a thing. It sent shivers down his back. "You mean they're atheists?" he exclaimed. "Atheist preachers?"

"Naw, they ain't atheists." Duane waved his cigarette and belched sour gas. He leaned against a porch post in the shade. "Take Jesus Christ, for instance. He a man or God hisself? What you think?"

Hank didn't have to think. "Both."

"There you are. Only those educated guys — " he jerked a thumb toward the front door, "they gonna tell you there never was a Jesus Christ. There was this cat named Jesus, grew up in Nazareth probably, became a rabbi, went on a radical binge and got executed. Then what we call Christ come after. Paul and other folks made up that second part. Like with Elvis. Elvis really wasn't Elvis, see? I mean, he was Elvis Presley, but he wasn't *Elvis*. That was myth. And it's still around, they making money off it. But Elvis the *guy*, he got fat on fried banana sandwiches and checked out on Overdose Air. Right?"

Hank wasn't sure to agree or not, wasn't clear on what he might be agreeing to. Duane didn't notice, or even wait, just kept on talking. "Same with Jesus. Heavy dude, no joke, had to be. Enlightened master, all that good shit. Him and Buddha'd probably hit it off righteous, they ever met. They'd groove, trade disciple jokes, slap skin, grab a few laughs. But if Jesus was to show up right now, hypothetically speaking, and got a peek at what got done — in his name, I mean, like he's some kinda consumer *product* — he'd shit bricks," and Duane flipped his butt into the yard, scratched at a black panther head tattoo, raising a small puff of flaked skin, saying, "Cause that ain't what the man was preaching, right?"

Hank didn't answer. He packed his lunchbox, frowning, suggested it was time to get back to work. Telling Duane he was welcome to take the inside duty again. Last day on the job, he'd just as soon hang out on the porch, enjoy the view. Take in the fresh country air. Maybe shoot the breeze with Ace if he came around. Hank speaking quickly, not looking at the guy when he spoke. Afraid to.

"Sure, pardner," Duane said. "Whatever. They'll keep me awake anyhow. Reckon I'll hit the toilet first."

Hank watched him go inside, pale blue-inked arms swinging loose, the lanky bones clanking in the unwashed uniform. Going to inhale another cigarette before assuming his post. Against the rules to smoke on duty. He'd never asked why, not being a smoker. But it seemed a good rule, like most. Why they had them.

Ace came out on the porch about three o'clock, said the meeting was wrapping up. He took off the straw hat, wiped his forehead with a blue bandana. The probing coyote eyes scanned the yard, the surrounding hills. "Yessir," he said, "we'll get back to some peace and quiet around here. Course, all the excitement come that first day. Ever figure out what ecumenical is?"

Hank said he thought so. Said he didn't much care for the idea. Or at least the results. He figured he'd rather listen to an old-fashioned gospel preacher anytime, hands down, he knew that much. "They get right to the point," he said, "no horsing around."

Ace nodded, whanged a juicy gob off the edge of the porch. "That they do. Grew up hardshell Baptist myself. Never have got over it."

"Well, that's good," Hank said.

"Maybe, maybe not. Listen, no need for you boys to hang around. Head on out if'n you want. An ol' rodeo wreck like me can handle it from here on out." He extended a gnarled brown hand for Hank to shake, wished him luck. Said he appreciated the backup. Said, "Keep it between the ditches, son," and then he was turned and gone.

Hank went out to his truck thinking they didn't make 'em like Ace anymore. Or if they did, you didn't meet many. He'd started the engine and backed up when the front door of the retreat center banged open and Duane came running, limbs scattering akimbo. Hollering, "Hang on there, hoss! You forgetting somebody!" He sidled up to the driver's window grinning. He fished a cigarette from his shirt pocket and lit it, drawing deep.

"They done broke up the meeting," he said. "Never did agree to anything, either. Them's our spiritual leaders, alright. Official position is no position. Believe that shit?"

"I believe it," Hank said. "I'm outa here."

"Well, let me get on around."

"I ain't got room." Said it flat out, meaning it.

Duane drew up short, spun back. A bewildered look passed over his bony features and settled in, as though he was in pain. "It's what I said at lunch, ain't it. About Jesus? I seen it scared you."

"Ain't scared," Hank replied. "Just ain't interested."

Duane blew out his breath and rubbed his jaw, stared off to the side. After a moment he swung back, fixed his gaze on Hank. He spoke quietly. "Listen, my friend, people gonna think what they told to think, and the bullshit runs deep. But what Jesus did say is we *all* the children of God. Gay, straight, it don't matter. Because the kingdom is right here, man," and he thumped his narrow chest with one fist, saying, "*that's* what Jesus said. *This* is the kingdom, man. Right here, right now," and dragging on his cigarette to spew forth a thin stream of smoke, he added, "same divinity in Jesus then is in you now. Or in me, for that matter. Don'tcha dig it?"

No, Hank didn't. Didn't much like hearing it, either. Words, just fooling with words. He had a good mind to pull out his baton and whack Duane over the head. Instead, he rolled up

the window and drove off. Left Duane standing there. Didn't
even look in the rearview. Screw him. The guy was a nut. Too
many drugs, most likely.
     Probably ought to report him to the supervisor, have him
check his police record.

     On the western fringe of Austin, at Oak Hill, he pulled off
the road at the first tavern he saw and went inside, ordered a
Lone Star longneck. Putting a dollar in the jukebox, he
remembered he'd forgotten to check the hillsides for whitetail
during the drive in, too distracted. He punched selections,
wondering if he'd missed seeing a buck, picked two Mark
Chesnutts and a George Jones ballad. East Texas boys. His
sister BeeBee, being in radio, had met both. She said Mark
was pretty young but George looked rode hard, as old as sin.
     He stood at the bar listening to the music, drinking. The
place was empty yet. When the bartender passed his way, Hank
asked him what he thought was a fair price to reimburse a man
for mileage on the job. The bartender, a slight humpbacked
geezer whose khakis hung off his hips, eyeballed him as if the
question was a trick, then said he wouldn't know in the least.
     "Well, how about that gay rights law the city's
considering," Hank said. He swallowed some beer. "What you
think about that? Think it's a bad idea?"
     The old man tugged at an earlobe, thinking, slowly wiping
the bartop with a dirty towel like he was composing an opinion
on Red China. Finally he said, "Feller lives to my age, he
figgers live and let live's about the only way to go." He rapped
the bartop twice with his knuckles and wandered away.
     Hank nodded. Yessir, now that made sense. It surely did.

Lawbreakers in Bethlehem

When the mayor appeared in the Dogwood Festival parade doffing his tan beaver Stetson from the back seat of a Buick convertible, Abner Huckaby rode through town the following day on a Briggs & Stratton riding mower. He circled the courthouse square saluting bystanders with a Jack Daniels gimmee cap. Front page photos of both men ran side by side in the weekly Bethlehem Bugle.

Later that year, the mayor led the Harvest Festival parade from the high cab of a John Deere diesel tractor, wearing Big Smith bibbed overalls bought expressly for the occasion. Next day, Abner Huckaby rigged axle and wheels to a one-share plow and rode it down Main Street behind a purblind mule. He wore Bermuda shorts and a Tiger Woods tanktop. Over one shoulder hung a bag of golf clubs, a slap at the mayor's only outdoor pastime. The next edition of the Bugle published pictures of both events on page one.

Each incident in turn displaced the usual topics of idle talk. Some folks grinned and chuckled; Abner sure had a sense of humor, poking fun that way at Mayor Boatwright, an insurance agent who took himself far too seriously. The mayor's supporters were less enthusiastic. Highly vocal, indignant, they contended such exhibitions of disrespect not only denigrated civic life but set younger people a poor example of the common courtesy any two adults should extend one another, especially when both adults held positions within the community.

Abner Huckaby wrote, edited and owned the Bugle — not

an elected position, but one of public trust. That ownership, in conjunction with the First Amendment, accounted in part for the pictures having been published. The other reason arose from an ongoing feud between the mayor, who believed Abner was reckless and no less than dangerous for the anti-business views he'd printed in the paper for more than two decades, and Abner, who reckoned the mayor was a publicity-seeking dimwit of small ability and dubious ethics who shouldn't be let near the town coffers, though he was serving his fourth term in office.

"The mayor is reminiscent of Nero, who stood in his glittering robes atop the Maecenas Tower, in full view of the populace, fiddling as Rome burned," Abner wrote in one editorial. "Entranced by the blazing inferno beneath him (and his reflection within it), he declaimed and sang arias while the city was consumed."

During the next council meeting, the mayor told his fellow officials, "The only thing consuming our fair city is heartburn. It's hard to digest news cooked up by a socialist lunatic turning firehoses on the torch of free enterprise."

Abner, sitting in the chambers taking notes, snickered at the tangled metaphors. The mayor ignored him.

And so it went. The years passed and neither man doubted the truth of his own views. They each accumulated evidence, piles of it, hard facts and unfounded allegations, two thick files of suspicions, hearsay and spurious scuttlebutt, each precious item perfumed with a whiff of scandal. Armed with these concealed weapons, either man felt certain he could demolish the other if he wanted. Yet through some unspoken compact of mutual restraint, neither had chosen to do so.

Moreover, outside the public parameters of city council meetings and the pages of the Bugle, the two carried on cordial relations. They said hello on the street, shook hands at the post office, were seen conspiring in whispers when they met by chance in the aisles of the Market Basket Foodstore. Both served as deacons at the First Baptist Church, Southern Convention. Each was a thirty-third degree Ancient and Accepted Mason, Scottish Rite, and an elected officer in the Bethlehem Optimist Club.

They were blood cousins on their mothers' sides.

Their wives were sisters.

Yet year after year, within the overlapping boundaries of their respective responsibilities, Abner Huckaby and Roy Boatwright waged war — a war limited in scope until recent months, when the photos appeared.

The mayor rightly considered the pictures provocative. But he had not survived the manifold vagaries of the political arena by committing rash acts, and after weighing alternatives, he judged circumspect restraint the better moral response. Aside from that single comment to the city council, he publicly said nothing, though the photos privately enraged him. He took comfort in his own patience, which his wife affirmed as proof he was a better man than his cousin. Roy Boatwright did not doubt it. Cousin Abner had been a loose cannon since childhood, and a heavy cross to bear. The public ridicule had hurt. Still, because he was a man of firm Christian faith, the mayor turned first one cheek, then the other.

But then came the Rodeo Week incident, when he had no other cheek to turn.

Mayor Boatwright expected something unseemly given Abner's antics after the Dogwood and Harvest parades. But as the mayor rode the tall palomino — a gentle horse, its owner assured — in the Rodeo Week parade, as he lifted his Stetson to the crowd along Main Street and squirmed in the saddle, the new Levi's rubbing his crotch raw while dark arcs of sweat collected beneath his armpits, he completely forgot his cousin. As honorary parade marshal, he rode in front. The people cheered. They gaily waved, clapped, gave him the thumbs up. He smiled and called out familiar names in a hearty voice, winked at the pretty girls. Behind him the parade fanned away to either side, awash in brittle autumn sunshine. A squadron of uniformed auxiliary deputy sheriffs on quarter horses followed him closely, hooves clopping loudly on the pavement, and behind them came a mounted brigade of teenage cowgirls wearing sequined tasseled shirts and jangling spurs, among them the future rodeo queen, and farther back yet the marching high school band playing a jaunty Sousa march, the big bass drums booming as scantily clad twirlers pranced and whirled, tossing silver batons spinning high into the air, hardly pausing to catch the sparkling wands falling behind their backs as an electrified crowd briefly held its collective breath.

The golden October sun, a pale blue cloudless sky, the festive marshal music, the clamoring communal noise, the hundreds of shining faces and grinning children — the perfection of it all in consort boggled the mind. Inspired, the mayor threw back his shoulders, ignored his physical discomfort. Behind him the parade reached farther back than the eye could see, and ahead lay the wide street lined with friends both known and unknown packed shoulder to shoulder and tall spreading shade trees fronting deep green lawns and the upthrust hopeful signs of thriving commercial enterprises whose very welfare depended upon his sensible and sober guidance.

The mayor had not felt so happy or complete in years. Maybe ever. The moment seemed to him the realization of a lifetime's achievement, the fruition of long voluntary exertion now commemorated by unanimous public acclamation. This victory was his, the tribute earned. He accepted it modestly, as was his duty, though his heart burst with joy.

It was only later he heard that during his unadulterated bliss, even as he basked in triumph, Cousin Abner was trailing up the parade astride a donkey. A small one, an ass. Wearing an aluminum foil crown atop his bald pink head, a white bedsheet draped about him like an ancient Semitic robe, held in place with safety pins, on his feet a pair of worn Birkenstock sandals dragging the pavement. Carrying a King James Bible under one arm. The mayor never saw it for himself, so later chose to disbelieve it. Not even a lunatic like Abner would dare pull such a stunt.

But he had, in fact, as the next edition of the Bugle proved. The mayor received a copy in his insurance office on Thursday morning. He gaped at the front page, collapsed into the chair behind his desk. His mouth hung open, his eyes sprung loose from their sockets. He thought he might vomit. Gripping the newspaper with both hands, he tore it in a sudden fit and crumpled it and threw the puckered wad to the floor with an awful grunt, as though he had seen upon the page the very image of Satan himself.

"Ain't that sumthin?"

He leaped at the words, jerked his head about to see his secretary Ronette standing in the office door. She leaned against the doorframe, stretched her mouth into a narrow upright oval and scraped the red fingernail of her little finger along the outer edge. "Kinda nutty. Don'tcha think?"

After a minute, he located his voice. "It's worse than that," he said hoarsely. "He's gone so far this time the whole town'll stand behind me. This here" — he gave the ball of newsprint a vicious kick — "this here is sacrilege!"

"Hit me that way, too," Ronette said. She was a twice-divorced mother of four kids and a backslid Pentecostal who didn't go to church. "They pretty much ruint me on organized religion," she often said, "but I still got my individual faith." Tall and lanky, she dressed like a hussy and wore more makeup than Mary Magdalene but the mayor trusted her judgment without question. Basically, Ronette ran the insurance agency.

"Think so?" he asked.

She lifted one eyebrow by way of comment and turned without speaking, disappeared into the front reception room. He fixed his eyes on the spot she'd vacated, studying it. Ten minutes later, he picked up the telephone and dialed city hall, got Lou Dawson on the line. "Chief, it's Roy here," he said tonelessly. "You seen the paper? Yeah, well, he finally crossed the line. I want you to pick him up, arrest him. That's right. Don't know which law he broke, but there's got to be one."

Within the hour, Abner Huckaby was a jailbird.

All things considered, he was not a model prisoner. He seized the upright bars of the cell and shook them, tried to pry them loose from their moorings, bellowing, "Guard! Guard!"

as if he'd seen every prison movie Jimmy Cagney ever made. He announced a hunger strike, set fire to a roll of toilet paper, banged a tin cup along the iron bars like a madman playing a washboard. He stood on the bunk shouting out the tiny window into the courthouse square below. People gathered there to listen. He roared his grievances, compared himself to the Man in the Iron Mask, to Sir Thomas More, to Galileo, to Saint Paul bagged by Nero's henchmen.

All this occurred within the first thirty minutes.

He raised a ruckus unlike any the nervous jailer, Hemp Murphy, had ever witnessed. "You reckon he gonna hurt hisself?" Hemp asked Chief Dawson, "cause I don't want no lawsuits asking me for a million dollars. I barely make my house payment."

The chief shrugged his beefy shoulders, leaned sideways to hawk a dark brown gob toward the spittoon. On balance, the chief thought the arrest a bad idea. Aside from the nuisance, there was his upcoming contract renewal to consider, and the endorsement of the Bugle always helped. Abner had changed position on that subject on the way to jail, had clearly stated so.

"How long we gonna keep him?" Hemp asked. He was shorter than the chief but twice as wide, a former high school tackle who'd never given up the weight battle because he'd never fought it. "I mean ... " his voice trailed away. The tiny porcine eyes in the big pumpkin face evidenced raw concern. "What's he charged with?"

"Reckon I'll offer him a phone call," the chief replied. He lumbered out the door down the ancient courthouse hallway past arched windowpanes overlooking the oak-leafed square, through another door into the jail, his heavy Wellingtons clomping on the floorboards. He stopped in front of the cell, gazed at the small, slender figure launched upright on the bunk gripping the window bars. Abner was yelling, his voice now hoarse and raw. "I'm Martin Luther King in the Birmingham jail! I'm —"

"Abner!" the chief shouted.

The man at the window stopped, cranked the pink, white-fringed head to peer over his shoulder, snarling, "If it ain't Pontius Pilate. What you want?"

"You got a phone call."

"Tell 'em I'm busy."

The chief tugged an earlobe, swiveled his head right and left searching for a spittoon. There wasn't one. He rolled the gob over his tongue, swished it into one cheek. "You get to make one," he said. "Who you wanna call?"

Abner hesitated. Not his wife. She'd throw a hissy fit, he didn't want to hear it. The daughter lived in Atlanta, where she was a corporate vice president for the Coca-Cola Company. How this had happened was a torment to Abner, who felt he'd somehow let her down and the job was her secret revenge. His son Eugene Debs, who had never been spiteful, was a lawyer with the Civil Liberties Union in Austin. Eugene was fighting the good fight.

"My boy," Abner said, squeezing one eye shut warily. "Only I'm not putting up any bond. You can forget that horse hockey."

The chief nodded patiently. "S'pose that's your choice to decide, if'n you like it here that much."

"That's not the point," Abner shot back. "I'll rot in jail before I put up one red cent ransom on such a ridiculous charge." He paused, frowning. "Just what is the charge?"

"Well, that shore is the question." Chief Dawson removed his straw cowboy hat, idly scratched his head with a big-knuckled thumb. "Far as I can tell, that ain't been decided yet."

"You sure are some kind of law enforcement officer," the small man retorted, climbing down from the bunk. "You oughta be ashamed of yourself, Lou. Let me outa here, I want to call my boy."

His son Eugene wasn't in but the secretary at the Austin office promised to get hold of him on his cellular. The boy called back within a minute. "Dad, what's going on? You in jail?"

"That's right, I'm a jailbird," Abner replied, glowering at

the chief and Hemp, who winced and stepped away. The two husky lawmen practically filled the small room, the jailer didn't have far to retreat. He backed into a corner straddling the wastebasket.

"They haven't decided," Abner was saying, "but I expect it'll be some trumped up charge a judge'll laugh out of court. A clear First Amendment violation. Might just go civil on them, sue for the courthouse deed, garnish some wages to boot."

Hemp kicked over the wastebasket and Abner yelled into the phone, "Hold on, hold on! I can't hear. Sounds like an inmate riot." Hemp upraised both enormous palms in self-defense and sidled out the room into the hallway. He heard Abner inside tell his son he planned to stay in jail without bond until a preliminary hearing. "They don't let me out on my own recognizance," he said, "I'll stay put until trial. Keep me a jailhouse diary, publish it in the Bugle. Blow them outa the water. Might win a Pulitzer." He hung up the phone.

After Hemp returned from locking Abner in his cell, the jailer told the chief, "Lord have mercy, that ol' man's gonna put us on the street. What other job I'm gonna do?"

"We got experience in the service sector," Dawson drawled. "Reckon we could sell cars."

"Ain't no salesman," Hemp grumbled. "I don't even like to buy stuff."

The chief bent over and pinged the spittoon, said, "Son, just what kinda American are you?"

The mayor managed to pry Judge Weaver off the golf course before lunch for a preliminary hearing. Once Chief Dawson informed him of his cousin's threats, Roy Boatwright began to wonder if he hadn't overreacted. The judge had acted aggravated on the telephone. There was no telling where Abner might claim his pound of flesh. Only a quick call to Pastor Wiley at the First Baptist bucked him up. The preacher reaffirmed the blasphemy of Abner's parade stunt, augmented further by the published photos. "I am a forgiving man," the preacher said, "as we all should be. But if a transgression of this nature goes without penalty, we might as well live in Sodom and Gomorrah. It is utter depravity, an abomination unto the Lord. Lucifer must be rebuked."

"That's right," the mayor agreed, "it's our duty. If not us, who else? If not right away, when?" He was paraphrasing one of his favorite sayings, which Ronette had clipped from Reader's Digest. "Only I'm not sure what to charge him with, reverend. Chief Dawson don't think disturbing the peace will stick."

"Call Bobby Reems."

The mayor mentally kicked himself. He should've thought of that. Bobby was the city attorney on retainer, a real estate lawyer mostly, but law was law. He thanked Brother Wiley, phoned Bobby at his office. The young lawyer didn't sound hopeful. "This looks like one of them things what falls between the legal cracks, you might say," Bobby suggested, "sorta like a small-stakes Friday night poker game, Mister Mayor. Or betting a six-pack on the Cowboys. More a matter of ethics or such as that, know what I mean?"

The mayor knew Bobby Reems played more than penny ante poker and bet more than six-packs. He was up to his keister in gambling debts, had almost lost his license over it. The lawyer was squeezing in a Twelve Step Gambler's Anonymous program between trips over the Louisiana line to the race track. But always talking about his Higher Power. Presumably that meant God. The mayor leaned back in his executive chair stretching the phone card, said, "Bobby, you're a God-fearing man. We got a town fulla fine churchgoing people we can't let down. Ol' widder women and children and taxpayers. Abner Huckaby made fun of Jesus Christ our Lord. Now what we gonna do?"

"Pray for him?" The lawyer giggled hysterically for a moment, abruptly grabbed hold. "Alright, mayor, okay, I'll see what I can work up. How much time we got?"

"Preliminary hearing in two hours. Judge Weaver, all we

could get. In a rush cause Abner's tearing up the jailhouse. The man's gone crazy."

"That's the defense I'd use," Bobby said, "but then I do real estate. I'll see you there. Sure wish it wasn't Judge Weaver." He hung up without explaining, though the mayor understood. Babe Weaver was one tough judge, a real stickler, prone to moody tirades from the bench.

Today was one of those days. Judge Weaver slumped glowering on the bench as Bobby Reems and the mayor settled behind one table and Chief Dawson brought Abner in wearing cuffs. "Are those necessary?" the judge snapped. The chief shrugged. He was in so deep it no longer seemed to matter. Abner was gonna flay his hide in the next Bugle sure as stink on horseplop. "Just routine procedure, judge," he muttered, "I can take them off."

"Do it."

Once the cuffs were removed, Chief Dawson took up position as sergeant at arms. Abner rubbed both wrists flamboyantly as the others watched, then sat down at the defense table assuming a wounded noble pose, somewhat reminiscent of Hank Fonda in "Gideon's Trumpet." But unlike Gideon, he harbored no abiding faith that Lady Justice might weigh the scales of impartiality without peeking.

Judge Weaver stared at him, waiting. He fixed his gaze back. The judge was a short squat woman in her sixties with tight curly gray hair and stabbing black eyes, her square bulldog face cast in a permanent scowl. She was a former collegiate golfer who wielded a gavel like a nine-iron. Now she raised the gavel and clobbered the bench side, which might have meant she was mad over getting called off the golf course except she always whacked it hard. "Alright, fellas, let's get this over with," she growled. "And where's your counsel?" she asked Abner.

He stood up. "I am representing myself, judge. And I ain't paying any bail, either, tell you that right now. I'm innocent."

138

She glared at him, said, "Well, I doubt that. Only it don't mean you're guilty, either. Is this about that little performance last week? The rodeo parade?"

"I presume so," Abner replied, "only you'll have to ask those boneheads over there," and he jerked a thumb across the aisle, "what I'm charged with. Last I heard they didn't know."

"Is that right?" She swung her gaze to the mayor and attorney. Bobby Reems was a skinny young man with longish sand-colored hair and an oversized Adam's apple, wearing a wrinkled blue seersucker suit. He leaped to his feet to say, "No, your honor, it sure ain't. Don't have a notion where the defendant heard that. We're ready." He flopped down, she immediately motioned him back up, saying, "Then why don't you let us in on the mystery, counsel? Just for the sake of argument."

Bobby grinned. "Yes, ma'am. And the prosecutor appreciates your patience, ma'am, as he ain't too accustomed to these criminal cases. The charge is libel." He sat down again.

"What!" Abner screamed. He shot to his feet. "Libel?"

"Sit down *now!*" Judge Weaver shouted. Abner abruptly took his seat. "Well now," she continued, turning to Reems and the mayor, who was yet to speak, "for the moment we'll just ignore the little issue of legal standing, not to mention several other minor legal issues the approximate size of a 747 that pertain to the matters at hand. We'll ignore all that, including a prodigious ignorance of the law that the city's counsel has thus far exhibited to the court," and she gave Bobby Reems a withering look, "not because the aforementioned issues are of no relevance but because the court chooses to dig into this affair a bit further. If only out of personal curiosity. Especially inasmuch as the aforesaid court has been dragged from the golf course on her day off. Do you get my drift?"

Bobby Reems wagged his head, belatedly lunged to his feet saying, "Yes, ma'am, and counsel appreciates the interest."

"Sit down," she replied, "you been watching too many lawyers on TV. Now, is this here the item you believe constitutes libel?" Judge Weaver raised a folded copy of the

Bugle with its two front page photos.

"Yes, ma'am, it is," Bobby Reems replied, half-standing in a crouch. He couldn't decide whether to stand or sit, he was pretty sure he should stand to address the court but she'd just told him to sit. Courtroom work surely wasn't his forte. But boy howdy, give him a real estate contract and ...

"I suppose you fellas aren't complaining about the photo of the mayor," the judge continued, "cause it shows him on a horse and I presume he was on that horse and the picture's more or less accurate, hasn't been monkeyed with. So I suppose you're claiming it's the caption under the mayor's photo that qualifies as libel, am I right?" she asked. "You sit tight, Counsel Reems, let the mayor answer. Mayor?"

Roy Boatwright said, "Well, your honor, now I'm no lawyer —"

"Neither is your counsel," she interrupted, "but that didn't stop him. This caption says, and I read verbatim, 'An ass on his way into Bethlehem.' Whereas the caption under the photo of Abner on a donkey wearing his ludicrous outfit says, 'On a noble steed, our master greets the waiting multitudes.' Now I presume these captions have been reversed, either by design or mistake, which isn't the first time our esteemed weekly rag has failed certain professional standards."

In her peripheral vision, the judge saw Abner rising to his feet to protest this attack and she banged the gavel sharply once saying, "You stand up and speak out of turn again, Abner Huckaby, I'll hold you in contempt," and he eased back down.

"So I presume, mayor, that you contend Abner has libeled you by printing a caption under your photo that appears to call you an ass, although the apparent correct caption wouldn't seem much more complimentary in the court's view. Am I right?"

The mayor frowned trying to decipher what sort of answer was wanted. In the end, he thought a person couldn't go wrong agreeing with a judge, so said, "Yes, ma'am. I mean, neither one was a compliment. Except that's not what we're charging."

The judge raised both caterpillar eyebrows. "Then just who do you contend Abner libeled? The horse?"

Bobby Reems leaped to his feet, the Adam's apple ratcheting up his throat with nervous excitement. "Jesus Christ!" he exclaimed.

"Don't curse in my courtroom, you idiot!"

The lawyer dropped into his chair. "No, ma'am," he said weakly. "I mean, well, what I mean is, Jesus Christ is the one got libeled. That's the charge."

"What!" Abner shouted, restraining himself in the seat with both hands. "Are you nuts?"

"That's your defense, not mine," Bobby Reems replied, grinning across the aisle. He grabbed the lapels of his seersucker jacket and pulled them together with businesslike dignity.

"Boneheads," Abner muttered.

Judge Weaver had closed her eyes, was silent. The others shut up and waited, uncertain what the silence meant. An explosion building, most likely. After a minute, she took a deep breath and spoke flatly, gazing towards Bobby Reems and the mayor. "If we can crawl back out of the hole we seemed to have fallen through into neverneverland," she said tartly, "the court would like to point out that libel isn't a criminal charge. It's a civil charge and therefore completely inappropriate for this court, counsel. I suppose you missed that class back in law school. On the other hand, my day is shot to hell and there's no point in sending you off to torment some other judge. So here's what we're going to do. We're gonna talk about it, just the few of us, and try to settle this matter here and now. You understand me?"

They all nodded.

"Good," she said, "cause this has gone far enough. I'd hate to think that news of this affair would get out and embarrass our humble county nationwide. Cause this is just the sort of thing the network TV news programs like to air as a humorous slice of life story. 'Country bumpkin mayor arrests country bumpkin newspaper editor.' That sort of thing. They'd use the pictures, too. Something to offset the wars and massacres and double-dealing Washington politicians that otherwise dominate the news, am I right?"

All but Abner nodded again. He agreed with the judge's assessment of the sordid state of network news but his sense of solidarity with all journalists everywhere prevented him from admitting it. He also knew she was right about the story getting picked up. Someone like Andy Rooney would love it. They'd all come off as imbeciles once that prattling curmudgeon was done.

"Now," the judge went on, "I'm no expert in the area of libel law but you —" she looked at Bobby Reems — "you obviously know nothing. Or just enough to be dangerous. Have you come prepared with any legal precedence in this case? Or maybe you intend to use Roman law. Or maybe some ancient Judaic code regarding graven images? Please enlighten the court."

Bobby Reems opened his mouth, shut it.

"What I thought," Judge Weaver said. "Cause if you intend to use American law, you might consider that the person libeled must be living and present. That's for starters. Also, if he's not a private citizen but a public figure, you have to prove malice. So, do you intend to bring Jesus to the witness stand? And assuming you do, is it your plan to have him appear in his incarnation as a person, or in his divine role as a part of the Holy Trinity? I'm assuming the latter, as the first would pose a practical problem unless my history is off. You might have a problem serving a subpoena either way. Which is it?"

Bobby Reems bent sideways and conferred with the mayor, the two of them whispering energetically, then the attorney said, "Yes ma'am, the latter, your honor. We intend to bring Reverend Ezra Wiley to the stand as witness."

Judge Weaver grunted. "Where is he?"

After another short consultation with his client, the lawyer said, "Over to the nursing home, ma'am, doing visitations. But he'll be at the trial." He paused, uncertain. The bump on his throat jerked nervously. "Plus he'll prove that malice part."

The judge rolled her eyes, turned to Abner. "And what has the defense counsel to say to this?"

Abner was so disgusted by the proceedings that he hardly found voice to speak. After a moment, he said, "Biggest bunch of malarkey I ever heard."

"I'm inclined to agree with the accused," Judge Weaver announced, "although that is somewhat unprecedented. On the other hand, his recent behavior is what precipitated this little crisis, so I'm also inclined to suggest he publish a public apology. Not for appearing in the parade as he did. Anyone in this fine nation has the right to make a fool of himself, that's what freedom's all about. At least that's the impression one has, if he's watching. But a printed apology for publishing the mayor's picture with the incorrect caption might help. How does the accused respond? It *was* the incorrect caption, wasn't it?"

Abner stalled. The idea of admitting any wrong in the matter chafed beyond endurance, especially as the captions appeared exactly as he'd intended. On the other hand, the so-called correct caption — 'On a noble steed, our master greets the waiting multitudes.' — wasn't bad. He could run the mayor's photo again with that caption, more or less get double value for his efforts.

"Alright," Abner conceded, "I'm willing to be fair about it, judge. I'll rerun the mayor's photo with the other caption and mention they got switched."

"No way!" shouted the mayor, struggling to his feet. "I ain't gonna be made a fool of twice!"

"Four times," Bobby Reems chimed in helpfully, "I mean, counting all them previous incidents."

The judge nodded. "I agree that reprinting the photo and caption might appear unnecessarily provocative," she observed. "Just a short correction and apology in text would seem sufficient. Does the accused agree?"

"If he don't, we're going all the way to the Supreme Court," Mayor Boatwright remarked, "isn't that right, counsel?" Bobby Reems flinched, fiddled with a jacket button. Good grief, he could see it now. Fumbling around in front of the highest court in the land, getting bounced right out. Man oh man. The mayor had to be bluffing. He bobbed his head, adding, "All the way to the top."

"That's it, that's it," Abner declared, slapping the table. "I've had enough of this. No way I'll stand by and let the First Amendment get bushwhacked. I'm not giving an inch, judge. What's more, I intend to file countersuit. I'll have the ACLU and the National Press Association behind me, you watch. These numskulls bit off more'n they can can chew. And I'm requesting you let me off without bail on my own recognizance."

Judge Weaver screwed up her face. "You're free to go. I told you this is no criminal case, you blockhead. You never should've been arrested." With a vicious swing of the gavel, she smited the bench. "Now get out of my courtroom, all of you. Now!"

They rose and left in a hurry. In the hallway outside, Abner said to the mayor, "She sure is mean." The mayor made a face and agreed. "Guess I'll see you at the council meeting tomorrow," Abner said. Mayor Boatwright said he reckoned so, the meeting was set for five o'clock instead of four o'clock as normal. "We don't have much business this week." The editor allowed he'd be there anyhow, and to say hello to the wife. "And yours," the mayor said.

The two of them shook hands.

Chief Dawson and Bobby Reems stood nearby, watching. It was the damnedest thing to witness. Later, outside on the sidewalk, Bobby asked the police chief, "Why you figger they act that way?"

"Cause about forty years ago Roy got the sister Abner wanted," the chief said, "and Abner got the one Roy wanted."

Bobby Reems rolled back on his heels, stunned. "You pulling my leg."

"Wish I was," the chief replied. He craned his thick neck to let fly a gob of tobacco juice into the johnson grass.

"Well, hell then, why don't they just switch?"

"And admit they made a mistake?" The chief smiled grimly. "Anyhow, they done forgot all about that." He hitched his gunbelt and stepped up the courthouse steps, throwing back over his shoulder, "Besides, what else they gonna do for entertainment in this little burg?"

The lawyer didn't say anything. But it occurred to him that he'd never found a problem staying occupied. Matter of fact, in an hour or so, after his Twelve Step meeting, he planned to get in the car and drive over to Louisiana, see what was shaking at Bayou Downs. Maybe win a little moolah. He was feeling lucky.

He lost every nickel he had. And then some.

The first horse he bet on, Beau Geste, crashed into the rail on the turn, jockey somersaulting into dirt. The second horse gave out near the finish, the third never got out the gate. By the fourth race he was coaxing dollars out of an ATM on a Mastercard he wasn't supposed to have. He'd got it on the sly under a client's name with the intention of never using it. Now he maxed it out at five thousand dollars, lost a grand on an absolutely sure quinella — even the tout sheet agreed — lost half the remainder on an exacta in the sixth. He knew the track was crooked, had taken that into account. He sat out the seventh, bamboozled, evaluating his strategy, decided to recoup all his losses on a superfecta in the last race. A spring-loaded Cajun sitting next to him, very friendly, talkative, said he was a former trainer. He knew the jockeys, a fix was in, a done deal. Sounded good to Bobby, so he bet his last two thousand. Afterward, the guy allowed something'd got screwed up. "Lost me them ten bucks," he griped, "how 'bout you?" Bobby Reems didn't answer.

On the drive back to Bethlehem he conferred with his Higher Power. It told him he was a fool, a lamebrain, a hopeless moron. It had spoke to him in this way before, he was used to it, though he was under the impression your Higher Power was supposed to be more supportive. "Call me all the names you want," he replied, "but a fella's gotta right to a little fun."

"Then you must be satisfied," the voice said. "How's the fella on that Mastercard gonna feel? Gonna be slap happy, you reckon?"

Bobby punched his Mustang over the two-lane tarmac

through the piney woods squinting into the sun, a methyl orange and scarlet fireball floating halfway down the horizon. The wind rushed in through the open windows scented with crisp autumn pine. In the rearview a pale horntipped moon dangled low. He admitted the man might not welcome the news. "Only I'll have it paid off before he knows."

"Sure you will," his Higher Power said, "all you have to do is win it back. How you plan to do that?" The voice sounded a tad sarcastic. It reminded him of Judge Weaver. Heartless old bat heaping all that ridicule on him. Right there in front of everyone, too, like he didn't have no dignity. Might as well've just gone ahead and beat him with a stick, or spit. Wasn't no expert on libel law anyhow, said so herself. But what did she know? Anything can happen. Win a big libel case like that, lawyer's cut would choke a horse. Lawyer down in Houston walked off with a cool ten million, it was just on TV. Chunk of change that size, now, you got a grubsteak. Fella could start over. Make a few investments, buy a place in Vegas. Could travel. Maybe take a run over to Monte Carlo, play that baccarat, have a little fun. A fella could make do with ten million, and that was a fact.

Once his debts was paid off.

"Better chance robbing a bank," the voice said, cleaving his cogitation, "because that libel case is a real stinker, you heard the judge. But if you settled it out of court, there might be some money in it."

"Abner Huckaby ain't gonna settle," Bobby replied. He twisted the wheel to avoid a crushed armadillo, the Mustang headed up the Sabine River bridge and crested the arc. The sun had set, the river below lay in pale moonlight, the land ahead a formless sea of shadow. He saw ahead the lights of the Dairy Queen blinking. "That ol' geezer's stubborn," he said, "he'd rather eat barb wire than settle."

"Never say never," the voice retorted. "He's probably in his office, working late. Can't know if you don't try. Where's your positive attitude?"

Bobby nodded thoughtfully. He sure couldn't argue with

that. He slowed the car, tapping fingers on the steering wheel. He concentrated, let the warm familiar feeling spread downward into his narrow chest and sunken belly, into his legs and out the arms into his hands as if someone was pouring a bucket of liquid hope through a hole at the top of his head. He grinned. Yessir, much better, way he was supposed to feel.

Now that was his Higher Power talking like it was supposed to.

Abner was in.

"So here's the deal. You go to court and it's gonna cost you ten, maybe fifteen thousand in attorney's fees," Bobby Reems said. "That's including any appeals, see? Get a judgment against you and it's more. We can settle it for five."

Bobby raised both hands palms upward as if to say, "And there you are," then leaned back in the folding chair, waiting.

Abner stared at the young man. They were seated close in his back office, a former broom closet with a rolltop desk buried beneath clutter and a single bare light bulb dangling overhead. A sagging plank along one wall threatened to collapse under a long row of dusty books — almanacs, dictionaries, yearbooks, familiar quote collections, encyclopedias of history, medicine and law. The lawyer, glancing upward, edged his chair away from the wall, was stopped by a careening stack of Bugle back issues.

"Five dollars," Abner said.

Bobby slapped a kneecap, grinned, said, "That's a good one." Except the editor didn't chuckle. The lawyer slumped. He poked at his Adam's apple with a thumbnail, said, "Naw, Mr. Huckaby, five thousand."

"You're nuts," replied Abner. "You tell Roy he's nuts. This is an insult, sending you over here."

"Well, you see, that's the thing," said Bobby. He scooted forward in the seat, shut one eye and dipped his chin, conspiratorial. "He don't know I'm here. Now, he wants to go ahead on this thing, only I don't. He's all knotted up, ain't thinking. So, if I was to just string it out, sort of drag my feet, you might say ... " He winked. "After a while he's gonna let it slide, too much trouble. Figger I deep six the whole thing, that oughta be worth something."

"Selling out your client," Abner snarled.

The lawyer's face twisted with pain. "Just bringing closure to a potential disaster, Mr. Huckaby. Why can't we look at it that way?"

Abner grunted. "Wait a second, I gotta go to the bathroom." He shoved his chair to one side and left. Bobby fidgeted, wondering if he hadn't lowballed the amount. Seven thousand seemed reasonable, actually, maybe ten. Probably too late, though. He checked his watch. Almost eight o'clock.

The editor shortly returned and sat down. "Okay, let's go over it again," he said, "I want to be clear." The lawyer relaxed, the deal was done. He laid out the arrangement, ad libbing a schedule as he went, made it sound rock solid. "On the money, now a cashier's check might be best if cash ain't feasible," he concluded, " but I'm flexible, nobody ever accused me of being otherwise." He patted his chest with both hands. "Whatever works for you."

"Well, I certainly appreciate that," Abner said, standing up. He walked the lawyer out the back door to the small shell lot where the Mustang waited nosed to a leaning tallow. Above, a ragged tuft of cloud snagged on a moontip. An owl promised romance in the distance. Bobby Reems fidgeted with his keys. "You know, I'd like to get this settled right away," he said, "no use putting it off. How's tomorrow sound?"

"You sure are a sorry excuse for a lawyer," Abner said. "Tomorrow'll be just fine."

Bobby Reems's trial was set for early December. At the preliminary hearing before Judge Weaver, she told him he must've studied up his lawbooks, he was in the right courtroom for once. "You got anything to say?"

The lawyer, bleary-eyed and tearful, contended his

intentions had been sound, it was the result that proved wobbly. "I was following my Higher Power," he said, "and it led me astray." As for the credit card thing, he'd planned to pay that money back.

The judge scowled, her black eyes shot with disgust. "That wasn't your Higher Power, you dolt! Bail set at five thousand, a number you'll remember," and she smited the bench with the gavel. The whack hurt his ears. "Next case!"

She could've set the bail at five bucks and he couldn't raise it. His single phone call had gone to ex-wife Noreen, who hung up, didn't even say hi. The trial was a month off. He went back to jail, slogging along beside Hemp Murphy, who seemed sympathetic. "That racetrack's shady as Blackjack Creek," the big man offered, "crookeder, too. What I heard? They dope them nags. I heard the New Orleans mafia runs it."

Bobby Reems said, "You interested in a Ford Mustang?" He rubbed the cuffs against his seersuckered crotch. What he wanted was a shower. "Low mileage, runs good. Make a price you like, no kidding."

They were going along the hallway past the tall arched windowpanes overlooking the courthouse square. The deep green oak crowns shading the lawn sparkled in sunlight. Hemp said, "Got clear title?"

"You bet," the lawyer replied. "Well, almost. Cover that in the price. I'm flexible."

Hemp admitted the wife would like a new car, said he reckoned his old GMC pickup would do for now, though, seeing as how it was paid for. Said he didn't like buying stuff, didn't like debt. He needed a truck with a bed to haul his dogs anyhow. "Them redbones tear up upholstery."

"That's alright," Bobby muttered, "someone else'll grab it." Thinking the loan company. He still couldn't believe Abner Huckaby had recorded that conversation on tape. Man, you couldn't trust nobody anymore. Still hadn't figured out how they'd learned about the credit card, though. Seemed like his bad luck had a life of its own.

"You seen the mayor?" he asked.

"Shore ain't," Hemp replied. "He's laying kinda low, what I heard. Wondering what Abner's gonna do."

Bobby Reems winced. "Think he'll write this up for the Bugle?"

"Don't see why not." Hemp rolled his enormous shoulders. "Puts everything else in there, don't he?"

Only for once he didn't. The coverage in the next edition of the Bugle was brief. Local attorney Robert J. "Bobby" Reems had been arrested on charges of credit card fraud, the trial was scheduled for December. A small snapshot showed the lawyer sitting on a picnic table in city park. He was gnawing at a barbecue rib, his lips stretched back like a hungry dog. Bobby guessed it came from Noreen. The story didn't go into details. Attempted bribery wasn't mentioned. He supposed some deal had been cut. Keeping the mayor's name out. Himself an incidental casualty. Christ, it was a wicked world, and no justice in it.

The lawyer dropped the folded newspaper to the cell floor, lay back on the bunk with a forearm over his face. Up to him, he'd just end it all now, tie his belt through the window bars. That'd put a stick in their spokes. Except his Higher Power wouldn't let him.

Down the street, in his office, the mayor had one foot propped over a desk corner as he gazed at the same Bugle picture, read the same words. Ronette lounged in a chair across the desk wearing a hot pink rayon blouse cut low, clipping her nails, showing beaucoup cleavage. "Still think you oughta sue his pants off," she said. "That was a bad thing he done."

The mayor grunted. He supposed she meant Abner. Sometimes it seemed Ronette had bigger cojones than he did. But then, she lacked an executive perspective. If he sued, Abner planned to go public with the whole sorry mess, call for attempted bribery charges, print the tape recording transcript. Make the city look bad. Plant the idea the mayor put criminals on the city payroll. Publicity like that would reflect on everyone. Bobby Reems had been a sore disappointment. He should've known, a lawyer claiming a Higher Power. Anyhow, sincere people used the word God, not Higher Power. They said it outright and plain, no skimping around like they was ashamed.

He flipped through the Bugle, wondering if he'd find a printed correction on those rodeo parade photos. Nope. Not that he'd expected one. That battle was done for, kaput. Cousin Abner had him bent over a barrel, the son of a bee. "Well, I'll tell you what, Ronette," he said, making the best of it, "someone in my position has to swallow a hard chunk of bone sometimes. I got to consider the big picture."

A crimson corner of her mouth dimpled outward, she dropped nail clippings in the trash. "That picture of Abner playing Jesus gave my momma a conniption fit," she drawled. "She claims she wouldn't even buy no Bugles no more if it weren't for the food coupons."

"An unbridled press comes with a cost," Roy Boatwright replied reasonably. "The forefathers done thought that out. Hard lesson to learn but I guess I learned it. Take criticism too personal and you can't find peace of mind. What's the bottom line to win a world war and lose your soul?" he added, more or less quoting Pastor Wiley.

Ronette uncrossed and recrossed her legs, the purple velour skirt riding high up her muscular thighs. She said, "Don't reckon I'm in danger of neither one. You still coming by this evening?"

The mayor nodded. "Right after council meeting. Wear that teddy thing, okay?" Thinking as far as he was concerned, Ronette was the best doggone secretary in the county, maybe the state of Texas. Even his wife agreed. Good women, both of them.

If that damned Abner found out about her, though, he could hang up his spurs.

In deference to the holiday spirit, during a special hearing

Judge Weaver offered to postpone Bobby Reems's trial until the new year. "I suppose you and your Higher Power'd rather spend Christmas in county jail than the state pen," she told him. "You can look out the window, see the pretty decorations. Better than getting your holiday cheer pressed face down to a Huntsville prison mattress, if you know what I mean. You'll meet some unusual fellas up there with interesting ideas. Am I right?"

Bobby said she sure was and thanked her. Who needed new friends?

The days continued balmy, often cloudstricken and gray, the usual southern Christmas weather. From his cell he watched city workers string colored lights along the square. He'd never noticed them going up before, only after. Now that he had the time, the process intrigued him. Up went giant frizzy green wreaths, silver and gold metallic streamers, oversized red and white candy canes tied to streetpoles. Atop the corner poles perched huge white plastic stars illuminated from within. He stood on the bunk in his socks and watched like a kid, excited. Once the workers finished, he waited anxiously. When they turned the lights on after dark, glittering jewels along the square, he giggled and whooped, then cried. He gazed at the blinking points of color through salty tears. Just to think a perfect child had been born straight from God only to save his crummy skin. It broke him up.

The next day a work crew backed a flatbed truck onto the courthouse lawn and began to unload a nativity scene. Hemp came into the cell and stood with him on the bunk to watch. The bunk frame groaned. "You believe in Jesus, Hemp?" Bobby asked.

"Shoot yeah," the jailer answered. "Ever'body believes in Jesus. Who else you gonna believe in?"

Bobby Reems admitted it was a good question. He himself had grown up Free Methodist, though it hadn't stuck. "You think Jesus is the same thing as your Higher Power?" he asked.

Hemp scratched his vast belly. "Well, I dunno, Bobby. Is them words capitalized?"

"You bet."

"Guess it could be then," Hemp allowed, "but don't take my word for it. I ain't no preacher. Want me to ask my wife? She reads Christian magazines, keeps up on that stuff."

"Naw, that's alright," the lawyer replied. He watched the workers lifting a big plywood cutout off the truckbed below. When they spun it around, he saw a wise man astride a camel. "I'm surprised Abner ain't put a stop to that manger scene," he told Hemp. "Separation of church and state, know what I mean?"

Hemp turned his head, showed a pained face. "He wouldn't do that now, would he? Wouldn't hardly be American."

Bobby said Abner might try, in fact he'd be willing to bet a clock-radio on it. He put out a hand, Hemp shook it.

The next day, Bobby lay on his bunk listening to the local AM station on his new clock-radio. Mac Bevils, the DJ who was ad salesman and manager as well as station owner, was blasting Abner Huckaby. Mac on a long harangue, almost hysterical.

"You think he's gonna win?" Hemp asked, meaning Abner. The jailer sat on a low wooden stool in the narrow walkway outside the cell. "Cause that nativity comes down," he added morosely, "my li'l kids gonna cry sumpin awful."

"I dunno," the lawyer admitted, "all depends on the judge. Wanna bet on the Cowboys-Redskins game this Sunday? Give you the cowpokes and three."

"How come?" Hemp asked, "you need anuther appliance? Crockpot maybe?"

Bobby said he didn't cook much. He turned the dial to a station out of Beaumont playing Christmas music and they listened to Rudolph and Jingle Bells and a black church choir rocking out Deck the Halls. "Them jigaboos sure can sing," Hemp said.

"Think so?" said Bobby. "Remind me to send you a tape of ol' field hollers when I get on the prison farm. Them high squeals gonna be me."

153

The Cowboys won by a touchdown. Hemp admitted that was why he never bet. You just never knew ahead of time. Bobby said that was a fact. He asked Hemp how long he'd been married. The jailer said twelve years.

"You happily married?"

Hemp, standing outside the cell, scratched an elbow and mulled it over. "Reckon so. Never think about it much."

"Think Abner and the mayor are happy? In their marriages?"

The big man wagged his head, embarrassed. "Shoot, how'd I know that? Must be, they got growed kids." His cloudy, unformed features gathered, he shuffled his feet. Then, after a minute, "Sorry about you and Noreen. She seems real nice."

Bobby said she was. Not mentioning the end, when she turned mean and said he was the worst thing ever happened to her. Meant it, too. Still, he hoped she might drop by for a visit. For old times' sake, spirit of the holidays. The whole town was acting generous and upbeat, he could feel it.

But she never did.

Bobby heard Mac Bevils hooting on the radio when Abner lost the nativity case in court. It probably wasn't a constitutional ruling, he told Hemp, but what the hell, people want the nativity scene. "Democracy's democracy," Hemp agreed, "gotta protect our rights. You gonna watch the Christmas parade?"

"Wouldn't miss it for the world."

The mayor had declined dressing up as Santa Claus this year. Rumor was he felt worried. If he dressed up and rode on the parade float as usual, Abner might pull another stunt. So the mayor had passed the duty to Chief Dawson, who also abstained, claiming it'd put his wife's nose out of joint. She was Jehovah's Witness. "Anyhow, that's how come I'm doing it," Hemp explained. He bowed his thick legs and grabbed his wide leather belt, hitched his pants, acting pleased. "Them kids a mine's excited."

"I bet they are."

"Oh yeah, peeing in their pants." Hemp rubbed a closed eye with his knuckle. "Listen, the wife says ask what you want for Christmas dinner. I'll bring it in to you."

Bobby Reems lay on the bunk considering the offer. Man, right when you decide the world's a snakepit, someone up and does something like this. Tears welled in his eyes, he mumbled an answer and rolled over to face the wall, hiding his face.

"What's that?" said Hemp.

Bobby raised his chin, said, "Whatever you're having, Hemp. Only about half as much, I reckon." Though what he'd really mumbled was: "Hold me, dear Jesus, I'm yours."

When the Santa Claus float passed on the side of the square facing the jailhouse window, the big guy in the red suit and curly white beard looked up from the float and waved right at Bobby. The lawyer waved back from his cell window.

Sometimes life sure did seem sweet.

He read the weekly Bugle, hot off the press, while eating Christmas dinner. Hemp had delivered it, hauling in a cardboard box with a picture of a remote control bulldozer on the side. "Gift for the youngest kid come in it," Hemp explained, "except the thing sucks up batteries. Cost me an arm and a leg. You priced batteries lately?"

"Not lately," Bobby conceded, "I been occupied."

The jailer set his teeth, offered an apologetic smile. "Yeah, s'pose so. Lookee here what the wife sent." Opening the box, he set out a saran-wrapped plate of roasted turkey and covered bowls of fried okra, mashed potatoes and cream gravy, French-style green beans, rice and broccoli casserole, steamed squash, a sliced cucumber, corn on the cob. Then cornbread and fried hush puppies wrapped in aluminum foil. Finally, a big hunk of sweet potato pie topped with spray whip and a six-pack of sweaty Pepsi colas. All together it covered the top of the folding card table.

"Good grief," Bobby said. "You eating with me?"

Hemp shook his head. "Naw, wish I could, Bobby, but I gotta get back. Trying to slap a swing set together. Directions in Jap or sumpin."

"Flip the page over, it's English."

"Reckon?" Hemp seemed doubtful. He pawed the floor with a boot toe, rubbed his neck awkwardly, said, "Got one more thing. Uhhh, here." He reached into a shirt pocket and pulled out a gift-wrapped present the size of a penknife and thrust it forward. "Made it myself."

Bobby took it. A thin green ribbon tied in a bow around pink and white Christmas paper, what looked like part of Santa's cheek. He opened it. A handcarved wooden whistle. Oak maybe, or ash.

"Blow it," Hemp urged, "got a sweet tone on it."

He blew. The sound was low and breezy, like a hard winter wind coming down a chimney. He blew it several times while Hemp watched, waiting. "Well, that's a fine sound," Bobby said, "just what I was wanting, too. Thank you kindly."

The big jailer palmed his nose. "All them kids got one, call 'em pocket bugles. Shoot, can't even hear in the house for the noise." He looked embarrassed. "Merry Christmas."

"You, too, Hemp. I ain't got no gift for you."

"That's alright. Just eat up." Then he left, and Bobby gazed at the fare. Looked like a magazine picture, all that food. A feast. Opening the newspaper to read back to front, as usual, he sat down on the bunk edge. Began eating and reading. The classifieds always interested him, what people were selling. Learn a lot about folks by what they sold off. Diamond engagement rings, stuff like that. Stories were buried in those ads, heartbreak and hope. He'd once seen a casket for sale. Talk about planning ahead. He ate and read, the radio on low, Christmas music. Mac was playing a joke song by Ray Stevens.

His hunger surprised him, he waded right through the food, was on the sweet potato pie and his third cola when he reached the front page. He stared at the photos with a mouthful of pie.

There was the mayor, dressed up in a bathrobe and flip-flops and a long wig, holding a shepherd's crook, playing Joseph in the Christmas play at First Baptist. The mayor gazed downward toward the manger. The caption read, "Bethlehem's newest father proudly watches his son, says he expects big things."

The other photo showed a closeup of a manger — it appeared to be a galvanized livestock trough — in which lay Abner Huckaby, naked but for a large white towel lapped around his pelvis, fastened in place by oversized diaper pins. Scrawny calves and feet upraised, kicking the air, he sucked on a baby pacifier, grinning. The caption said, "Bethlehem's newest youngster reads the Bugle, says you should, too."

Bobby Reems swallowed and burped. He reckoned someone'd be hunting up a lawyer about now, looking for some justice. Thinking, good luck. Man oh man, he sure was gonna miss this little burg. He figured he had a one in five shot of surviving Huntsville. Bad odds anyway you looked.

He set the paper aside, finished the sweet potato pie, wiped his mouth on a paper towel.

Shortly, he laid back on the bunk with the whistle to his lips. It really did have a sweet tone. Pocket bugle. Kind of cute. He blew again and again, as loudly he could, like he was calling down Judgment Day. Calling down his Higher Power — God, Jesus, whoever.

Telling Saint Peter he was on the way.

Soldiers for the Lord

She sat slumped on the folding metal chair swinging her legs and chewing a fingernail, watching Uncle Booster show the tall fat man in camouflage fatigues a gun. The gun was a square black ugly thing with a short barrel that looked like a pipe and Uncle Booster was explaining how to pull out a pin to make it shoot faster, without stopping. "Only I cain't do it for you," he said, "it ain't legal. Got to do it yourself."

The fat man wore a canvas hunting cap that matched his fatigues, had thick gray whiskers and dark red bulging cheeks marbled with purple veins. He laid the weapon across one palm and lifted it up and down, weighing it. He smiled. His forehead was beaded with sweat.

"What kinda clip I can get?" he asked. "A hunnerd?"

Uncle Booster thrust both hands into the back pockets of his khakis and rocked forward, stretching his calves. "Least that," he said. He threw his chin over his left shoulder. "See that ol' boy over there, end of the aisle. Seems like he was handling the big clips. Don't sell 'em myself. Liability."

The man snorted and looked away as if that single fact confirmed a world gyrating off its axis and half gone to hell. "Goddamned lawyers," he growled, "between them and the guv'ment we losing every right."

The child stood up and leaned against the folding table, her hands gripping the molded vinyl edge. In front of her at chest level spread a crowded but carefully arranged assortment of automatic pistols and revolvers and longer guns with plastic

158

stocks, boxes of bullets and horn-handled Bowie knives, leather holsters, rifle scopes, weapons catalogs and books on ordnance, ballistics, handloading, marksmanship. Her shoulder bumped the thigh of her uncle, who reached an arm across the table and retrieved the gun.

"Yessir, you're right," he agreed, "Sure can't argue with that. But they ain't gonna get all mine. Can turn me into a criminal, but they can't take what they don't know I got."

She looked up and saw Uncle Booster wink at the other man, who in turn grinned and pulled a package of Red Man from a shirt pocket. He shoved it open with enormous hairy fingers ending in thick yellow nails. He withdrew a wad of tobacco and stuffed it into one cheek. "I hear that," he said, nodding at the weapon in her uncle's hands. "How much?"

Her attention wandered and she didn't listen to them dicker. Her eyes roved the high orange-colored metal rafters stretched overhead like bridge struts, down the inclined plane of seat rows cascading forward off the walls below the "East Texas Gun & Knife Show" banner, over the vast expanse of the convention center filled with dozens of tables like her uncle's and with hundreds of people, mostly men and boys, fathers and sons, roaming the aisles examining the merchandise. Their voices rose like murmurs of smoke, swirled above the floor in a muffled roar.

The girl put her hands over her ears and sat back down in the folding chair. She bent forward, elbows on knees, bored. She wore jeans and pink plastic sandals and a Shania Twain T-shirt. Her hair was bobbed short and held back off her forehead with two carnation barrettes.

"Amanda, take this, child, you must be starving."

She raised her head to see Aunt Lois holding a bun with a Polish sausage wrapped in a napkin toward her. "I put mustard on it. You like mustard?"

The girl nodded and took the sandwich.

"Here's some chips and something to drink."

She laid the sausage and bun in her lap, accepted the bag of Fritos and can of Dr Pepper. The can was very cold and she set it on the floor beside the chair. She opened the bag of Fritos with her teeth.

"That there's my niece," she heard Uncle Booster say. She glanced up. He was speaking to the fat man, who was inspecting the ugly black gun again. "Not but six years old and she's a orphan now," he said, "cause my brother wouldn't listen. And that's a fact."

"Unh-unh," Amber said softly.

"What?"

"Now, don't you go talking that way, Booster," said her aunt. Uncle Booster was short and thin with a big Adam's apple and reminded her of a turkey gobbler, while her aunt was short and heavy with a blunt round face and white doughy skin. "She's still got her momma."

"And her daddy's in the ground," her husband replied flatly. He turned toward the other man, who was watching with interest, the weapon in his hands momentarily forgotten. "If he'd listened to me and had one of those," Uncle Booster declared, thrusting his chin toward the gun, "he'd be walking and breathing and some other sumbitch wouldn't be. Simple as that."

The man grunted as though someone had poked him in the belly. He stroked his beard. "Some nigger shoot him?"

Uncle Booster took off his gimmee cap with the Colt Arms insignia and bent his head down sideways, wiped it on his flannel shirt sleeve. "We don't know," he replied, his tone a mixture of resentment and disgust. "Sumbitch is still loose. My brother Topper was a trucker. They found his body on a picnic table at a rest stop outside Houston. Truck was gone."

"Hijackers," the big man decided. "Happening more'n more, what I hear. He wasn't carrying?"

"What I'm saying," Uncle Booster replied between his teeth. "Topper wouldn't listen. Ex-marine and a Gulf War vet and he wouldn't arm. Now his little girl's an orphan."

Behind the Polish hot dog Amber mumbled, "No'm not."

"'Cept for a mother that I won't comment on, you are," he shot back, his eyes jumping. "Just think about who you're with, little girl, explain that to me."

"Booster, that's enough," said Aunt Lois.

Her uncle acted as though he hadn't heard but pointed toward the ugly black thing in the fat man's hands and said, "You gonna buy that? It's a good price."

"Dunno yet," the man answered, placing it on the table. "Just got here, need to look around. I'll stop back, let you know."

"You do that. And check out the fella on the end down there. He's got them clips."

After she finished eating, Amanda told her aunt she needed to use the restroom.

"Know where it is?"

"Yes ma'am."

"All right, go on, then come right back."

She went down the aisle toward the end of the exhibition hall where the restrooms were, watching the faces of the men and boys huddled over display tables. Many of them wore baggy camouflage pants and olive green T-shirts, hunting vests and fold-up knives cased on their belts. Most wore boots, either black combats or laced leather workboots with thick soles, and hunting caps or gimmee caps advertising outdoors products. They'd come to an inside shopping place dressed for traipsing through the woods, but that did not impress her as strange. It was how men dressed.

She wondered which one of them might've killed her father. She covertly scrutinized each face.

At the end of the aisle she paused to study a pudgy young boy in a Cub Scout uniform who was bent over a small glass case looking at pocket knives. When the man behind the table said, "I got good deals on Bucks," the tall man beside the boy said, "Old Timer's what we want." She moved on to the restrooms, making double certain she entered the door with the outline of a lady.

When she came out shortly she turned right instead of left

and passed a woman sitting behind a long table shoved against the wall. The surface of the table was covered with colored bumper stickers and she stopped to look. They had messages like "Bible & Gun, Don't Leave Home Without 'Em" and "Jesus Supports the NRA".

"Hey there," the woman said.

Amanda didn't speak but cocked an eye and twisted sideways, fixing her attention on the stickers. She idly scratched a mosquito bite on one arm.

"I'm a soldier for Jesus myself," the woman said. "How about you? You go to church?"

Amanda nodded, brushed the woman with short furtive glances. She was older than Aunt Lois, and taller, with reddish brown hair piled high atop her head and green eyes and wrinkles. She wore a floral print dress with long sleeves and was eating a Butterfinger candy bar.

"What kinda church you go to?"

Amanda shrugged.

"You don't know? Is it Baptist?"

Amanda frowned, then shook her head.

The woman smiled. She cupped one elbow in the other hand propped on the bulge of her stomach and waved the candy bar when she spoke. "What's it called?"

"Faith Tabernacle." Amanda fingered the corner of a lemon-lime bumper sticker, squinted at the drawings of a cross and a rifle printed on it. "With my aunt we go to the 'semblies."

"Assembly of God?"

She dipped her chin.

"You a Trinitarian," the woman observed. "Myself, I'm Oneness. You know what that means?"

Amanda nodded, then shook her head no, then said, "My daddy's done dead. They shot 'im."

The woman stopped chewing. "My Lord." Her sharp features moved around as if she had a thousand questions and didn't know where to start. "Somebody shot your daddy? Where'd this happen?"

She closed her eyes, remembering. "Houston."

"Well, I'm not surprised," the woman said matter-of-factly, "that's a big evil city. Full of niggers and Mex'cans tryin' to get sumthin for nuthin. They'll shoot anybody. Someday God's gonna destroy it all. What's your name?"

"Amanda."

"Well, that's a right nice name, Amanda, and you sure are cute. I know you miss your daddy." When the child didn't reply the woman said, "Well, at least you still got your momma," and then her green eyes suddenly rattled in their sockets and her face fell and she said, speaking low, "You still got your momma, don'tcha?"

"Yes ma'am," Amanda said. "She's checkin'."

"She's what?" The woman's eyebrows bunched together. "She's chicken?"

Amanda rolled her shoulders and with both hands fiddled with a stack of bumper stickers, her eyes focused on the tabletop beyond them. "Checkin'," she repeated, "at the Wal-mart."

"Oh," the woman said, leaning her head back, "a checker. Well, Amanda, I'm sorry about your daddy. Here, you want a candy bar?" She reached down beside the chair into her purse and brought out a Butterfinger, gave it to Amanda, then bent forward from the waist to peruse her merchandise. She picked up a bumper sticker and held it out. "You take this and tell your momma to put it on the car."

She mumbled thanks and wandered away down the aisle, looking at the sky-blue sticker with black letters. It said, "Be a Soldier for the Lord, Nail Satan," but she did not understand all of the words and tucked it under her arm. She unwrapped the candy bar and began to gnaw at the chocolate, waiting for later to bite into the caramel center. The bittersweet taste exploded on her tongue and enveloped her mouth like laughter.

After a few minutes she knew she was lost. She walked along the aisle between unfamiliar tables through a forest of legs. The towering men bantered or huddled close in negotiation. Down below, awash in the smells of gun metal and oil and worn boot leather, she felt her way along. She saw the fat bearded man but was afraid of him and did not ask directions. He stood beside another big-bellied man with crossed hairy arms and they both were laughing. As she passed behind the two men she began to shake and it occurred to her that it might've been the fat bearded man who'd done it. She pictured him holding the black gun, smiling. Or maybe both of them. Uncle Booster had said robbers were cowards and liked to work in pairs.

She scooted past shuddering and came to the end of the aisle by the concession stands selling cold drinks with hot dogs and chili and popcorn. She turned left and then left again into the next aisle. Halfway down she saw Uncle Booster and Aunt Lois seated behind their sales table. She quickly squeezed between it and the table next door and her aunt said, "I was wonderin' if you got lost. Where'd you get a candy bar?"

"A woman," Amanda said. She held up the bumper sticker. Her uncle angled his head to read it and said, "That's from Janet Crowder out of Lufkin, she handles them stickers."

"Well, she doesn't know Janet Crowder from the First Lady," Aunt Lois commented, the words rising with indignation. "Is that who gave you the candy bar?"

Amanda didn't know the woman's name. "Yes, ma'am," she said. She bit off a chunk of caramel and chewed, felt it sticking to her teeth.

"And what did I tell you about talking to strangers?"

She didn't say anything.

"Didn't I tell you not to talk strangers? Didn't I tell you not to take anything they offered? Didn't I?"

Her aunt sounded angry so she backed away rubbing one ankle against the other and shrugged. But the woman reached out and grabbed her by one arm and jerked her near, swiftly spun her around and smacked her several times hard on the backside with an open hand, saying, "Next time you listen to me," then, more loudly, her voice strung tight as fence wire, "That's how children get kidnapped, you hear me? That's how they get raped and killed! Now you have a seat and don't move without my say-so." She abruptly released her grip and pushed the child toward the empty chair. The woman was breathing hard, panting red-faced as if the whipping had worn her out. "I said did you hear me?"

Amanda nodded and went to the folding metal chair and sat down. The backs of her thighs stung and she dropped her chin to her chest. After a moment her eyes filled with tears and her mouth twisted upside down and she began to weep. She cried quietly so as not to draw attention but heard Uncle Booster say, "Ain't no call to beat on a child just cause you're scared."

"And what's your idea?" Aunt Lois answered. "Just let her talk to anybody 'til someone takes advantage? I'm trying to set an example."

"Teach her to handle a gun then," said Uncle Booster.

"She's too young."

"What you think," he replied tersely. "Ain't never too young to defend yourself."

An hour later she was bored of listening to her uncle talk with men who stopped by the table and she still had not looked at her aunt, who sat nearby needlecrafting a Bible verse into a wall hanging. It was John 3:16, and she'd so far completed "For God so loved the world." Her aunt complained to no one in particular that she wished she'd chosen something shorter, her fingers were getting sore.

Amanda reached into her knapsack for the book her mother'd brought from the Wal-mart. It was a story book with pictures entitled *The Miracles of Jesus*. She opened it and began reading the one about an old woman whose son had died. She was coming out of the gate of a city. Behind her some men were carrying the body. They were going to the cemetery. Jesus saw them and said stop. He told the woman not to cry. Then he touched the dead son, who stood up and began talking. He didn't even know he'd been dead. In the colored drawing, Jesus was holding his arms out to either side and the mother was kneeling, kissing his robe.

Amanda swung her legs and concentrated on the picture, fingering the small gold heart she wore around her neck, the one her father had given her for Christmas. He'd bought it in St. Louis, he said, at the jewelry section of a truck stop, and he'd paid a pretty penny.

"Got any Old Timers?"

She heard the question and looked up, saw the tall man with narrow shoulders and the boy in the Cub Scout uniform standing across the table. Uncle Booster said, "Got a few, yessir. What kind you lookin' for?"

"Pocket knife for my boy," the man replied. His face was flat and wide and clean shaven with large dark eyes. He wore a starched cotton dress shirt and new jeans with a sharp crease down each leg. Beside him the boy's greedy eyes scanned the tabletop, searching. "My first good knife was an Old Timer," the father said, "thought I'd get him one." He smiled. "Tradition and all that."

Uncle Booster bobbed his head indicating he certainly understood, saying, "Tradition's a fine family thing. If we don't keep it alive, who will?" He picked up a small cardboard box and opened it but paused then and looked up. "Reckon I know you from somewhere. You live up in Bethlehem?"

The tall man said he did, he'd just recently moved there. "Name's Harmon," he said, putting out his hand, "Lloyd Harmon," and he tilted his head toward the boy, "My boy Lloyd Junior."

She watched her uncle shake the man's hand. "Booster Pratt," he said. "Live up that ways myself, we got a place on the river. You the new man over at the water works?"

"That's right."

Uncle Booster nodded wisely, stroking his jaw. "You the fella who lost his wife to them burglars down in Beaumont. Read about it on the news."

Amanda saw the man's shoulders flinch and his dark eyes retreated for a moment, drawing inward, then he put one hand out to rest on the boy's shoulder and said, "Yes, that's right." The boy's gaze roving the wares spread before him never altered.

"Well, those boys'll get the death sentence," her uncle said, rapping the table three times with his knuckles. "Don't you worry about that. This is Texas, we don't mess around, nossir. Those boys'll get what's comin'."

Aunt Lois said, "Booster, show the man a knife." She held the wall hanging and big threaded needle in her lap and gave the man a sad sympathetic smile, as if to show him she understood both his loss and her husband's lack of manners.

Her uncle didn't reply but removed a small pocket knife from the open box he held in one hand. "This'uns one of the smaller ones," he said, offering it over, "but if it's too little we can work our way up on size."

The man took the knife and turned it over in his palm, inspecting it, holding it low so the boy could see.

"Reason I mention it is 'cause I lost my own brother pretty much the same way," Uncle Booster said. "This here's his little girl, she ain't but six." He jerked a thumb sideways toward Amanda, adding, "Her and her momma live in Bethlehem. They still grievin', yessir, it was quite a loss."

She saw the man now gazing at her uncle, a quizzical expression perched like a preening crow on the wide flat face. Then he swung his dark eyes onto her and she looked away down at the open book in her lap.

"You just come on over to the house for supper one night," she heard her uncle say, "bring the boy there, too, and I'll introduce you. Her momma works at Wal-mart, you probably already seen her and didn't know it."

"Booster!" Aunt Lois cried, drawing the name out long. She had a pained look on her face, which had turned bright red.

"You hush up," her husband said, not bothering to turn around, "I'm extending this man a invitation. He's new to town. You're gonna find Bethlehem's a friendly place, Mr. Harmon, real neighborly. We're good Christian people. What you think of that knife?"

"I like it," the boy said, his pudgy face practically nuzzling the knife in his father's hand. "It's like the one you had, ain't it?" His voice sounded both demanding and whining at once.

The man said it was and while he and her uncle settled on a fair price, Amanda studied the boy who was opening and closing the shiny steel blade. She stood up and leaned against the table to see closer. His hands were white and fat and he held the knife in his fist like a tiny sword. When he saw her watching he shot his arm out and thrust the blade toward her, grinning. He couldn't reach across the table but she stepped back anyway. His small black eyes seemed as vacuous as a pig's.

"Don't," his father said, laying a big hand on the boy's arm. "Put it in your pocket."

The boy bit his lower lip frowning but put the knife in the front right pocket of his trousers.

"Yessir, you got a fine boy there," Uncle Booster said.

The man glanced up with raised one eyebrow as he counted dollar bills from his wallet. "He'll do." He gave the money to her uncle.

"Thank you, sir. Prechate it. And like I said, stop over one night to supper. I'll show you a thing or two about the river. You like to fish? That river's got some good cats if you know how to find 'em."

The man said, "Thank you," and Amanda watched as he and his son drifted down the aisle to stop at another table. She didn't think he was the one who killed her father. He looked worried though. She wondered if he'd killed someone else.

Uncle Booster sighed and sat down next to his wife, saying, "I'd a tried to sell 'im a gun but I reckon he's got plenty by now. Know I would."

Aunt Lois squinted at the needle and pushed it carefully through the cloth. "He's the one they tied up to watch, ain't it?"

"That's him. Tied up the boy, too."

"Good Lord have mercy, it's a wicked world." Her aunt

leaned forward to see around Uncle Booster and said, "See there, Amanda, that's just what I'm talking about."

But she'd already picked up the picture book and pretended not to hear.

It was late afternoon and she stood outside the convention center doors on the concrete apron watching people load up their trucks and vans. The horizon to the south was bruised purple with massive storm clouds and the white sun hung low in the west and the wind carried the charged smell of rain. Her uncle passed pushing a dolly loaded with cardboard boxes into the parking lot toward the pickup. Her aunt was inside packing.

She adjusted the nylon straps holding her knapsack and stepped back when two men came outside and halted right beside her. "You call the congressman?" one said.

"Better believe it," the other replied. "Tol' him he better stop them damn gun laws. They takin' this country down."

"He'll do what he can."

"Tol' him I'm registered to vote, too. He got the message." The man leaned to one side and spit brown tobacco juice.

Amanda drew farther away toward the glass doors, listening. Both men wore hunting clothes and scuffed leather boots and one had a rifle slung over his shoulder. He said, "Ain't him I'm worried about. He's with us. It's them others."

"Yankees mostly."

"That's right. All they need's another nut to go shootin' up a school. Scare ever'body, work up the sympathy. Hell, they ain't enforcing the laws we got."

"Naw, they ain't. Wish someone'd go after a few congressmen. Save us the trouble. Lookit that storm comin' in."

Both men gazed southward. Amanda followed their aim and regarded the clouds, saw lightning flash down to flicker over the dark swollen bellies in thin pulsing veins of hot light. She chewed a fingernail, thinking it could've been them, the two men standing there. She believed they could shoot someone and not be bothered, they'd probably like it.

There was a movement behind her and she turned to see the tall man with the boy in the Cub Scout uniform come through the doors. The man saw her and stopped, looked at her blinking as if he'd walked from darkness into a bright room and for a moment he couldn't clearly see. Then he nodded once and went on. The boy lingered behind, and when his father was safely away he pulled out the pocket knife and opened the blade. It glinted in the sunlight. He turned his back so his father couldn't see, stepped close to her. "See that?" he said, speaking low. His small pale face twisted with fury. He bared his teeth like a death's skull. With a short violent thrust he stabbed the air. "That's what I'm gonna do," he hissed, "I'm gonna kill 'em."

"Lloyd," his father called, "let's go."

The boy's flat black eyes peered into hers as he folded the knife and shoved it into his pocket. Amanda shivered. She was clutching the gold heart on the chain around her neck. Then the boy wheeled and ran to catch up to his waiting father. She watched them walk across the lot and climb into a blue and white truck and drive away.

A few minutes later Uncle Booster said the truck was loaded and Aunt Lois came out and said, "Dear Jesus, look at that sky, it's about to storm." She asked Amanda if she needed to use the restroom before they left. She shook her head no.

She crawled into the back of the pickup cab and sat in the fold-down jump seat behind the passenger's side with the knapsack on her legs. Out the back window she could see the green tarpaulin her uncle had stretched over the boxes in the bed. When he pulled onto the highway she unzipped the knapsack and pulled out the picture book and began to read the story of the woman with a dead son. She read slowly, looking up once to ask, "You think that man's gonna come visit?"

"Who's that?" said Uncle Booster.

"She means that Mr. Harmon and his son," said her aunt. The woman craned her neck about but couldn't turn that far so she said over her shoulder, "I doubt it. He didn't look like the social type."

"Imagine he's lookin' to get married," said her uncle, "man with a kid needs a wife." There was a crash of thunder overhead and the rain began to fall in huge drops that burst against the glass and he turned on the windshield wipers. "Hoo boy," he said, "we got outa there just in time." He looked at Amanda and grinned. "How'd you like to have a brother?"

"Oh, you be quiet now," said Aunt Lois.

"Well, it ain't such a bad idea," he protested. "Man's got a good job, looks after his boy. Good lookin' boy, active in the Scouts."

"Just lookit that rain."

"Comin' a gully washer, all right."

"Reminds me of Noah."

"You say that ever time."

"Cause it does."

In back, Amanda had stopped listening. She ignored the voices and the rain splattering against the truck cab and the steady beat of the wiper blades and concentrated on the story. When she finished reading it she looked at the picture of Jesus for a while, then closed her eyes. She was back in the church during the funeral, sitting on the front pew between her mother and aunt. The preacher at the pulpit was talking about Jesus and below him down in front was the casket, only a few feet from where they sat in the pew. Her father lay inside the casket wearing a suit, his skin pale as a wax. Her mother and aunt were weeping but she was waiting for Jesus to come up the aisle and touch her father only he never did. So she rose from her seat and went forward herself. At the casket she looked over the side and reached down and caressed her father's cheek. His eyes opened and he smiled, then he sat up and looked right at her. He seemed surprised. "Why, what I am I doing here?" he asked.

"You was dead," she said.

He grinned. "Amanda, you're funnin' me. And look at you all dressed up, dumplin'. You look pretty as an angel."

She meant then to tell him he looked nice in a suit but was interrupted by a hand on her shoulder. She opened her eyes and saw it was her aunt groping back over the seat.

"Ma'am?"

"I said I know you're lookin' forward to seeing your momma, child, didn't you hear me?"

"No ma'am."

"Well, you're probably tired. All that people watchin' you did. Ever see such a crowd before?"

"No ma'am."

"Well, it's always like that. I bet you enjoyed yourself."

"Sure she did," said Uncle Booster, "had a big ol' Polish sausage for lunch and a free candy bar for dessert and a spanking. Cain't beat that."

"My Lord, I don't know why you got to bring that up," fussed Aunt Lois. "Always dredging up unpleasantness. She's got enough to deal with."

"Ain't no use hiding from the facts," he replied. "People hiding from the facts is what's wrong with this country. You take Topper, for example. If he'd only —" and he looked back over his right shoulder to make sure Amanda was listening but saw that her eyes were shut and she lay slumped against the back window. "Well, I'll be," he said, "she passed right out on us."

"I'm not surprised," said his wife, "didn't you hear me say she's tired?" She crossed her arms in her lap and looked out the window, satisfied. "Nuthin tires a child like a good time. If you'd pay close attention for once, Booster, you might notice something."

We've Got a Deal for YOU!

An old adage says that none of us live the life we'd intended. That's always seemed true to me, and even more so the older I've become, but the summer Sharon Beaudry returned into our midst drove the truth of it home for even a blind man to see.

In Bethlehem most folks take paths laid out far in advance by a natural complicity of social rank and personal inclination, so that the daughter of a doctor either marries a doctor or becomes one herself, just as the ambitious son of a sawmill hand is more likely to advance into the carpentry trade than the profession of architecture. No one in our small town ever appeared much surprised by these events, so they were not shocked when Sharon, the only child of Jasper Beaudry, the owner of the Ford-Nissan dealership, returned from a four-year hitch as an Assembly of God missionary in Africa and joined her father's automotive sales business.

By then, Jasper had become an old man nursing various ailments and was ready to relinquish the business into more vigorous hands. Sharon was the natural heir. So the daughter took over the dealership while the patriarch piddled with the rose bushes in his yard or played an occasional round at the Sabine Country Club. The only splinter in his eye after a lifetime of hard work and commercial success was the young woman's religion. Jasper was Episcopalian and did not think much of holy rollers who spoke in tongues and leaped shouting from the pews, who laid convulsing in the aisles while a

173

sweating peckerwood preacher beat on a pulpit and threatened them with hellfire and brimstone.

Which was what his daughter, Sharon, had taken to.

"Leave it be," Jasper's wife Bonnie told him, "be thankful for what she is, not what she isn't." Bonnie was his second wife and not Sharon's natural mother, who'd died of leukemia in her early thirties when the daughter was a small girl and Jasper, who'd postponed a youthful marriage out of consideration for empire building, had reached his mid-fifties. Within a year of her death he'd remarried. Now Jasper was seventy-five and suffering from arthritis, a swollen prostate, a bad heart and unpredictable attacks of dizziness on hot afternoons. His second wife Bonnie was twenty years younger, still healthy and trim, and though she'd never pursued any ambition higher than the presidency of the Ladies Book Club, she covertly admired her step-daughter's independent streak and encouraged her.

"Your father's a strong-willed man," she counseled Sharon, "and he'll walk right over you if you let him." But she knew the words were meant more for herself than for Sharon, who evidenced no shortage of will or any reluctance to oppose her father's sporadic harangues. When Jasper forgot and started in, Sharon likely as not would stand and walk out, saying, "Call when you remember who we are, Daddy," leaving the old man mumbling in his teeth and Bonnie secretly thrilled. She herself had never possessed the nerve.

Sharon was in high school when she attended a tent revival meeting with a friend and came home a convert. A tall, slim, pale-skinned girl with thick brown hair down her back and square shoulders — an all-district basketball player and volleyball team captain — her gray eyes sparkled with unconcealed joy as she described her conversion experience, the moment she kneeled at the altar in the sawdust and the Spirit moved her, the electricity sweeping over her face and shoulders and down her back as she wept with happiness and her mouth flew open to loosen colored ribbons of unknown tongues.

To her father's dismay, she abruptly quit the basketball and volleyball teams, withdrew her membership in the Episcopalian church and began attending the integrated Assembly of God services held three times weekly in a small clapboard building on a country road near Blackjack Creek. In the evenings when she sat on the back screened-in porch reading the Bible, Jasper would wander out with a gin and tonic over shaved ice with a wedge of lime and sit in the porch swing sipping his drink to watch, waiting for her to look up and explain herself. Instead, she'd say, "Hello, Daddy," smiling, and ask after his health, then after a short exchange of pleasantries return to her Bible. It drove him crazy.

After high school graduation Sharon attended the University of Texas at Austin for two years, taking the bare minimum of requisite courses so that she could pack her schedule with classes in philosophy and religion. Once she'd taken all the courses of interest she promptly announced she was quitting college and going to Africa to perform missionary work. That night Jasper got drunker than a pipefitter on payday, then seriously studied taking his Browning twelve-gauge automatic and putting the Assembly of God preacher out of his misery. The man was a full-time pump mechanic for a pipeline company and preached on the side, an unlearned and unschooled cracker Bible-thumper with more professed righteous humility than Jasper could stomach. Dawn found the father sitting in his Lincoln Continental on the street facing the preacher's trailer, stinking of whiskey and sweat, the loaded Browning cradled in his lap. Then the man came out and climbed into his F-150 pickup and drove away. Paralyzed with shame, Jasper watched the truck disappear down the road, a Beaudry Ford insignia on the bumper, and knew how a person felt when his life had overreached the limits of his own design or intention, when he was most apt to drive over to Wal-mart and buy a laminated plaque with the Serenity Prayer and hang it on the bathroom wall.

Sharon was gone for four years except for two visits home, and on those occasions spent most her time traveling the county visiting churches raising money for the mission in Africa, for medical and educational expenses and the missionary church itself. Jasper could never remember the name of the specific country — one of those places that had changed its name following one civil war or another — because in his mind Africa was Africa, any dark place in it as dangerous as any other, filled with half-naked savages with bone-pierced noses shaking spears and elephant hide shields dancing through the midnight hours to boogaloo drums when they weren't busy spreading the AIDS.

When she appeared in Bethlehem for both visits home with ruddy cheeks and clear gray eyes, lovelier than he'd remembered, Sharon seemed older than her years. The carriage of her head and shoulders indicated a staunch purpose that made her father feel vaguely inconsequential, as though his life had been spent pursuing a frivolous goal and a meaningless end, a project paltry by comparison to what others were accomplishing elsewhere outside the cloistered riverbottom domains of Bethlehem and East Texas. It made Jasper feel small, and the resentment that filled his thoughts made him feel smaller, and the only thing he could think to do to regain any estimation was write the substantial donation checks his daughter requested, which he did marveling at his own gullibility as a man and a father. His wife Bonnie sat in a chair watching, hands clasped in her lap, unabashedly taken by the scene she witnessed, an indulgence paid for later when her husband lashed out at her in belated anger. He was not well. His weakness only made him feel worse.

Then Sharon returned from overseas one June in the fourth year and announced she was interested in assuming the family business. Jasper didn't ask why. He was overjoyed. He believed he'd encountered the sort of grace his minister frequently mentioned, a state of undeserved redemption that previously existed, in Jasper's experience, as no more than an abstract religious concept used for padding sermons while causing no moral challenge or offense to well-heeled parishioners. Despite poor health, a bounce appeared in his step that had been missing for years. When he subsequently discovered his daughter knew far more about the automotive dealership than he'd ever imagined, that complex financial and logistical matters he would have expected months or even years for her to comprehend were mastered in short order, he shook his head and marveled. Sharon was a natural businesswoman, he plainly saw, and he spent less and less time at work as she shouldered the responsibilities, until the late summer day arrived when he realized he had not been into the office for almost two weeks and she had not called once for advice.

The only remaining fly in the ointment, he believed, was that Sharon remained as devoted as ever to the Assembly of God faith. She attended the small country church on Sunday mornings and evenings and each Wednesday night for the weekly prayer meeting. During the summer revival, she went every night for two weeks. For a successful business person to reject the more mainstream congregations for a low-end holy roller church given to loud emotional outbursts and bizarre scriptural interpretations just didn't make sense, Jasper privately complained. What's worse, the church had whites and coloreds worshiping side by side. The whole situation seemed more than a little vulgar if not positively scandalous in a town like Bethlehem, so carefully stratified by class and race.

"Look on the bright side," his wife Bonnie counseled, "she could still be over there in darkest Africa."

"She practically is."

"Now Jasper, count your blessings."

And so he did, as he always had, for his account books never missed a stroke. But if Jasper had known his daughter's plan, what lay in store for the business he'd spent a lifetime creating, he might have wept.

In hindsight, the first hint of it appeared the Friday afternoon Jasper's longtime acquaintance Durwood Brooks, who owned the leading insurance agency in town, called on the telephone complaining Sharon had tried to gig him on a car purchase.

"How you mean?" Jasper asked, tipping his gin sling for a swallow. He'd spent the morning working his prize roses, his hands and elbows ached with arthritis. Now he sat resting on the back porch overlooking a vast rolling lawn of St. Augustine and azaleas, rose beds and pecans trees and magnolias, watching two hummingbirds squabble over Bonnie's sugar water feeder. They buzzed one another like tiny fighter jets, making rat-a-tat sounds like machine guns. Jasper had never noticed before that hummingbirds made noises, and it amazed him. It seemed the sort of thing a man his seventies would know.

"I've always bought from Beaudry," Durwood carped, "*always*. And I've always bought at wholesale plus a hundred. Am I right?"

"That's right." He'd always sold cars to Durwood Brooks practically at cost out of courtesy, one local businessman to another — plus Durwood was a fellow Episcopalian — and had considered the insurance man driving a Beaudry vehicle a kind of advertising.

"Only now your daughter says no dice. It's five hundred or I can go elsewhere."

Jasper cocked an eyebrow.

"And I know for a fact she sold a new Escort right at wholesale to Johnny James who runs that sorry nigger barbecue stand out on Sarah Jane Road. He come in here for the insurance."

"Maybe he was just bragging," Jasper offered, knowing it wasn't true. Johnny James was an amiable old black man who'd raised ten kids without ever needing to bail one out of jail. Selling pork ribs and chicken and cold potato salad, he'd managed to produce a brood with seven college graduates and three military lifers. Yet he was not a boastful man.

"And maybe your daughter's just sticking it to me," Durwood retorted, "only I ain't the only one. Ask around, Jasper, take some time. Find out who's getting the deals and who ain't." He hung up the phone with a sharp click.

Jasper held the silent receiver to his ear, thinking. The

summer smell of hot damp grass and roses and honeysuckle wafted over the porch on a slight breeze. It was a slow lazy day, the sort of day he'd meant to enjoy in retirement. He dialed the dealership, asked Gloria the receptionist for his daughter. Sharon came on the line.

"Durwood Brooks just called me madder'n a hornet," he said. "Claims you tried to stick him on a buy. He says you sold Johnny James a car right above cost."

After a minute, when he realized his daughter had no intention of responding, Jasper said, "I told Durwood he probably just misunderstood."

"That's more or less right," Sharon replied crisply, "if you mean that Mr. Brooks doesn't understand economics. Have you ever wondered why we sell cars at discount to people with money and demand maximum price from folks who slave for every penny they earn?"

Jasper sipped the gin sling, frowning. He had a certain sense of where the conversation was heading and felt fairly sure he didn't want to follow.

"Now, consider a situation where folks with money pay a fair market price," his daughter continued, "and folks struggling to make ends meet pay what's fair for them. You might see how a situation like that could arise."

"Un-huh," he said quietly, "I think I see it rising."

"I thought you'd understand," she said. "If Durwood Brooks calls again, tell him to come back in and talk. We'd like to keep his business."

"You bet," he replied, "been buying from us forty years."

"There you are," Sharon said, "he knows how to find us."

She hung up.

Jasper freshened his drink and sat in the chair and watched the hummingbirds joust, contemplating his retirement, wondering whether he dared go to church on Sunday. Another thing about hummingbirds, he noticed, the male was more colorful but the female was bigger. He'd never paid much attention to that little detail, either. All of a sudden it seemed significant.

*   *   *

During the next week, he got several more angry phone calls and saw Lester Guidry, who'd spent twenty years as a minimum wage stock boy and carryout at the Market Basket Foodstore, driving a brand new Beaudry Nissan Sentra down Main past the barber shop. Twice he noticed elderly black women who worked as maids in the neighborhood — he didn't know their names, but he'd seen them come and go for years — parking shiny Beaudry compacts along the street. And when Thomas Edison Jones, his yardman, showed up for the weekly trim and edge, he arrived in a new Beaudry Ford Ranger pickup, his ancient Briggs & Stratton lawnmower and landscaping equipment in the back.

Bonnie stood on the drive with both hands on her hips and exclaimed, "My goodness, Thomas Edison, that sure is a pretty truck!"

"Yes, ma'am, it sho'ly is." The burly yardman tenderly stroked the fender, his flat broad face, as black as polished ebony, reflected in the bright red paint. "She a fine young woman, dat Miss Sharon. Fust new vehicle I ever done had. Never could get no loan, no'm, I laxed the credit."

"Well, congratulations," Bonnie said, "I'm proud for you," and she turned to Jasper, who stood nearby idly stroking his jaw, and said, "Honey, there's a phone call for you. In the kitchen. I told him you'd be right there. I think it's Mr. Hebert from the bank."

"What's he want?"

She arched her eyebrows and opened both hands wide and he went inside and picked up the receiver off the kitchen counter. "George Thomas?"

"Morning, Jasper. Looks like another hot one."

"Yes, it does."

"Humid, too." The bank president hesitated. "Well, I know you're busy, Jasper, so I'll get right to it. I'm seeing new Beaudry Fords and Nissans all over town, only none of 'em getting financed here at the bank. We've been scratching the other's back a long time, Jasper. What's going on?"

"Well, you know, George, I've been stepping back and Sharon's pretty much running the show. You asked her?"

"No, I haven't. I don't really know Sharon, and she hasn't been by to visit."

"Ask her to lunch. You tried that?"

The banker cleared his throat. "Listen, Jasper, I've been hearing things. But I'm not one to pass rumors, nossir, so I'll just stick to bank business. We'd like to finance some of those cars you're moving."

"Sharon's moving."

"Right. We'd like the business."

Jasper stretched the phone cord across the kitchen and took a glass from the cabinet, topped it with ice from the freezer. At the sink he turned on the tap and filled the glass with water. He took a long swallow.

"Jasper?"

"I'm here, George Thomas. You know half these people you wouldn't even approve, not likely. Not unless they had a house for collateral. I reckon Sharon's taking them through Ford Finance or some such big outfit that's willing to risk. Probably getting low finance rates, too."

"That's what I hear." The banker's voice was cold. "You take business out of town that way, it hurts the local folks. Local folks get hurt, it hurts you, Jasper. What goes around comes around, you know that."

"You oughta ask Sharon to lunch."

"If I can be direct, Jasper, I don't expect she and I'd find a lot in common, her being young and a single woman. Plus you know I go to First Baptist." He cleared his throat again. "Some of the other fellas in the Chamber feel the same way. We'd like to see you back down at Beaudry running things."

Jasper gritted his teeth.

"Either that or you sit down and have a heart-to-heart with your daughter. Not that I want to interfere in family, nossir. But talk some sense into her, set her straight," and then, after a moment, "This is a small town, Jasper. Even smaller than it looks."

He leaned on the counter and gazed out the kitchen window at the hummingbird feeder and the tiny zipping birds, then past them over the back lawn, his rose bushes and the expanse of bright green grass, saw Thomas Edison pushing his beat-up mower toward the far hedgerow. "Tell me, George, if I sent my yardman, Thomas Edison Jones — you know him?"

"He does my yard, too."

"If I sent him down to the bank, would you finance him a new Ford Ranger pickup?"

"Well, that all depends. Of course, I'd be prudent, take a look at his credit record," the banker replied. "If he's got one."

"What I thought," said Jasper. "Listen, George, you tried to buy a Beaudry vehicle lately by chance?"

"No, no I haven't. But Durwood Brooks did. He's talking it all over town. Not the kind of advertising you want, either."

"Appreciate the call, George. I'll talk to Sharon, but I'm not sure you can handle the business she's turning. You have a good'un." He hung up the receiver and tossed the water and ice into the sink, muttering, "You greedy sumbitch."

He went out the back door and across the sun-drenched yard to Thomas Edison, who shut down his mower and wiped his perspiring face with the towel draped over his shoulder. "Yessuh?"

"You try to finance your truck at the bank?" Jasper asked.

The black man poked out his lower lip and looked away. He slowly wagged his head. "Nossuh, no use in tryin' dat, suh. I axed befo' and dey turn me down. Only Miss Sharon, she fixed me up."

Jasper nodded. "Thank you, Thomas Edison." He turned on his heel and marched back up the lawn, stoop-shouldered and bent, hands thrust into his back pockets.

They had lunch at the Pioneer House, an old former homestead outside town on a knoll overlooking the Sabine River. Two young men from Houston had bought the place and rebuilt the interior with cypress beams and split log walls, put in a decor leaning toward antique iron farm implements, leather mule harnesses black with oil and age, old oak-staved barrels worn smooth as driftwood cut in half for planters overflowing with geraniums and wildflowers. The place offered a home-cooked fare of country-style meats and vegetables.

Jasper and Sharon sat at a table near the back window. Outside enormous live oaks and beeches shaded the slanting grounds all the way down to the water's edge. Jasper sipped his ice tea, Sharon her lemonade, they perused the dining room, mostly empty an hour before noon.

Watching a waitress mop the floor by the service counter, Jasper said, "George Thomas at the bank called. Says he and some of the business folks in town want me to take the dealership back."

She tilted her head. "That's certainly your prerogative."

He looked at his daughter. She wore a long black skirt and white rayon blouse, her thick brown hair pulled back into a ponytail. She sat upright, her square shoulders straight, hands folded in her lap. Her gray eyes gazed directly into his.

"It isn't what I want," he said.

"That's certainly your prerogative, too."

Jasper raised his hands and snorted impatience, set his fingertips on the table's edge. "What I'd like to know is what a young woman who'd use a word like 'prerogative' is doing in a holy roller church full of redneck illiterates." His voice rose, almost pleading. "It don't make any sense, Sharon."

"Is that why we're here, Daddy? Because if it is, I have things to do."

He exhaled loudly, shook his head. "No, I wanted to talk about the business."

"All right."

His eyes wandered over her head to the side wall on which hung an assortment of old pioneer photographs in oval frames, the faded brown surfaces fissured with tiny cracks. Here and there a landscape, a log cabin or baygall overshadowed by tall cypress draped in Spanish moss, but most of the pictures were of men in overalls and women in homespun cotton dresses

183

staring into the camera with rough country faces, stern and unsmiling. His own grandparents, Zack and Myrtle Beaudry, were up there. He quickly turned his eyes back to his daughter.

"Sharon, this just isn't right. You're embarrassing me to death, girl." He spoke in a rush, as if concerned to get it said before second thoughts rushed in, muzzled his mouth.

"Well, Daddy, you'll just have to get over it."

He rubbed the corner of one eye with a forefinger. Geez, she was tough. "What are you doing down there?"

"I'm running the business."

"We gotta be losing money."

"No, sales are up."

"You mean units sold is up. But we ain't making any money on 'em."

"Sure we are, Daddy. Volume's compensating for discounts. We're making as much money as we ever were."

He drummed the tabletop, stumped. "Well, hell."

"Don't curse at me. Would you like to see the books?"

Flustered, he gazed out the window toward the river's muddy edge, saw an egret feeding in the shallows. It's slender neck uncoiled, the pointed yellow beak pierced the water. "This ain't no way to run a dealership, that's all I'm saying."

"No? Tell me, Daddy, if Jesus was running Beaudry Ford-Nissan, how do you think he'd do it?"

Jasper rolled his eyes. "Don't be ridiculous. The business is dirty."

"Not this one. Not any more."

"Well, it's a silly question. Jesus would never run a car dealership."

"He is this one."

He stared at his daughter, his mouth set firm, attempting to process at once what she'd just said and what she'd said only previous to that, something about the dealership not being dirty "any more." The implication in the statement frightened him.

"Listen here, Sharon, when I said the business is dirty — "

"You were being honest," she said, interrupting. "And I

appreciate that, Daddy, I really do. I know it isn't easy. You built the business from scratch."

He wiped his chin in the palm of his hand, the shaved whiskers against skin sounded like sandpaper. His eyes shot left and right wildly, as if unstrung from their sockets.

"But that was then," she continued. "Now it's time to clean up and fly straight. Fortunately, because of your years of hard work, we can afford to do that," and she paused a moment before adding, "But I'd do it even if we couldn't."

He winced.

Then the waitress came carrying a large tray holding bowls of mashed potatoes and gravy and green beans and okra, glazed carrots, turnip greens, a platter of corn on the cob and another of cornbread. She set down a large bowl of fried chicken and empty dinner plates. "You ready for refills on the drinks?"

"Yes, thank you, Mabel," Sharon said. "Dad?"

He nodded. When the waitress strode away, a large elderly woman wearing heavy-soled white nurse's shoes, her iron-gray hair pulled back in a tight bun, he asked, "How you know her name?"

"She goes to my church. Mabel Crowder's a widow raising three young grandkids on waitress wages."

"You sell her a car yet?"

Sharon smiled. "Enjoy the meal, Daddy. And stop worrying. If that's all you've got to do I can find you a better job."

"I'm trying to retire."

"And you deserve it," she said, spooning green beans onto her plate, "now I'd like to hear how you've been spending your time."

He told her about the hummingbirds.

But he couldn't let go. Three days and several more irritating phone calls later, Jasper put on his blue seersucker suit and a lemon tie and drove over to the dealership, parked out front. The lot spread over two acres to either side and behind the showroom floor and office building, row upon row of shiny Ford and Nissan cars and pickups sparkling in the midday sun. The inventory. He scrutinized the nearer vehicles, ascertaining they were properly detailed and prepped and ready to roll out. His eye roved to the large sign rising on a steel column by the road — "Beaudry Ford-Nissan" — and the white banner with big red letters hanging over the showroom entrance: "We've Got a Deal for YOU!"

The moment he stepped inside he was cornered by Vic Dooley, the sales manager. "Mr. Beaudry, we got problems."

Jasper sighed. "What is it, Vic?"

The young man picked at his mustache, a trim blond line of bristles that reminded Jasper of a dirty toothbrush, then glanced back over his shoulder and said, "Could we talk in my office? Private like?"

Jasper followed the dapper salesman into the small cubicle, where Vic shut the door and began to complain. "She's changing all the rules, Mr. Beaudry. What we supposed to do?"

Taking a seat, Jasper said, "What rules you mean?"

Vic perched on a corner of his desk and explained how salesmen now had to list all the costs up front when pricing a potential sale. "And I mean *everything*. Items like taxes and dealer prep and extended warranties, stuff we always add on at the end, you see, once the customer's already bought the vehicle in his mind, when he ain't likely to back out on us," and he frowned mournfully, plucking at the end of his mustache. "It just don't seem hardly fair, Mr. Beaudry."

Jasper scratched his jaw and listened. The salesmen, Vic continued, were no longer permitted to lowball or slip in unrequested options. Nor could they bump customers up to a higher priced car once they'd stated the amount they could afford to spend. If a customer made an offer, salesmen weren't allowed to say they'd have to discuss it with the sales manager, then go out back and smoke a cigarette while the customer waited and worried. Do that several times and a customer gives up, Vic said, and pays the higher price. He threw up his arms. "I mean, now the boys got to come tell me every offer, Mr. Beaudry!" The sales manager went on to list four or five other proven sales techniques that were no longer acceptable at Beaudry Ford-Nissan.

When he finished, Jasper said, "Tell me, Vic, are you making a living? Have your commissions dropped off?"

The young man hesitated, picked a piece of lint off his trousers. "Well, no sir, not as a whole. Unit price is down but volume is up. We're just having to work harder. But it ain't easy standing on your feet all day hustling cars, Mr. Beaudry. And changing the rules on us, well, it ain't half the fun it used to be."

"Why?"

"Sir?"

"I asked why."

Vic frowned, confused. "Well, I mean ... shoot, you know how it is, Mr. Beaudry, you the one taught us. Taking a customer over the hurdles, it's like a game. You ain't sure who's gonna win but you play the angles, give it your best."

Jasper nodded, remembering. "And if you can't play the game it's only a job, right?"

"Right," Vic agreed.

"So that's what you've got. A job."

"Sir?"

"I said you've got a job, son. You're in the service industry. Give service, and give it with a smile."

The young man looked away, blinking, popping his lips as if this concept was too innovative and complex to comprehend all at once, then he shrugged and climbed off the desk, straightened his belt and sports coat lapels. "Yes sir," he said, "that's what I'll do. But what we supposed to do about these rule changes?"

The older man shook his head as if confronted with a deficient intellect and stood, put his hand on the doorknob to leave. "What you do's up to you," he said, "but I reckon if it was me, I'd try and adjust. Like it or not, rules have a way of changing on a person." He opened the door and stepped outside, then put his head back in. "By the way, son, you a Christian?"

"Well, I was raised Baptist." Vic tugged at his tie, then his mustache. "Only I don't go regular."

"Might try going then," Jasper said, "it might help your adjustment. You take care now," and he shot the young man with a cocked thumb and forefinger and added his trademark parting line, "Move those vehicles, pardner, they look lonesome out there."

He hated it, though. The morning he came to the church to speak with me his face was drawn, the lines around his eyes tight with fatigue. He appeared as though he hadn't slept well, and confessed as much. I was seated in the small cottage in back where I kept my reference books and prepared sermons. In those days I was a young Episcopalian minister fresh out of seminary, in my first church. But I was already learning how in the confrontation between fine ideas and social convention, principle was apt to be crushed beneath pragmatism, a lovely red rose snipped rudely from the bush and posed on a mantel to admire as it wilted.

My study was in disorder and the day was mild so I suggested we sit outside. Several wrought-iron chairs rested in the grove of longleaf pines surrounding the cottage. There in the summer morning shade, with bluejays calling back in the wind-rustled trees, he told me what had happened, what he foresaw. Jasper Beaudry was deeply troubled, and though some of the anxiety pertained to his own reputation and the future of the business he'd built, he told me he'd made his peace with that probability. It was concern for his daughter Sharon that worried him.

"These ol' boys in town are going to eat her alive," he said. He interlaced his gnarled fingers and squeezed. "They got ways she don't even know about, couldn't imagine. It's dog eat dog and those boys run in a pack. Under all those smiles and howdy-do's, they're one mean bunch." He leaned forward, elbows on knees, his hands cupped around his sagging mouth.

I nodded without speaking and waited for him to continue. As I said, I was a young man, and inexperienced, but old enough to know that simply listening covered a lot of ground and often compensated for wisdom I did not yet possess. Then, as now, I believed on faith that a person will see the truth of his own predicament, and discover the path he must travel, if given a sympathetic ear.

The man then began to explain the methods by which he'd built his dealership, narrating the sordid story of a life devoted to material success, of virtues sacrificed to personal and social gain. The details shocked me. Though I knew on principle that greed was a bad thing, and often preached so, my knowledge was general in nature and I hadn't the slightest awareness of the specific strategies by which ambitious men wreak havoc on the unsuspecting — and on one another. That morning Jasper Beaudry removed the scales from my eyes and it dismayed me. By the time he left, I had not the slightest doubt that I was the one who learned most from the encounter, although he, preoccupied with his own distress, did not notice.

"Anyhow, that's how it's done, and that's how I done it," he said. "I don't dispute but Sharon's doing the right thing, least according to the book. But nobody else is. Business is business. They'll come after her. She's only got two cheeks to turn, then what happens?" He looked right at me.

It was the sort of question for which a minister ought to have an answer. And while I did, in theory, I realized that the specificity of the circumstances he described called for a concrete response, which I did not have. Like him, I could see Sharon Beaudry turning her cheek time and again as avaricious men slowly destroyed her by means I could only vaguely comprehend.

Jasper took a deep breath and sighed. He pulled himself upright on the chair, rubbed his eyes with the heels of his hands. "They're gonna crucify her," he said, "that's what."

I gazed past him, past the nearer pines toward the water oaks flanking the small branch which bordered the back property line, thinking about a fellow student at seminary who one day turned to me in the library and said, "You ever considered the fact that Moses, the Buddha, Mohammed,

Confucius, they all lived to a ripe old age? That only Jesus died young, and by violent means? Why you think that is?" They were good questions, and the conceivable answers worrisome. Then my attention was drawn back to Jasper Beaudry, who was speaking.

"Not much I can do about it, either. I'm an old man, won't be around much longer. She's all grown up." He crossed his arms and legs and sighed again. "I guess you know she goes to that holy roller church. Bible thumpers and tongue speakers," and he glanced my way, saying, "You've been to religion school, what can you tell me about that bunch?"

I told him what I knew about fundamentalism, the literal interpretation of scripture, the dangers I saw in it, and the hard drive of evangelicals to spread the Gospel as they understand it, the motives behind their zeal, the anger too often found beneath a veneer of compassion. As far as charismatic worship itself, I added, speaking in tongues, or glossolalia, has some basis in New Testament scripture, the books of Acts and First Corinthians, though I was not personally familiar with the experience. "There are some in the mainstream churches who've begun to practice it," I said. "They seem to find some value in charism, say it strengthens their faith."

He grunted and glanced at his watch, abruptly stood up saying, "I better be moving along. I thank you for your time, pastor."

We walked over the sunblazed yard together to the side lot where his Lincoln was parked, me apologizing for not having more advice to offer. He put a hand on my shoulder and shook his head. "You did fine, son. Needed someone to listen mostly, and that you did. I appreciate it." He opened the car door and got in, me standing alongside watching. He hit the electric button and the window rolled down. "What I told that sales manager? About adjusting to the rules changing?"

I nodded.

"Reckon I was preaching to myself, yessir." He smiled sadly, turned on the ignition and began to pull away.

"God bless you," I called, and he turned into the street,

leaving me alone with a profound sense of inadequacy, a feeling which during the many years since has become a familiar if uncomfortable pastoral companion. I watched his car disappear around the corner and wondered what would become of him, what would happen to his daughter.

Several months later I learned. By then the events were behind them, but that was when Jasper stopped by the church again for a private visit. What I'd heard until then came through the grapevine so I treated it warily, although an article in the weekly newspaper, the Bethlehem Bugle, had announced in October the sale of the Beaudry Ford-Nissan dealership to a Beaumont businessman. What follows is the version Jasper Beaudry told me —

He'd been seated on his back porch one September morning on the tail end of summer. Having finished tending his rose bushes, he sipped a glass of ice tea and watched the hummingbirds skirmish. The small dashes of color buzz-bombed one another off the feeder by turns, ruby throats clicking like a car starter on a dead battery. After observing them for a hour or so he drifted off into a state of mild inattention, a self-forgetting. That's when the idea crawled up his spine and exploded in his brain like a slow-motion nuclear mushroom. He immediately phoned Sharon at the dealership and arranged to meet her for lunch at the Pioneer House.

Her first response was refusal. They sat at the same table by the back window overlooking the spreading oaks and beech trees and the grounds inclining downward toward the low brushy bank of the river. "No, Daddy, I'm sorry," she said, "but I can't just abandon our customers."

"Whatever happened to my prerogative?"

Her shoulders jerked as if someone had poked her in the back.

"Never mind," he said quickly, waving a dismissive hand, "sorry I mentioned that. Anyhow, I've already spoken with Jack Burke at the Ford dealership down in Beaumont. He runs a low-margin high-volume business, that's his strategy. Same as yours. Jack says he'll take care of it. He'll deal with the folks you been dealing with. Jack'll sell a car to anyone, whatever it takes."

Sharon shut one skeptical eye. "Out of the goodness of his heart."

"Are you kidding? Jack's heart is blacker'n coal." Jasper smiled. "But we'll help him get settled in up here, help him get established."

She drummed the tabletop with her fingers, her gray gaze serious. "Okay, then what."

He laid it out. Sharon would get fifty percent of the proceeds, he and her step-mother Bonnie would get the other half. He planned to split his share with Bonnie, she'd end up with twenty-five percent. "Of course, we don't really need it," he said. "I've got some investments salted away, more than enough to live on. For Bonnie, too, when I pass on. So our share'd come to you down the road eventually." He shrugged nonchalantly. "Bonnie and I talked, decided to give it to you now."

"Come again?"

"Said you'll get the entire proceeds from the sale." He crossed his arms and leaned back in his chair to make room for the waitress, who arrived with the tray of bowls and platters. "Hello, Mabel, how are you?"

"I'm fine, Mr. Beaudry," the large woman replied. She bent her knees to unload the tray, glanced at him from the corner of one eye. "How're you, sir?"

"Can't complain. Sharon tells me you have three fine grandchildren."

"Yes sir, I do." She set down the food, carefully arranging the bowls in the middle for each of them to reach.

"And have you recently purchased a new automobile from Beaudry?"

She gave Sharon a quick look. "Yes sir, I have."

"Good, good. I hope it's performing to satisfaction."

"Yes sir, it is," she said, "thank you for asking," and she

walked away giving a quick curious glance over her shoulder.

"My goodness, Daddy," Sharon said, "aren't we on our best behavior today."

Jasper chuckled and forked a chicken leg from the platter. "By the way, Bonnie sends her regards, asks if you'll join us for dinner tomorrow night. Said she wants to make a gumbo."

"Of course." She placed both elbows on the table edge and propped her chin on clasped hands, scrutinizing her father. "You want to tell me what's really going on here?"

"Why, you don't want to sell?"

"No, I don't."

"What if you was to put the money to good use? Good works, that sort of thing."

"I'm already doing that."

"I mean something else."

"Such as?"

He gazed out the window at the river, the silty brown current running low at summer's end. A crowjack winged low over the surface, lifted and disappeared into the woods. "Such as a mission in Africa. A school, a hospital."

When she did not seem surprised but only studied his face, her eyebrows lifting thoughtfully, the old salesman recognized a closed deal.

"And a church," she said.

He opened one hand palm upward and dipped his head, conceding the point. "And a church. Though Bonnie and I'd like to earmark our part for the school and hospital, if you agree."

Sharon smiled, raised a forkful of green beans to her mouth. "Why of course, Daddy. After all, you do still have *some* prerogative."

Jasper shook his head and grinned.

"Well, my goodness," she murmured, as though speaking to herself, "this has certainly moved along faster than I'd expected."

*　　*　　*

This all happened some years ago, as I mentioned, and I'm pleased to say that these strange events unfurled to a good end. Sharon Beaudry built a successful mission in Kenya, and later, I'm told, yet another mission in Zaire, the former Congo. She named both schools after her father, Jasper Beaudry, and the hospitals after her mother and step-mother.

By then I'd left Bethlehem and moved on to other churches, a larger one in Tyler, where I married and began my family, then still a larger congregation in Houston, where I still tend my flock with adequate results — at least they haven't voted me out — and grow roses in the parsonage garden. When Jasper died of heart failure several years ago, I heard about it from a former parishioner and sent some of the roses to the funeral. I soon received a kind note from his wife, Bonnie. She wrote that she planned to move to Zaire and help with Sharon's mission school as a teacher. She sounded very excited, and I had the impression she saw herself embarking on a strange, exotic adventure, something she'd never expected of herself.

A month or so later I received another letter, this one postmarked Zaire, from Sharon. She narrated the principal events in her recent life — she'd had a close brush with marriage, she said, but did not specify what forestalled it — and closed with a paragraph that explained the reason for her correspondence. Her father had visited her in Kenya the year before his death. In passing, he'd mentioned that a short conversation with me is what planted the seed for his inspiration to sell the family business and finance Sharon's mission work. She thanked me.

I had no idea what Jasper Beaudry meant by this remark — and still don't — but concluded once again that grace works in mysterious ways.

More recently, I had the occasion on a driving trip with my wife and children to pass through Bethlehem. Upon seeing the old Beaudry automotive dealership, I pulled off onto the shoulder of the road. The sign now saying Jack Burke Ford-

Nissan was larger and the showroom had expanded, but otherwise the place appeared unchanged. I even recognized the banner over the showroom entrance. The original one must have been replaced more than once during the intervening years, but the slogan remained the same. In large red letters the banner proclaimed, "We've Got a Deal for YOU!"

My wife joked that the slogan would make a good title for a sermon. Yes, it certainly would, I told her. But Sharon Beaudry had already used it.